A CANDY APPLE COLLECTION

Volume 1

The Accidental Cheerleader

The Boy Next Door

Miss Popularity

SCHOLASTIC INC.

New York Toronto London Auckland Sydney
Mexico City New Delhi Hong Kong Buenos Aires

If you purchased this book without a cover, you should be aware that this book is stolen property. It was reported as "unsold and destroyed" to the publisher, and neither the author nor the publisher has received any payment for this "stripped book."

No part of this publication may be reproduced, stored in a retrieval system, or transmitted in any form or by any means, electronic, mechanical, photocopying, recording, or otherwise, without written permission of the publisher. For information regarding permission, write to Scholastic Inc., Attention: Permissions Department, 557 Broadway, New York, NY 10012.

The Accidental Cheerleader
ISBN-13: 978-0-439-92928-8 • ISBN-10: 0-439-92928-8
Copyright © 2006 by Mimi McCoy.

The Boy Next Door
ISBN-13: 978-0-439-92929-5 • ISBN-10: 0-439-92929-6
Copyright © 2006 by Laura Dower.

Miss Popularity
ISBN-13: 978-0-439-88814-1 • ISBN-10: 0-439-88814-X
Copyright © 2007 by Francesco Sedita.

These books were originally published by Candy Apple.

ISBN-13: 978-0-545-08835-0
ISBN-10: 0-545-08835-6

All rights reserved. Published by Scholastic Inc. SCHOLASTIC, CANDY APPLE, and associated logos are trademarks and/or registered trademarks of Scholastic Inc.

12 11 10 9 8 7 6 5 4 3 2   8 9 10 11 12 13/0

Printed in the U.S.A.   40
This collection first printing, May 2008

Text design by Steve Scott

A candy apple collection

Volume 1

Three sweet, complete novels!

CHAPTER
One

"Check these out!" Kylie Lovett exclaimed.

She yanked the hanger off the rack and held the jeans up to her waist. They were dark indigo with a flare at the ankles. A dragon embroidered in red and gold thread crawled down the left leg.

Her friend Sophie's hazel eyes widened. "Ooh, *serious* shivers," she said. "Shivers" was Sophie and Kylie's word for anything that was so cool it practically sent chills down your spine.

She looked at the price tag. "Make that serious shivers and *on sale*. I swear you have the best shopping karma of anyone I know, Kylie."

Not like me, Sophie thought with a sigh. She found it practically impossible to find stylish clothes that fit her tiny four-foot-nine-inch frame. At twelve years old, she was still the same height she'd been

1

in fifth grade. As far as Sophie was concerned, the Juniors section in the department store might as well have been called Too Big for Sophie Smith.

"Never fear," Kylie told Sophie. She plunged her hands back into the rack and rapidly began to sift through the hangers. A second later, she pulled out an identical pair of jeans in a smaller size.

"Last pair," she declared. "And they look like they might fit you."

Sophie grinned. "You rock, stylie Kylie."

"Anything for my girl."

Draping the jeans over their arms, the two girls made their way toward the fitting rooms. In a week, school would begin, and the store was crowded with kids hitting the back-to-school sales. Sophie glanced around to see if she recognized any faces from Meridian Middle School, but no one looked familiar.

Whenever she thought about school, Sophie felt a little jolt of excitement. This year she and Kylie would be in seventh grade. Sophie thought seventh grade seemed like the perfect age. You were no longer a scared middle-school newbie like the sixth-graders, and you weren't *about* to be a scared high-school newbie like the eighth-graders. You were right in the middle, and Sophie was a right-in-the-middle kind of person.

When they reached the dressing rooms, the bored-looking attendant took the clothes and counted the hangers.

"There's only one room open," she informed them, handing the jeans back. "One of you will have to wait."

Kylie's eyes widened. "Oh, no, ma'am. I'm afraid that's impossible."

The woman folded her arms and raised her eyebrows.

"You've heard of color blindness, right?" Kylie went on, undeterred. "Well, my friend here," she pointed at Sophie, "is pattern blind. She can't tell paisley from stripes. A real fashion disaster." She leaned in closer to the woman and lowered her voice. "For everyone's sake, it's probably better if I go with her."

The attendant frowned. But before she could say anything, Kylie grabbed Sophie's wrist and sashayed past her to the open dressing room.

As soon as they'd shut the door to the tiny cubicle, the friends burst into giggles.

"Pattern blind?" Sophie said.

Kylie shrugged. "It was the first thing I thought of. No offense or anything."

"None taken."

Sophie sat on the bench to untie her sneakers.

Kylie kicked off her flip-flops and yanked the dragon jeans up under her short, flounced skirt. Then she undid the skirt and let it fall around her ankles, all before Sophie had even managed to take off her shoes.

"Judy Lovett's speed shopping rule number one: Wear slip-on shoes for quick changes," Kylie advised. "In the time you spend untying laces you could be scoring a bargain."

Sophie rolled her eyes and yanked off her shoes. Kylie's mom was a real estate agent. She was always zipping around town trying to sell expensive houses to people. She was a pro at shopping on the run. Kylie's mom could find, try on, and purchase an entire outfit in under seven minutes. Sophie had seen her do it. It was pretty impressive, but in her opinion it wasn't a very fun way to shop.

A moment later she'd donned the smaller pair of dragon jeans. The two friends stood squeezed together, side by side in the mirror.

Although their jeans matched, the girls who looked back at them couldn't have been more different. Kylie was five inches taller than Sophie. She had big green eyes, a wide mouth, and golden hair that sprang from her head in tight ringlets. "Striking" was the word Sophie's mom always used to describe Kylie. She wasn't beautiful exactly, but there was something about her face that made you want to keep looking. It always seemed to be on the verge of a hundred different expressions.

Sophie thought her own looks were pretty average. Bobbed brown hair, small nose, freckles. Nothing striking there, Sophie thought, except for her cheeks. They turned raspberry red whenever she felt even a tiny bit embarrassed, which for Sophie was about ten times a day.

Sophie sucked in her cheeks like a super-model and turned sideways to get a better look at the jeans.

"Those jeans fit you perfectly, Soph," Kylie said.

They *did* fit perfectly. The cuffs just covered the tops of her feet, and the legs were fitted but not too snug. The dragon's body ran up the side in a long, undulating wave.

Sophie turned and checked out her other side. Something about the jeans made her look taller, she thought.

"Yours look good, too," she said, checking Kylie in the mirror. Then again, everything looked good on Kylie.

Kylie did a little spin, examining herself from all angles. "Sold!" she declared.

As she changed back into her shorts, Sophie looked again at the price tag on the jeans. Even on sale, they were expensive — almost fifty dollars with tax.

Sophie did the math. For fifty dollars, she could probably buy four T-shirts. Or a sweater and a bunch of socks. Or she could go to the movies eight times and still have money left over for popcorn. Or . . .

"Just get them, Soph," Kylie said suddenly. She was standing over Sophie with her hands on her hips, smirking. "Stop thinking about everything you *should* buy and just get them. They look great on you."

Sophie grinned. She and Kylie had been friends since first grade. They could practically read each other's thoughts. Kylie knew that if Sophie had a dollar in her pocket, she would spend ages trying to decide whether to buy one pack of gum, two candy bars, or ten watermelon chews — and Sophie knew that if Kylie had a dollar in her pocket, she would probably lose it before they even got to the candy store.

But Kylie was right this time, she thought. She had to buy the jeans. They would be the perfect thing to wear on the first day of school.

Sophie giggled. "Come on," she said. "Let's pay for these and go get something to eat. I'm starving."

At the register, Sophie pulled out her credit card and handed it to the cashier. She felt a twinge of pride remembering the day a few months before when her parents had given her the card. "You're old enough now to be responsible," her dad had said, solemnly placing it in her hands. Sophie's parents weren't rich, and she knew her father especially worried about money, so it made her that much prouder to know that they trusted her.

As Sophie signed the credit card receipt, Kylie spun a display rack of jewelry around. "Ooh!" she said, stopping at a pair of dangly earrings. "Shiverlicious!"

She took the earrings off the rack and set them on the counter next to her jeans. A moment later, she added a bracelet. Then she took a tiny bottle of glittery nail polish from a nearby display and added that to the pile, too.

The young woman behind the counter rang up Kylie's purchases.

"Hmm," said Kylie when she saw the total. She pulled some bills out of her wallet and counted them. She counted them again. She searched around in the bottom of her purse.

The cashier tapped her long orange fingernails against the register, waiting.

Kylie picked up the earrings, bracelet, and nail polish. "I'm just going to put these back," she told the cashier.

The woman sighed and retotaled Kylie's bill.

The minute she had heard that Sophie had a credit card, Kylie had rushed to her parents and asked for one, too. They said no before she'd even finished her sentence. They knew better. Kylie was very impulsive — when she saw something she liked, she bought it. She could max out a credit card in a single trip to the mall.

As they exited the store, Sophie swung her shopping bag and did a happy little skip. "Total score!" she exclaimed. "We are going to look so great on the first day of school."

"Absolutely," Kylie agreed. Then she frowned. "But we can't *both* wear them on the first day."

Sophie stopped swinging the bag. "Why not?"

"'Cause it's not *cool*. We can't be all matchy-matchy on the first day of seventh grade. Everyone would think that we're big losers who have to do everything together."

"Oh." Sophie hadn't thought of that. In sixth grade, she had seen lots of friends wearing the same necklaces or jackets or sneakers. And besides, she and Kylie *did* do everything together.

But maybe Kylie knew something about seventh grade that she didn't.

"And since we can't both wear them on the first day," Kylie went on, thinking aloud, "I guess it's only fair that neither of us do."

"I guess." Sophie wondered what she would wear instead. The whole point of this shopping trip had been to find her first-day outfit.

They had almost reached the food court. Sophie could smell french fries and cinnamon buns. She started to head toward a pretzel stand, but Kylie grabbed her arm.

"Can we go into the Cut Above?" she asked, pointing to the store across from them. "Just for a second?"

Sophie shrugged. "Sure." The Cut Above sold crazy, expensive gadgets, like chairs that massaged you while you were sitting in them and alarm clocks that woke you up with recordings of real bird sounds. She wondered why Kylie wanted to go there. But before she could ask, Kylie had turned and was making a beeline into the store. Sophie hurried after her.

"Look at this," Sophie said when they were inside. She picked up a robotic dog. "'The perfect pet,'" she read from the box. "'Never needs to be fed or walked. Odor-free. Hair-free. Noise-free.' How about fun-free? What do you think, Kye? Should we get it for your mom?"

Kylie didn't answer. She was staring at something across the room.

Sophie followed her gaze. Three boys from Meridian were gathered around a plasma TV against the opposite wall, playing a simulated golf game. The tall one, Scott Hersh, was the football team's star quarterback. The other two guys, Jake and Dominick, were his best buds. They would all be eighth-graders this year.

Now Sophie understood why she and Kylie were there. Kylie had a crush on Scott. Half the girls at Meridian did. Last year Scott had won the district all-star award for football, and he was part of the most popular clique at school.

As Kylie stared, Scott glanced in their direction. Quickly, Kylie pretended to be examining the display in front of her. It was a table of electric nose-hair clippers.

"I don't know if I'd get those if I were you," Sophie said, sidling over to her. "I hear Scott Hersh likes girls with really long nose hair."

Kylie smiled sheepishly. She set down the nose-hair clippers and moved over to the next display. KARAOKE IN YOUR OWN HOME! the sign read.

10

"I love karaoke!" said Kylie.

She began to fiddle with the dials on the machine. A second later, the opening phrase of a pop song burst from the speaker. Kylie picked up the mic and started to sing.

Heat rushed to Sophie's cheeks as if someone had lit a match underneath them. Why did Kylie have to live out her pop idol fantasies right now, she wondered, when three of the most popular guys at Meridian were playing simulated sports just twenty feet away?

A few people in the store turned to look. Sophie glanced over at the boys, but they were still absorbed in their game.

Kylie's eyes were shut tight and she had her head thrown back, singing like a true pop diva. Sophie sighed. She loved her friend's outgoingness, but sometimes she wished she didn't have to be so . . . well, *outgoing*. Hanging out with Kylie could be sort of like riding a roller coaster. Ninety-nine percent of the time it was a blast, but every now and then she did something that made you want to scream.

Out of the corner of her eye, Sophie saw Scott and his friends turn around.

They're coming over here! she thought. *What should I do?*

For a brief instant she considered unplugging the karaoke machine. Then she realized that, without music, Kylie would just keep singing, which would be even more embarrassing.

Stop freaking, Sophie told herself. *Just calm down.* After all, she didn't even know these guys. Who cared what they thought?

But the truth was, Sophie cared. She didn't like to attract attention, good or bad. She might not be the most popular girl at school, but she wasn't the biggest geek, either. She thought of herself as a nice, normal person, and she thought other people probably saw her that way, too. At least, she hoped they did.

In Sophie's opinion, an impromptu pop concert at a high-end home electronics store did not make her seem like a nice, normal person. Kylie might as well have hung a flashing sign over their heads, LOOK AT US! in neon lights.

Sophie closed her eyes and willed the moment to be over as soon as possible.

A second later, it was. As she opened her eyes, she was just in time to see the boys' backs as they headed out the door of the store.

CHAPTER Two

Sophie leaned against her locker and checked her watch for the third time that morning. Eight-fifteen. Kylie was late.

The hall was starting to fill with students. Noise echoed through the corridor as they hollered greetings, excited to see one another after the summer. A few kids Sophie knew said hi as they passed her. They all were wearing bright clothes in the latest fashions. They sported new haircuts and dark tans, and the ones who'd gotten their braces off flashed extra-wide pearly white smiles.

The first day of the school year wasn't really like school at all, Sophie thought. It was more like a commercial for school. All the kids wore cool clothes and looked happy, the teachers acted nice, and the classes actually seemed interesting. It was

13

like watching a movie preview that turns out to be way better than the movie itself.

As she waited for Kylie, Sophie eyed her own lime green corduroys. She wished she'd worn something else. The pants were too heavy for the warm late-summer morning. But she'd promised Kylie she wouldn't wear the dragon jeans, and these were her only other new pants.

"Sophie!"

Kylie rushed up, her blond curls bouncing like hair in a shampoo commercial. She threw her arms around Sophie as if they hadn't seen each other in years, even though they'd talked on the phone just the night before.

"Sorry I'm late," Kylie said breathlessly. "I missed the bus, so my mom had to drive, but she couldn't find the car keys. Boy, was she mad —"

She broke off when she saw Sophie staring at her. "What?" Kylie asked.

"Your jeans," Sophie said.

"What?" Kylie looked at her legs. "Did I spill something on them? What is it? Toothpaste?" She craned her neck, looking for stains.

"You wore *the* jeans," Sophie said, eyeing the red-and-gold dragon on Kylie's left leg. "Kye, we agreed that *neither* of us would wear those on the first day of school. Remember?"

14

Kylie's eyes opened so wide Sophie could see white all around her irises. "Ooooops! I totally forgot, Soph. I was running late, and my mom was yelling at me to hurry. So I grabbed the first thing —"

"Whatever. Forget it," Sophie said, cutting her off. *It's just like Kylie to forget her own rule,* she thought.

"Really, Soph, I forgot. You aren't mad, are you? They're just jeans."

"Right," said Sophie.

The thing was, Sophie knew Kylie hadn't meant to break her rule. She sometimes did things without thinking. Sophie knew that. She was used to it.

So why did she feel so annoyed?

She tried to shrug off the feeling. Sophie didn't like to make a big deal out of things. "So, what do you think of my locker?" she asked, changing the subject.

Her locker was in the sunny southeast corridor on the second floor. Normally, seventh-graders were assigned lockers on the lower floors. But this year their class was bigger than usual, so some of them had been given lockers in the upstairs hallways, near the eighth-graders.

"You're lucky you got a good one," said Kylie. "Mine's across from the cafeteria. The whole hallway smells like barfburgers." Barfburgers was what Kylie called school food, whether it was a burger or not. She claimed it was all made from the same mystery substance, and it all made you want to barf.

"Yeah, it's nice up here," Sophie agreed, looking around.

Kylie suddenly gasped. "And I just saw something that makes it a whole lot nicer! Scott sighting, dead ahead."

Sophie turned. Across the hallway, Scott Hersh was leaning casually against a row of lockers, talking to a friend. As they watched, he turned and put his bag inside the locker directly across from Sophie's.

"I cannot believe your locker is right across from Scott Hersh's!" Kylie's whisper was so loud, Sophie was sure Scott could hear it on the other side of the hallway. "You are the luckiest girl alive."

"I guess."

Sophie didn't get why everyone was so into Scott. He was good-looking, she supposed. He had deep brown eyes and a scar above his lip that gave him a cute, crooked smile. But Sophie thought he seemed aloof and unfriendly. He didn't talk much, and when he did it was only with other football players.

"Trade lockers with me," Kylie pleaded.

"Nope," said Sophie.

"I'll be your best friend."

It was an old joke between them. They had already been best friends for almost as long as either of them could remember. "You wouldn't send your best friend down to barfburger hall, would you?" asked Sophie.

Kylie sighed. "You're right. I could never do that to you. I guess it just means I'm going to be here *all the time*."

"Fine with me."

Just then, there was a ripple in the flow of hallway movement. Several kids turned to look as a quartet of girls strode down the center of the corridor.

In the lead was a petite girl with almond-shaped eyes and long wavy black hair that reached halfway down her back. Everyone in school knew Keisha Reyes. She was head of the cheerleading team and the most popular girl at Meridian. The red-haired girl to her right, walking so close that she matched Keisha's steps, was her best friend, Courtney Knox. Following on their heels were two blonde girls — Amie and Marie Gildencrest, the only identical twins at Meridian Middle School. Courtney, Amie, and Marie were all cheerleaders, too.

As they walked down the hall, the girls shouted greetings to the other popular eighth-graders. Keisha had a perfect smile, Sophie noticed. It was wide and full of even, white teeth. Courtney, on the other hand, looked like she was pouting even when she wasn't. Sophie thought it was because of all the lip gloss she wore.

"Heeeey, Scott!" Keisha called flirtatiously as she passed.

Scott flashed his crooked grin and waved at her.

Someone called Sophie's and Kylie's names. A boy's voice. Confused, Sophie pulled her gaze from the cheerleaders and looked around. There was Joel Leo making his way toward them through the crowded hallway.

Joel had moved in down the street from Kylie the year before, at the beginning of sixth grade. They had become friends riding the bus together. Sophie had gotten to know him a little, too, when she took the bus home with Kylie after school.

"Joel-e-o!" Kylie exclaimed.

"Hey, Joel," said Sophie.

"What's up, guys?" he said. "How was your summer?"

"Oh, you know, the usual," Kylie answered, with a bored wave of her hand. "Jetting to Hollywood. Shopping in London. Sunbathing in Saint Trapeze."

Joel smiled. "You mean Saint-Tropez?"

"Yeah, there, too," Kylie said.

Joel and Sophie laughed. "We mostly hung out at the pool," Sophie told him. "What about you?"

"Yeah, I didn't see you around," Kylie added.

"I was in California helping out on my aunt and uncle's farm," Joel told them. "They grow organic kiwis. Weird, huh?"

"Weird," Sophie agreed. "But it sounds kind of cool, too."

"It was pretty cool. They paid me six dollars an hour to pick fruit, and I got to eat all the kiwis I wanted. I don't really like them, though. Kiwis, I mean. They're all furry."

"Gross!" Kylie said. "So you spent the summer eating furry fruit? Sounds like a blast."

Joel smiled. "Naw, most of my family lives around there, too. I have some cousins who are pretty cool. They taught me how to surf."

The way he said "surf" gave Sophie a little chill. She tried to imagine Joel eating tropical fruit and surfing in southern California. It seemed incredibly exotic compared to hanging out by the pool. Sophie always found Joel slightly mysterious. He didn't look like most of the other boys at Meridian. His hair was long and a little shaggy, and he wore T-shirts for bands that Sophie had never heard of. Even his name was unusual. Joel Leo. If you took off the *J* it was the same spelled forward and backward.

What impressed Sophie most, though, was how laid-back Joel seemed. She couldn't imagine starting middle school in a new town where you didn't know anyone, but Joel didn't seem to mind at all. In sixth grade, he'd been just as friendly with the math nerds as he was with the skaters and the soccer players. As far as Sophie could tell, he wasn't part of any clique. He got along with a lot of different kids.

Sophie noticed how his teeth stood out white against his brown face. *He got tan over the summer,* she thought. *He looks good. In fact, he's cute. Way cute.*

As quickly as the thought came, Sophie pushed it away. Kylie and Joel were neighbors, and their parents were friends. She knew their families sometimes had dinner together, which in Sophie's mind practically made them related. If Kylie found out she had a crush on Joel, she'd never hear the end of it.

The bell for first period rang loudly, startling Sophie out of her thoughts.

"Well, I better go," Joel said. "I'll see you guys later." His eyes rested on Sophie for a moment. She felt the beginnings of a blush creep into her cheeks.

"Later, Joeleo," Kylie said cheerfully.

"Bye," Sophie murmured.

"Hey, by the way, Kylie," Joel said as he walked away, "cool pants!"

Kylie beamed. Sophie gritted her teeth, hating her lime green cords.

Later that day, Sophie stretched her legs across the seat in the last row of the bus. She worked the flavor out of a piece of cinnamon gum.

Kylie was sprawled out on the seat in front of Sophie, and Joel lounged in the seat across the aisle. Sophie was going over to Kylie's as she usually did after school, and both Kylie's and Joel's houses were the last stop on the bus route. The bus was mostly empty now, so they had taken over the back rows of seats.

"I heard Keisha was dating a high-school guy over the summer," Kylie reported.

Kylie had spent the last fifteen minutes reviewing the summer gossip she'd picked up at school. Most of it centered around Keisha Reyes.

"I heard she dumped him right before school started," Kylie went on. "And he spent every night for a week calling her on the phone, crying and begging her to get back together. Can you imagine? A high-school guy!"

"What grade in high-school?" Joel asked.

"I'm not sure. Ninth, I think."

"Big deal. If he's in ninth grade that means he was in eighth grade last year. Which means he's practically the same age as Keisha," Joel pointed out.

Kylie shrugged defensively. "It's just what I heard."

"Anyway, I'm tired of hearing about Keisha Reyes. She's a snob," said Joel.

"Maybe people just *think* she's a snob because she's a cheerleader and she's pretty and popular. Maybe she's actually really nice. She has nice hair," Kylie pointed out.

"That's great logic, Kylie," Joel said. "Just because someone has nice hair doesn't mean she's a nice person."

Sophie sighed and let her attention drift. She wondered what it would be like to have a guy beg you to get back together. The crying part sounded awful, she decided. But it still would be nice to have a guy like you so much he called every night.

Sophie had never had a boyfriend. Not a real one, anyway. In fourth grade a boy named Tyler had asked her to go out with him, but they didn't go anywhere and it didn't really mean anything. But she knew having a boyfriend was different in middle school. Girls held their boyfriends' hands. They hung out by their lockers and went to the movies. They even kissed.

She glanced across the aisle at Joel. He was wearing a black T-shirt that said THE RAMONES in bold white letters. A loop of his long light brown hair fell against his cheek. He tucked it behind his ear. Unconsciously, Sophie brought her hand to her face and tucked her own hair behind her ear.

Joel felt her gaze and looked over. When he met Sophie's eyes, he smiled. Quickly, Sophie turned her attention back to Kylie.

"Anyway," Kylie was saying, "I guess we'll know what they're all like pretty soon. We're probably going to be spending a lot of time with them."

"Spending a lot of time with whom?" Sophie asked. "What are you talking about?"

"Keisha and the other cheerleaders," Kylie told her. "Tryouts for the team are next week. I think we have a shot at making it."

"You're trying out for cheerleading?" Sophie was surprised. Kylie hadn't mentioned it before.

Kylie's smile could have lit up a football stadium. "Nope. *We're* trying out. I signed you up, too!"

There was a squeal of brakes as the bus lurched to a halt at Joel and Kylie's stop. Sophie sat bolt upright and stared over the seat back at her friend. "You did *what*?"

CHAPTER Three

"No. No way. Absolutely not." Sophie squeezed her eyes shut and shook her head from side to side as if trying to erase the idea from the air with her nose.

For the last twenty minutes, Kylie had been telling her how great cheerleading would be. But Sophie wasn't buying it.

"Come on, Soph. It will be fun," Kylie pleaded.

"Fun? Yeah, the way total humiliation is fun," Sophie fumed.

Sophie, Kylie, and Joel were sitting on the deck in Kylie's backyard. A bag of potato chips, a two-liter bottle of soda, and a pack of cherry-flavored licorice whips sat open on the patio table in front of them. Sophie's parents hardly ever bought junk food, and normally she loved eating at Kylie's. But right now she was too angry to be hungry.

25

"I cannot believe you signed me up for cheerleading tryouts without even asking me, Kye. Do I *look* like a cheerleader? I mean, I can't even talk in class without blushing." She glanced at Joel and, as if to prove her point, turned beet red.

Joel didn't seem to notice. "But you used to go to gymnastics meets, right?" he asked casually, reaching into the bag and scooping up a handful of chips.

Sophie had taken gymnastics lessons, all through grade school. She'd won all-around second place in the last citywide meet she went to, just before she quit.

She shrugged. "Yeah. So?"

"So didn't you have to compete in front of lots of people then?"

"That was different," said Sophie, willing her cheeks to return to their normal color. "All that mattered was whether I landed a back handspring or not. I was being judged on my skills, not my hair or clothes or how cool I was."

"It isn't all that different," argued Kylie. "And anyway, you won't be in front of the entire school. The only people who see the tryouts are the coach and the eighth-grade cheerleaders."

"Oh, *only* the eighth-grade cheerleaders. *Only*

the most popular girls in school." Sophie rolled her eyes. "No way, José. Do it without me."

"I *can't* do it without you. You have to try out with a partner. That's the rule."

Sophie located a stray chip on the table. She stabbed it with her thumb, breaking it into pieces. "So find another partner."

With a little huff, Kylie sat back in her chair. "If I'd known you would freak out like this I would have."

Sophie said nothing. She continued to pulverize the potato chip.

Kylie tried a different tack. "Soph, remember last year, when we did the school play?"

The year before, Kylie had gotten a small role in the school play, and she'd convinced Sophie to do backstage crew. It had been Sophie's job to make sure all the actors were in their places and to pull the rope that opened the stage curtains. She remembered the tingly feeling of excitement she'd had standing in the wings with everyone just before they went on.

In fact, most of the exciting things Sophie had ever done had been Kylie's idea. When Kylie ran for class president in fifth grade, she'd made Sophie her campaign manager. It had even been Kylie's idea, back in first grade, to take gymnastics classes together. Kylie had quit after only a month, bored by the endless exercises. It was Sophie who'd gone on to become a gymnast.

But all that was different, Sophie reminded herself. Controlling the curtains backstage was not the same as cheerleading.

"Sophie, I could never have gone onstage every night if I hadn't known you were there watching," Kylie told her now. "And I can't imagine doing this without you, either. It just wouldn't be as fun. So, will you do it? Please? I'll be your best friend."

Sophie swept the chip crumbs off the table and into her open palm. Then she leaned over the edge of the deck and tossed them onto the grass. She thought about how she always went along with Kylie's ideas.

Kylie watched her, waiting for an answer.

"No," Sophie said at last.

Kylie's face tightened. She scraped her chair back and stood up. Without a word, she marched into the house, sliding the screen door shut behind her with a bang. A moment later, Sophie heard the television come on in the Lovetts' living room.

"I think you should do it," Joel said suddenly.

Sophie looked over at him in surprise. "What?"

"I think you should try out."

"Why?" She'd assumed that Joel thought the tryouts were a bad idea, too. "I'd be the worst cheerleader ever. I'd probably make the crowd want to cheer for the other team."

"No, you wouldn't," Joel said. "You'd be good at the cartwheels and handsprings and stuff. Besides, Kylie isn't asking you to be a cheerleader. She just wants you to be her partner for the tryouts."

"But I thought you thought cheerleading was lame. You just said Keisha Reyes is a big snob."

"I said Keisha Reyes is a big snob," Joel replied. "That doesn't necessarily mean I think cheerleading is lame. Look, if you don't make the team, it's no big deal. After a week, no one will even remember that you tried out. And if you do make it, well, you'll be with Kylie, just like she said."

"Kylie only wants to be a cheerleader so she can hang out around Scott Hersh all the time," Sophie blurted.

Joel studied her for a second. "I don't see what's wrong with wanting to hang out with someone you like," he said softly.

Sophie chewed her lip. She felt outnumbered. It was two against one in favor of Sophie Smith trying out for cheerleader. Or make that, cheer*loser*.

"All right," she said with a sigh. "I'll think about it."

"Sophie, you have to *smile*!" Kylie exclaimed. "You look like you're directing air traffic, not rooting for a touchdown."

Sophie stopped midcheer and dropped her arms. "I *was* smiling," she snapped. "Wasn't I?"

"Not unless you call this smiling." Kylie grimaced as if she'd stubbed her toe.

It was Saturday afternoon. The girls were in Kylie's backyard, practicing their routine for the cheerleading tryouts.

Every day after school that week, Sophie and Kylie had gone to training sessions held by the eighth-grade cheerleaders. All the girls who wanted to try out were supposed to pick one cheer and develop a routine with a partner. Tryouts would be the following Monday after school.

With a groan, Sophie flopped down on the grass and covered her face with her arms. "I'm no good at this," she said. "I am going to totally humiliate myself."

"No, you're not," Kylie replied. She marched over, grabbed Sophie's hand, and pulled her back onto her feet. "Now try it again. From the top."

Kylie sat at the edge of the deck, and Sophie stood on the lawn, facing her. "Ready, o-kay!" she shouted.

"We're the Mules, we can't be beat. So clap your hands and stomp your feet. . . ."

She began to go through their routine, lifting her knees, bending her arms into stiff, precise shapes. Sophie actually liked the movements. They reminded her a little of the dance steps in a gymnastics tumbling routine.

"We're the Mules, we make the rules, we trample all those other schools. . . ."

"Bigger smile!" Kylie called out.

It was the smiling that Sophie found hard. She felt like a big dumb Barbie doll with a phony smile plastered across her face.

She stretched her lips wider to show she was trying.

"Now you look like a dog that's about to bite someone," Kylie told her.

Sophie stopped cheering and glared. "I *feel* like I want to bite someone," she said meaningfully.

"Okay." Kylie stood up. "You take a break. I'll practice and you can give me pointers. Be brutal. I can take it."

The girls traded places.

"Ready. O-KAY!" Kylie shouted. She started to move through the cheer.

Watching her, Sophie thought it looked like a completely different routine. Where Sophie tried to be precise and angular, Kylie looked like she was made of rubber. Her kicks wobbled. Her curls bounced. Her arms flapped like wet spaghetti. But Sophie had to hand it to her. Kylie's smile was perfect. From her expression you'd think she'd never had more fun in her life.

By the time she'd finished, Kylie was panting. "What did you think?" she asked between breaths.

"You need to keep your legs straighter on your kicks," Sophie advised. "But otherwise you looked really good."

Kylie plopped down in the grass beside her friend. "I was thinking. We need to have a big ending. Something that will make the judges be all, like, 'Wow!'"

"Like what?" Sophie asked.

"Well, you could do some gymnastics trick," Kylie suggested. "An aerial cartwheel, maybe. Or even a back handspring."

Sophie frowned. "I don't know. They didn't say anything about tumbling at the practices. It seems kind of show-offy."

Kylie rolled her eyes. "Duh, Sophie. Cheerleading *is* show-offy. That's the point. To show off your cool moves and get the crowd psyched."

"Well . . ." Sophie plucked a handful of grass from the lawn. "What would you do?"

"I could do a cartwheel or something. If we're both doing it at the same time, it won't really matter."

"Can you even *do* a cartwheel?" asked Sophie.

"Sure."

"Show me."

Kylie got up from the lawn. Raising her arms over her head, she took a step as if she was about to cartwheel. But at the last second she pulled back. She took another step and faltered again.

"On the count of three," said Sophie. "One, two, *three!*"

Kylie placed both hands on the ground and kicked her legs in the air.

She looks like a donkey trying to buck something off its back, Sophie thought. *Or a cat falling headfirst out of a tree.* One thing was certain, it was no cartwheel.

Kylie righted herself. "I know. Not perfect. But you can coach me, right?"

Sophie sighed. It wouldn't be easy to teach Kylie how to do a cartwheel in a day and a half. But she could see that her friend had made up her mind.

And if they were going to do stunts at the

end of their routine, Sophie thought, they ought to look good. Better than good. They ought to look perfect.

She stood and brushed off the back of her shorts. "Okay," she said, positioning herself next to Kylie. "This is how you start."

CHAPTER
Four

Monday morning, Sophie woke with a feeling of doom.

It stayed with her while she showered and dressed. At breakfast, it turned her cornflakes to glue in her mouth. It made her forget to bring her book to Spanish class, and in social studies, it even made her forget her own last name. She had to think for a minute before she wrote it at the top of her paper.

By the time she and Kylie made their way to the gym after school, the feeling was so strong Sophie was certain it was visible — an ugly gray cloud clinging to her like fog.

"I'm so nervous!" Kylie whispered as they walked through the gym doors.

Sophie nodded. "Nervous" didn't even begin to

cover it. She felt like she was about to walk the plank.

Any minute now, the cheerleading tryouts would begin. Sophie, Kylie, and a group of other seventh-grade girls stood at the back of the gym, waiting for the coach to arrive.

From where she was standing, Sophie could see patches of blue sky out the high gym windows. The weather had finally cooled into the kind of clear September day that normally made her want to spread her arms wide and shout for joy. At that moment she would have given anything to be outside.

She would have given anything to be anywhere but here.

In the center of the gym, the six eighth-grade cheerleaders were sitting at a table that had been set up on the half-court line. Courtney, lip-glossed and perfectly coiffed, as usual. The twins, whose blond hair was braided into identical pigtails. At the end of the table sat the two other girls, named Alyssa Craig and Renee Ramirez. Alyssa was pretty, with arched eyebrows and black hair that curled up at the ends in a smooth flip. Renee was very fair with dark hair she usually wore pulled back in a ponytail. And of course, there was Keisha Reyes, right in the center where she always was.

They were the most popular girls, the royalty of the school. And any minute now they were going to give their undivided attention to shy little Sophie Smith.

To distract herself, Sophie started to go over their routine again in her mind. They had spent all day Sunday in Kylie's backyard practicing over and over until Mrs. Lovett claimed their shouting was giving her a headache and drove them over to Sophie's house to practice there instead. When Sophie had gone to bed that night, she could still hear the words of the cheer ringing in her ears.

The trickiest part was the stunt at the end. The way they'd rehearsed it, Sophie did an aerial cartwheel in one direction while Kylie did a regular cartwheel the opposite way so they crossed each other. It had taken half a day of coaching to get Kylie's cartwheel into shape. When she finally nailed it, Sophie couldn't have been prouder than if they'd actually made the team.

Still, all that practicing hadn't made Sophie any more confident. She knew she wasn't cheerleader material. Even her parents didn't think so. At dinner her father gently reminded her, "It's the effort that counts." And when her mother had come to kiss her good night, she'd told Sophie how proud she was already. Sophie knew that was all code for "We still love you even if you don't make the team."

Sophie closed her eyes. She hid her hands behind her back so no one would see her cross her fingers as she made a wish.

Please, please, please, don't let me make a fool of myself, she pleaded.

She jumped as the door to the gym banged open. A short blond woman walked briskly into the room. She wore a yellow T-shirt that said CHEER ALL OUT OR DON'T CHEER AT ALL. Two other women followed her in.

The blond woman clapped her hands for attention, which wasn't necessary. All talk had stopped the moment she entered the room.

"Okay, ladies!" Her voice seemed to reverberate through the entire gym. Sophie was surprised that such a loud voice could come from such a tiny person.

"I'm Madeline Charge, the adviser for the Meridian Middle School cheerleading squad. If any of you have older sisters, you may already have heard of me. I've been coaching this team for more than ten years, and I like to say that every year our cheerleaders get better."

She flashed a brilliant white smile around the room.

Sophie stared. She had never seen an adult who seemed as perky as Madeline Charge. She just *looked* like a cheerleader, right down to the pink polish on her perfectly painted fingernails.

"Before we begin, I want to introduce you to our two guest judges," Ms. Charge boomed. "This is Ms. Biers. She coaches the Meridian High School cheerleading team." She gestured at the blond woman, who nodded. "And this is Ms. Lytle, captain of the Meridian Community College cheerleaders." Ms. Lytle raised her hand and waved. "Please give them a round of applause. We're very lucky to have them with us today."

The seventh- and eighth-graders dutifully clapped. Ms. Biers and Ms. Lytle beamed like contestants in a beauty pageant. They were very good at smiling, Sophie noticed.

"And of course," Ms. Charge went on, "you already know our other judges, the eighth-grade cheerleaders."

The girls smiled smugly from their chairs.

"So, let me tell you all how this is going to work," said Ms. Charge. She held up a worn-looking baseball cap and explained that each of the teams would draw a number from the hat. That would be the order in which they went. "Got it?" she bellowed.

Around the room, girls nodded.

"Let me just remind you of the rules. When it's your turn to go, take the floor with your partner, say your names, and then start your routine. Your routine shouldn't be longer than one cheer. And no props, including boom boxes. I want to hear you girls shout. Got it?"

They had it. The girls started to shuffle around, straightening their shorts, tying their sneakers, combing their fingers through their hair.

"I'm not through yet, ladies," Ms. Charge boomed. The shuffling stopped. "We have twenty-eight girls trying out," she told them. "There are six open spots on the team. You might end up on the team and your friend might not, or vice versa. I asked you to try out in pairs today because cheerleading is all about teamwork. And teamwork means that you respect your teammates whether they win or lose. I don't want to hear about sore losers or sore winners. Got it?"

There were a few tentative nods.

It was just like adults to stand around giving lectures about teamwork when all the kids wanted to do was get on with the game, Sophie thought. She rolled her eyes at Kylie to say, "Do you believe this garbage?" But Kylie wasn't looking. Her eyes were glued on Madeline Charge like she was the greatest thing since sliced bologna.

"All right," Ms. Charge said, clapping her hands again. "Let's do this!"

She held up the hat. Several girls hurried over to pick numbers.

Kylie nudged Sophie. "Go ahead, you get it," she whispered.

Sophie was glad to move. Her legs felt stiff from standing in one place for so long. She walked over to Ms. Charge and fished a slip of paper out of the beat-up old hat. On it was written the number four.

Four? Four was too soon. Four meant there were only three pairs of girls ahead of them. Sophie's heartbeat quickened. She took a few shallow breaths.

As Sophie turned to bring the slip back to Kylie, she tripped. Her arms flew out and she barely managed to catch herself before sprawling face-first on the floor. Several people turned to look, including Ms. Charge.

Ms. Charge raised her eyebrows and waggled a finger at Sophie's sneakers. Looking down, Sophie saw that one of her shoelaces was untied.

Cheeks burning, she knelt to tie her shoe. *Perfect,* she thought, *now everyone thinks I'm a klutz and a slob.* Again she wished she were anywhere but here.

Sophie stomped back over to Kylie and handed her the slip of paper.

"Great! Four is perfect!" Kylie said brightly. She didn't mention that Sophie had just made a total fool of herself.

Sophie stared at her friend. What had happened to Kylie all of a sudden? How could she act like everything was great and perfect when everything clearly was awful? She was already acting like a cheerleader, and they hadn't even gotten through tryouts yet!

The judges took their seats in the folding chairs behind the table. Keisha passed out clipboards and little pencils.

"How do I look?" Kylie asked Sophie. She was wearing white shorts, a pink T-shirt, and tennis socks with matching pink pom-poms at the heels. She'd parted her blond curls into two springy pigtails that flopped alongside her head like the ears of a cocker spaniel. They looked goofy but cute, Sophie thought.

"Good. Cheerleaderish," Sophie told her. "How about me?" She'd put on a yellow T-shirt and purple track pants. They were supposed to represent purple and gold, the school colors, though the violet of her pants was too dark and her yellow shirt wasn't quite yellow enough.

"Great," Kylie said. "You look great."

"Okay, pair number one, you're up," Ms. Charge bellowed.

Pair number one turned out to be two girls named Trisha and Kate. Sophie knew them. Everyone did. From the first day of middle school, they'd established themselves as the most popular girls in the class. Sophie wasn't even sure how. They just had it — whatever "it" was.

"Dang," Kylie whispered, eyeing Trisha and Kate's identical purple polo shirts. "We should've worn matching outfits. I didn't think of that."

"Ready, let's go!" Kate and Trisha hollered in unison. They started into their cheer. Their moves were tight and their smiles pert. Their claps made crisp popping sounds.

Sophie glanced over at the judges. Keisha and Courtney were smiling as if they were watching their own little sisters. She knew then that Trisha and Kate were in.

When they were finished, Ms. Charge smiled. "Thank you," she said. She wrote something down on her clipboard. Sophie noticed the other judges writing, too.

Next up were two girls who were pretty and well liked. One of the girls had straight blond hair that she'd pulled into a high ponytail. Sophie thought

43

she looked like a younger version of Madeline Charge.

When they were done, Madeline smiled and thanked them, just as she had Trisha and Kate.

"Pair three," she said when she finished writing on her clipboard.

For a second, no one stepped forward. The girls who were waiting their turn began to look around. Had a group forgotten their number?

Suddenly, there was a flurry of movement. Two girls burst from the sidelines, doing round-offs and back handsprings. When they reached the center of the floor they stopped.

"Amy Martin!" one shouted, standing like a soldier at attention.

"Angie Biggs!" the other shouted.

"Ready, O-KAY!" they cried in unison.

Sophie recognized Amy and Angie, but she never knew which was which. Though one had brown hair and the other was blond, they were both blandly cheerful in a way that made it impossible to tell them apart. Sophie had never paid much attention to them before. But now she couldn't tear her eyes away from them.

They must've been practicing for weeks! she thought. Their movements were perfectly in sync.

Their voices seemed to meld into a single, unified shout.

As they reached the end of their routine, Amy sprang into the air, flipping backward in a standing back tuck, while Angie spotted her. When Amy landed, both girls slid into splits, their arms raised over their heads.

The eighth-grade cheerleaders clapped and whistled. The seventh-graders stared with expressions of dismay. Sophie knew how they felt. How could any of them hope to make the team when this was what they were up against?

Madeline Charge looked like she'd just won the lottery. "*Thank you,* ladies," she said, beaming. "That was very good."

She made a note on her clipboard. Sophie imagined her drawing a big star next to Amy's and Angie's names.

"Okay. Group four, you're up," the coach said.

For a second, Sophie thought she wouldn't be able to move. She felt as if someone had injected ice-cold water into her arms and legs. Then Kylie gave her a little nudge, and before she knew it, she was out on the floor.

"Kylie Lovett!" bellowed Kylie in a good imitation of Ms. Charge.

"Sophie Smith," squeaked Sophie. Her mouth felt as dry as the Sahara.

Ms. Charge looked up from her clipboard. "Volume!" she commanded.

Sophie blushed. "Sophie Smith," she managed in a slightly louder voice. She took a deep breath.

"Ready, O-KAY!" Sophie and Kylie said together.

They had practiced their cheer so many times over the weekend that Sophie could have done it in her sleep. Instead, she concentrated on smiling. She grinned so hard her cheeks started to cramp.

In what felt like seconds, the cheer was over and they had come to the tumbling finale. Sophie was upside down in midair when she realized that Kylie wasn't cartwheeling alongside her. Righting herself, she saw that Kylie was frozen, her arms in the air and her eyes wide.

Oh no! Sophie thought. *She's chickening out!*

To stall for time, Sophie did another aerial cartwheel. To her relief, Kylie started to move. But she didn't cartwheel. Instead, she put her hands on the ground and did a big, clumsy somersault, the kind a toddler would do, straight toward the judges.

Kylie came out of the roll with a giant grin on her face. Behind her, Sophie dropped to one knee.

"Gooooooo, Mules!" they shouted.

Sophie quickly got to her feet and hurried over to the sidelines. Kylie was right behind her.

"Wasn't that great?" said Kylie, her eyes shining.

Sophie didn't think so. The eight-grade cheer-leaders were laughing, and so were some of the seventh-graders. She looked over at the judges. The three women had their heads together, talking.

They hadn't talked after any of the other pairs. Not even after Amy and Angie. What were they saying? Had Sophie and Kylie been *that* bad?

Just then, Ms. Charge glanced over at them. When she saw Sophie looking at her, she smiled.

Sophie felt sick to her stomach. The judges were laughing at them, too. Now she was sure of it.

When Sophie got to her locker Tuesday morning, Kylie was waiting for her.

"They've posted the results," she told Sophie. "The list is right outside the counselor's office. The anticipation is *killing* me."

"You could've looked without me," Sophie pointed out. She wasn't in any hurry to see who'd made the team. It still made her cringe to think about the tryouts the day before.

"I'm too nervous. We have to go together. Come on." Kylie grabbed Sophie's arm.

Sophie let herself be dragged down the hall, still wearing her backpack. Kylie hadn't even given her a chance to drop off her things in her locker.

By the time they got to the counselor's office, the crowd around the posted sheet was three girls deep. Sophie would've preferred to wait her turn, but Kylie was already shouldering her way through. Sophie reluctantly followed in her wake.

The list was printed on yellow paper. Sophie felt her heartbeat quicken as she began to run her eyes down the names.

Then her heart almost stopped. There, right at the end of the list, it said SOPHIE SMITH.

She read her name over and over again, hardly believing her eyes. Then, slowly, her disbelief gave way to another feeling. *I made it,* she thought. *I made it! I got picked over all those other girls. Kylie and I are going to be cheerleaders!*

She turned to Kylie, ready to celebrate. But the look on Kylie's face stopped her.

Kylie was frowning.

Sophie turned back to the list. She'd seen Kylie's name, hadn't she? Yes, there it was, at the very bottom of the page.

"Oh!" Sophie said with a little gasp.

The list read KYLIE LOVETT — MASCOT.

CHAPTER Five

"A *mule*!" Kylie moaned.

Sophie, Kylie, and Joel were sitting at one of the outdoor tables in the school quad, eating lunch. Kylie had just finished filling Joel in on the results of the tryouts.

"I mean, do I *seem* like I'd be a good mule?"

Sophie hesitated, thinking of the donkeylike kick Kylie had done in her backyard the day before the cheerleading tryouts. Kylie gave her a wounded look.

"No," Sophie said quickly. "You're nothing like a mule."

"There's nothing mulelike about you. Except for your hooves. And your long ears. And your stubborn personality," Joel teased.

Kylie stuck her tongue out at him. "I went to see Ms. Charge after first period," she told them. "And I was, like, 'Why am I the mule?' She said it was because I was funny at the tryouts. They liked my spirit. She acted like that was a good thing."

"Being funny and spirited *are* good things," Joel pointed out.

Kylie sulked. "What a stupid mascot. Why can't it be the Meridian jaguar? Or the Meridian eagle? Or . . . or the Meridian goddess!"

"They don't make goddesses into mascots," Joel told her.

"But it's a good idea, right?" said Kylie. "I mean, I'm not just thinking of me. Having a mule as a mascot makes the whole school look dumb."

"Mules are strong. They're hardworking. They never give up," said Sophie.

"They're also ugly," Kylie grumbled.

"But in a cute way," said Joel.

"Well, maybe you can tell Ms. Charge that you want to be the Meridian goddess this afternoon," said Sophie. "The first practice is right after school."

Kylie plucked two french fries from her lunch tray, swabbed them around in a pool of ketchup, and popped them in her mouth. She chewed for a moment, then pushed her tray away.

"Ugh. I'm not hungry. This whole mule thing has ruined my appetite. Here, you guys have my fries."

Sophie and Joel reached for fries at the same moment, and their fingers touched. Sophie felt an electric sort of tingle her fingertips. Quickly, she pulled her hand away.

"Anyway, I'm not going," said Kylie.

"Not going where?" Sophie asked distractedly. Under the table, her fingers could still feel the brush of Joel's skin. She avoided looking at him.

"To practice. Forget this stuff. I tried out to be a cheerleader, not a mule."

"But" — Sophie was aghast — "but we're supposed to be doing this together! You promised!"

"Well, you don't have to go, either," Kylie pointed out. "You don't even *want* to be a cheerleader. In fact, why don't you quit? Give the spot to someone who really wants it."

"No!" Sophie said, louder than she'd intended. Kylie and Joel both looked at her. She blushed and lowered her voice. "No. We can't just not show up. We tried out and we made it and now we have to do it. That's just how it is." Sophie always followed through on her commitments. She prided herself on it. And she wasn't going to stop now just because Kylie didn't feel like being a mule.

"Fine," said Kylie, a bit huffily. "I'll go to practice. Jeez."

"Give it a chance," Sophie told her, nodding. "That's what I'm going to do. I'm just going to give it a chance."

"STAR. That's a word I want you to remember. You are all Meridian Middle School STARS."

Madeline Charge stood before the cheerleaders, hands on her hips. Today her T-shirt read THERE IS NO "I" IN "TEAM."

The girls sat on the outdoor bleachers, shielding their eyes against the afternoon sunlight. They could hear the boys' football team practicing at the far end of the field. There was an occasional muffled *thud* as the boys banged into one another in their gear.

"Can one of you explain to our new teammates what STAR means?" the cheerleading coach asked, addressing the eighth-graders.

Courtney raised her hand. "Studies. Teamwork. Athleticism. Responsibility," she said primly. She smiled like the teacher's pet.

"Thank you, Courtney. That's right. Studies. Teamwork. Athleticism. Responsibility." Ms. Charge ticked them off one by one on her fingers. "These are the things that you have to focus on to be the best cheerleaders you can be."

Sophie sensed a lecture coming on. She tried to make herself more comfortable on the hard metal seat.

"First of all, *Studies*," Ms. Charge boomed. Even outside, her voice carried. "You all must maintain a C average. We do grade checks once a week. If anyone falls below a C in any class, we have a conference with your teacher. If you don't pull your grade up within a month, you're off the team. Got it?"

The cheerleaders nodded.

"Teamwork." Madeline paced back and forth in front of them like a drill sergeant. "Cheerleading is not about one person being the center of attention. When you're all in a pyramid, the person at the bottom is just as important as the person at the top."

Blah, blah, blah. Sophie hated lectures. She only ever heard them at school, where the adults acted like kids were social morons. Her parents never lectured. If they were disappointed with her, they said, "How do you think you could have done that better?" But they weren't disappointed very often.

Next to Sophie, Kylie snapped her gum. She'd been fidgeting the whole time Ms. Charge was talking. Sophie noticed that Kylie didn't seem to find the coach quite as fascinating as she had at the tryouts.

"Athleticism," the coach went on. "You girls are athletes, and I want you to think of yourselves that way. It's fine to wave pom-poms, but your kicks better be up by your ears or no one cares."

It was true that the girls who had made the team seemed to have been picked more for their athletic skills than their popularity. Trisha and Kate were in, of course, and so were Amy and Angie. But the pretty girl who looked like Ms. Charge hadn't made it, and neither had some other popular girls who'd tried out. The other seventh-grade cheerleader was a girl named Joy. Her eyebrows arched in a way that gave her a constant look of happy surprise, and she had impressed everyone at the tryouts by doing a perfect toe-touch jump.

"Responsibility," Ms. Charge went on in her megaphone voice. "You're expected to show up at practice on time and ready to cheer. If you have to miss a practice, I want to know *before*. Don't come to me with excuses later. I don't want to hear them."

54

Ms. Charge looked from one face to the next. "You are the STARs of Meridian. But you are all part of the same constellation. One STAR shouldn't outshine the others."

Kylie pretended to stick her finger down her throat. She made a retching noise just loud enough for Sophie to hear.

"Okay. Enough talk," Madeline said, "Now, are you ready to cheer?"

"Yeah!" the other girls cried.

"Uh, Ms. Charge?" Kylie raised her hand. "What should I be doing while everyone else is ... cheering?"

"Oh, Kylie, our multitalented mascot. You can run drills with the rest of the girls today if you like," said Ms. Charge. "Come see me after practice, and we'll set up a time for you to get your costume."

As the girls got up from the bleachers, Keisha sidled over to Kylie. As usual, Courtney followed at her side.

"I just wanted to say I think you will be a *great* mascot," Keisha told Kylie.

"Really?" Kylie looked pleased.

Keisha nodded. "You were hysterical yesterday at tryouts. It took a lot of nerve. I mean, I could never have gotten up there and embarrassed myself like that in front of a bunch of people. But you made it look totally natural."

Kylie's smile froze. "Thanks," she said uncertainly.

"Anyway, I just wanted to tell you that." With a little smile, Keisha and Courtney walked over to the other cheerleaders to warm up.

Kylie turned to Sophie. "I *embarrassed* myself yesterday?"

"I'm sure that's not what she meant," Sophie said quickly. "She probably just meant that your somersault was original."

Kylie glanced at Keisha's retreating back. "She sure had a nice way of saying it."

The girls spent the next hour doing strengthening exercises. They ran stairs on the bleachers. They did sit-ups and stretches. They worked on their high kicks, cartwheels, and jumps.

By the time they were ready to start learning a cheer, Sophie was sweating. It felt good. She realized how much she'd missed working out since she'd stopped doing gymnastics.

Ms. Charge, who had gone to the equipment room to get the pom-poms, left Keisha in charge of teaching the cheer. As the girls got into rows,

Keisha singled out Kylie. "Not you," she said. "You can't stand in the front row."

"Why not?" asked Kylie.

"Because you're not a cheerleader," said Courtney, coming to stand next to Keisha.

"But if I'm here, I might as well learn the cheer. What if you need a sub or something?" Kylie pointed out.

Keisha wrinkled her nose as if Kylie were something stuck to the bottom of her shoe. "Only the cheerleaders do the cheers. That's why they call them *cheerleaders*."

Kylie pressed her lips together. She didn't move.

Sophie glanced around at the other girls. They were all watching. Alyssa, one of the eighth-graders, had her arms folded and a look of disgust on her face, but Sophie couldn't tell if she was disgusted with Keisha or Kylie.

Keisha gave an exaggerated sigh. "If you really want to learn the cheers, you can stand over there." She pointed to a spot behind the back row.

Kylie looked at Keisha for a second. Then, tossing her curls, she lifted her chin and walked to the spot where Keisha was pointing. Sophie started to follow.

"Not *you*," Keisha said, stopping her. "You have

to stand in front. Otherwise, you won't be able to see anything. You're so small."

Sophie gave Kylie an apologetic look and returned to the front row.

Keisha and Courtney taught a short cheer. Sophie, who was standing between Amy and Angie, was surprised that they already seemed to know it.

"We learned it at cheer camp," Angie explained when Sophie asked.

"You went to cheer camp this summer?" Sophie asked, astonished. In their school district, girls couldn't try out for cheerleading until seventh grade. How could they have gone to camp if they weren't even cheerleaders yet?

"Every summer," Angie told her. "It's not a team cheer camp. It's more like pre-cheer camp for girls who want to be cheerleaders. I've wanted to be a cheerleader since I was five."

"I've wanted to be one since I was four," Amy chimed in from Sophie's right. "My mom was a cheerleader, and my grandma was a cheerleader, too. It's kind of a family tradition."

"Stop talking," Keisha barked. Amy and Angie hushed at once.

Amy and Angie had been going to cheer camp since they were in kindergarten? That explained why their tryout routine had been so good. For the rest of the practice Sophie watched them out of the corner of her eye. There was more to Amy and Angie than she'd thought. Granted, it was a little weird that they'd been practicing to be cheerleaders since before they were even in grade school. But Sophie admired the fact that they were so dedicated.

Finally, Ms. Charge reappeared and announced, "That's it for today. See you all here at the same time tomorrow."

As Sophie and Kylie headed over to the bleachers to collect their things, Kylie said, "Cheerleading is harder than I thought."

Sophie grinned. "Before you know it, you'll be doing back handsprings."

"*If* I come back," Kylie reminded her.

"Kylie!" Ms. Charge walked over to them. "I wanted to find time for you to try on your costume. Can you come by the equipment room next Monday after school?"

Kylie hesitated. At that moment, the boys' football team began to straggle off the field, helmets in their hands, their hair tousled and sweaty. Kylie's gaze landed on one tall figure. Her eyes lit up.

"Sure thing," she said, turning back to Ms. Charge.

"Perfect." Ms. Charge smiled her toothpaste-commercial smile. "See you next week, then."

"Don't we have practice tomorrow?" asked Kylie.

"You don't have to come to all the cheerleading practices," Ms. Charge told her.

"But how will I know the routines?"

"You don't have to know every routine. Mostly what you do is . . . improvise. Run around. Do spirit waves. Make the crowd laugh."

"Make the crowd laugh," Kylie repeated. "Right."

When Ms. Charge was gone, Sophie turned to Kylie. "But if you don't come to practice," she began, "that means . . ."

Sophie looked over at the other cheerleaders with a sinking feeling. *That means I'm on my own.*

CHAPTER Six

"One, two, hit!"

At the signal, Sophie pushed off Amy's and Angie's shoulders with her hands. Both Amy and Angie were standing in deep lunges. With her right foot braced on Amy's thigh, Sophie lifted her left foot off the ground and brought it up to the top of Angie's thigh. Now she was standing atop their bent legs, balanced between them. Sophie locked her knees and raised her arms in a V.

She held there for one second ... two seconds ...

Sophie wobbled. Her foot slipped, and she fell onto the grass.

"Nice try, ladies," barked Ms. Charge. "Angie, your lunge needs to be deeper. I should be able to balance a glass of water on top of your thigh.

Sophie, straight arms! I want to see V for Victory, not U for Unsure. And Alyssa," she turned to Sophie's spotter, who was standing behind Amy and Angie. "Where were you? Let's try it again."

As Amy and Angie set up again, Sophie shook out her legs. After a week of practicing straight cheers, Ms. Charge had started them on stunts, like the thigh stand. Sophie had been surprised by how hard even the easy stunts were. If everyone wasn't doing her part perfectly, the lift didn't work. She was beginning to understand why Ms. Charge was so gung ho about teamwork.

Because she was the smallest person on the team, Sophie had been made a flyer, which meant that she got lifted in the stunts. Keisha and Renee, who were also petite, were the other two flyers. The rest of the girls were bases, who lifted the flyers into the air, or spotters, who helped support them in the lifts and made sure they didn't fall.

"You're doing great," Alyssa told Sophie. She nodded at Renee, who was practicing with another group. "Last year, it took Renee weeks to get this down. You learn fast."

"Thanks," Sophie said, blushing.

"Ready to try again?" asked Alyssa.

Sophie nodded and moved to her spot behind

Amy and Angie. She placed her right foot on Amy's thigh and her hands on both their shoulders.

"One, two, hit!" counted Alyssa.

This time Sophie's foot slid off Angie's thigh before she'd even straightened her legs. Alyssa caught her waist to keep her from falling.

"I think it's time for a break," said Ms. Charge.

Inwardly, Sophie groaned. These were the words she dreaded more than any others, even more than the command "Stairs!" which all the girls hated. She would have happily run fifteen minutes of stairs rather than take a five-minute break with the other cheerleaders.

The girls headed for the bleachers to grab bottles of water and sports drinks.

Sophie pulled a bottle of strawberry-kiwi juice from her backpack and surveyed the scene. Keisha and Courtney were sitting side by side in the grass. Trisha and Kate sat right across from them. Ever since cheerleading practices had started, Keisha, Courtney, Trisha, and Kate had become a tight foursome. In fact, the two popular seventh-graders seemed to have edged out the twins in Keisha's favor. Amie and Marie sat slightly to the side, talking more to each other than anyone else. The other three seventh-graders, Angie, Amy, and Joy, hovered around the edges of the group, drawn like iron filings to a magnet. They were all clearly in awe of Keisha.

Alyssa and Renee also sat at the edge of the group, swigging from Gatorade bottles. Unlike the rest of the cheerleaders they didn't even seem to be trying to be part of Keisha's group. Sophie had noticed they usually sat together during breaks, and she had never once seen them sitting with Keisha's posse at lunch.

During these breaks, Sophie was always in agony over where to sit. No matter where she landed, she felt left out, too shy to chime in on the conversation without feeling stupid. For Sophie, this was the worst part of practice. She wished, not for the first time, that Kylie were here with her.

At last she decided to sit next to Joy. She had just settled on the grass when she heard someone say, "Hey, Itsy-Bitsy."

It took a second before Sophie realized that Keisha was talking to her. Keisha hadn't paid much attention to her, except to give her directions when they were practicing cheers.

"Can I have some of your drink?" she asked Sophie. "I love strawberry-kiwi."

Sophie handed over the bottle at once.

Keisha raised it to her lips, then stopped and

gave Sophie a sidelong glance. "You don't have cooties, right?"

Cooties? Sophie thought, baffled. Who talked about cooties in middle school? Still, she didn't want Keisha spreading any rumors that Sophie Smith had cooties. "No," she told her somberly.

Keisha rolled her eyes. "I'm *kidding.*"

"Oh."

Keisha took a long drink. When she was done she gave Sophie an appraising look.

"You're pretty," she said. "You have nice eyebrows. But your hair would look better if you parted it on the left side. And you definitely should use mascara. I don't need it. My eyelashes are naturally long and thick, so it would look weird. But yours are really short."

Sophie wasn't sure what to say, so she just nodded.

"I'm going to call you Bitsy," Keisha decided. "For Itsy-Bitsy, because you're so little." When Sophie didn't say anything, she added, "That's better than if I called you Weensy for Teensy-Weensy, right?"

Courtney laughed, and so did Trisha and Kate. Sophie smiled uneasily. She couldn't tell if Keisha was making fun of her or not.

"All right, ladies! Let's get back to work!" Ms. Charge hollered.

"Thanks for the drink, Bitsy. You're sweet." Keisha handed back the bottle of juice. There was only an inch left in the bottom.

Sophie didn't care. Keisha Reyes had told her she had nice eyebrows. *And* she had said she was sweet. *And* she'd given Sophie a nickname! For the first time since Sophie had started cheerleading, she felt sort of like she belonged.

Maybe, she thought, *I'm starting to fit in, after all.*

Friday night, Kylie and Sophie sat curled on the sofa in the Lovetts' living room. Sophie struggled to keep her eyes open as Kylie flipped through the TV channels, looking for something to watch.

Sophie almost always slept over at Kylie's on Fridays. Usually Sophie could stay up all night watching old black-and-white movies. But now it was only ten o'clock, and she was already yawning.

"There's nothing on," Kylie complained. Kylie was a pro channel-changer. She could never settle on one thing. Even if she liked a show, she still had to keep changing channels to see what else was on. If Sophie wanted to watch an entire movie uninterrupted, she usually had to wrestle the remote out of Kylie's hand.

At last, Kylie shut off the TV. "Let's go to my room," she suggested. "We can paint our nails."

On the way to her bedroom, the girls stopped by the kitchen. Kylie took a box of chocolate chip cookies from the cupboard and two cans of soda from the fridge. As an afterthought, she grabbed a bag of pretzels and a jar of peanut butter. Loaded with provisions, they made their way to Kylie's room.

"So," Kylie said, settling herself on the floor. She popped open her soda and twisted the cap off a bottle of purple nail polish. "Tell me how awful cheerleading is."

"It's really not so bad." Sophie picked up a bottle of pink polish and looked at the name on the bottom. Pink Decadence, it was called. "Some of the stunts are hard. But other than that it's okay."

Sophie set down the nail polish and went over to Kylie's mirror. Flipping her hair away from her face, she examined her stubby eyelashes. "Do you have any mascara?" she asked, sifting through the mess of pens, barrettes, tubes of lip gloss, and other junk atop Kylie's dresser.

"No," said Kylie. "Mascara is gross. Your eyelashes are supposed to keep stuff *out* of your eyes. If you put gunk all over them, it kind of defeats the purpose. Anyway, I thought your mom wouldn't let you wear makeup."

"She won't."

Sophie's mom didn't wear any makeup, and she told Sophie she couldn't wear it until she was sixteen. She liked to say, "If you're going to cover your beautiful face with that junk, you'll have to wait until you can drive yourself to the store to buy it."

"I was just curious to see how it would look," Sophie told Kylie. She flipped her hair out of her eyes again.

Kylie glanced up from the toenail she was painting. "What's up with your hair?" she asked.

"It's just something I'm trying."

"Well, you look like a spaz the way you keep jerking your head like that."

"I haven't trained my part yet, that's all," Sophie told her. "So it keeps falling in my eyes."

"Why don't you just use barrettes like you normally do?"

Sophie shrugged. "Barrettes are boring." She was trying to train her hair to part on the left, like Keisha had suggested, but it kept flopping into her eyes. Sophie actually kind of liked it like that. She thought it made her look sophisticated.

"So, tell me about the last practice," Kylie said. "What did Miss Superego do this time?" Kylie came to practice only on Mondays. Most of the practice she sat around waiting for them to finish a cheer so she could jump into the final pose.

Sophie couldn't blame Kylie for hating the practices; she would have been bored just sitting around, too. But it gave Kylie plenty of time to watch the other cheerleaders. She was the one who'd first pointed out to Sophie that Trisha and Kate were in with Keisha, and the twins were out. The way she made it sound, you'd think she spent every Monday afternoon watching some crazy after-school special, and not just the Meridian Middle School cheerleading practice.

"Who are you talking about?" Sophie asked coolly. She knew whom Kylie was talking about, but she didn't feel like going along with her.

"Are you kidding? Keisha, of course. She's got, like, an ego the size of Lake Michigan."

"I guess she can be bossy. But she *is* head cheerleader. It's kind of her job to be bossy."

"Not just bossy. She's sick with power. Joel calls her the Tyrant."

"When were you hanging out with Joel?" Sophie's face felt warm. She hadn't forgotten the tingle she felt when her fingers had brushed Joel's at lunch that day.

Kylie shrugged. "Earlier this week, when you were at practice."

69

Sophie waited for Kylie to say more. But Kylie was still thinking about the cheerleaders.

"And what about Courtney?" she asked, digging into the box of cookies. "She acts like she's some kind of beauty queen, but she follows Keisha around like a dog on a leash. That's what we can call them. Keisha and Leasha." Kylie laughed.

Sophie frowned. It seemed mean to talk about Courtney behind her back. Courtney had told Sophie she had perfect fingernails. And once she'd loaned Sophie a hair band and hadn't asked for it back. "Ms. Charge says Courtney has the best high kick on the team," she said, feeling she needed to defend her in some way.

"Ms. Charge is a kook," Kylie said through a mouthful of cookies. "'You are all STARs,'" she mimicked. "'But you are all part of the same constellation.' Give me a break."

"Why are you being so negative all of a sudden?" asked Sophie, unable to hide her exasperation. "You were the one who wanted to be a cheerleader in the first place."

"That was before I found out they were all tyrants and followers and kooks."

"Oh? So where do I fall in?"

"Come on, Sophie. I'm not talking about *you*."

"Right."

"Don't freak out. I was just kidding."

Sophie stood up. "I think I'm going to go to bed," she said.

Kylie looked at the clock on her nightstand. "But it's only ten-thirty."

"I'm really tired from practice this week." Sophie crawled into one side of Kylie's double bed and pulled up the covers.

There was a moment of silence.

"You're not much fun tonight," she finally heard Kylie mumble from the floor.

Yeah, well, Sophie thought, *neither are you.*

CHAPTER
Seven

The following week, Sophie was standing at her locker, when she felt a tap on her shoulder. She turned around — and shrieked.

A giant mule face with crossed eyes and buck teeth was hovering just inches away from her nose.

"Gooooo, Mules!" Kylie shouted from inside the head.

"Gosh, Kye, you scared me," Sophie said. She put a hand over her fast-beating heart.

Kylie pulled the costume off her head. "I know. It's frightening," she said. "Ms. Charge couldn't let me into the equipment room after school, so I had to get this now. It doesn't even fit in my locker. I'm going to have to carry it around until the game this afternoon. Of course," she added, eyeing Sophie's uniform, "it's no match for your outfit. Isn't that skirt against school regulations?"

Sophie blushed as she tugged at the hem of her pleated cheerleading skirt. Kylie was right. School rules said that skirts and shorts couldn't be more than two inches above the knee. But when Sophie held her hands at her sides, her skirt barely reached her fingertips.

"I guess they make an exception for cheerleading uniforms," she said unhappily. "Please don't make a big deal about it. It's embarrassing enough as it is."

If Sophie had ever had second thoughts about cheerleading, she was having them now. It was one thing to spend your afternoons tumbling and practicing cheers. It was another to show up for math class wearing a skirt so short it required matching underwear.

Kylie leaned against the locker next to Sophie's and stared across the hallway. "Look how cute he looks in a tie," she said dreamily.

Sophie didn't need to ask whom she was talking about. She glanced over at Scott. He had traded in his usual T-shirt and jeans for a blue button-down, khakis, and a yellow tie. The first big game of the season was that afternoon. Just as the cheerleaders wore their uniforms on game days to show their school spirit, the football players dressed up to show how serious they were about the game.

"Here I am, the love of his life, standing right across the hall," Kylie complained. "I can't believe he hasn't noticed me yet."

Sophie couldn't believe it, either. Kylie was kind of hard to miss. Especially when she was holding a two-foot-high mule head.

"Why don't you go say something to him?" she suggested.

"Like what? 'Marry me?'"

"I was thinking more like, 'Hi, how's it going?'" said Sophie.

Kylie frowned. "I can't just walk up and start talking to him." Suddenly, her face brightened. "Oh! But maybe I could pretend to drop something by his locker! And when I stood up, he'd be standing right there, and I could be, like, 'Hey!'"

"That's not a bad idea," Sophie said.

"You think?"

"Go get 'im, girl."

Kylie took a deep breath and started to head toward Scott's locker.

"Kye?" said Sophie.

Kylie turned. "What?"

"Maybe you should leave the mule head here."

"Oh. Right."

As Kylie set off to make her love connection, Sophie went back to searching for her math book in her locker.

"Hey, Sophie."

Sophie looked up. Joel was standing by her locker door. "How's it going?" he asked.

"Um, fine." *Dang!* Sophie thought. Of all the people in the school, Joel was the last person she wanted to see her in her cheerleading outfit.

"So, are you ready for your first game?" he asked.

She shrugged. Thinking about the game made her even more nervous. "Yeah, I guess. Whatever," she mumbled.

Joel's smile dimmed a notch. "Oh. Well, I just wanted to let you know I'll be there."

Joel was coming to the game? Joel was going to watch her cheer? Whenever she'd pictured herself actually cheering, it had always been in front of a faceless crowd. But of course, that was dumb. The people who would be at the game would be all kids she knew. Like Joel.

"Cool," Sophie said unenthusiastically.

Before Joel could reply, they were interrupted by a commotion across the hall. Sophie turned just in time to see Scott's books go flying from his hands as he tripped over Kylie, who was kneeling right in front of his locker.

Sophie and Joel winced.

"Oh!" Kylie sprang to grab one of the books at the same time Scott did. Their heads collided. As Scott put a hand to his bruised forehead, Kylie got hold of the book. "Here ya go," she said with a radiant smile.

Scott gingerly took the book. He quickly collected the others before Kylie could get to them and walked on down the hall, shaking his head.

A moment later, Kylie came stomping back over to Sophie's locker. Her face was crimson.

"That," she said, "did not go well."

"Let's get fired up!"
Clap-clap-clap-clap.
"We are fired up!"
Clap-clap-clap-clap.

As the football players took the field, the Meridian Middle School cheerleaders tried to get the crowd energized by clapping their hands.

"Really fired up!"
Clap-clap-clap-clap.

As she cheered, Sophie ran her eyes over the crowd in the bleachers. She told herself she wasn't looking for Joel. She was just looking. But when she spotted him sitting with a few other guys from their class, her stomach did a little flip.

"Let's go, Mules!"

Kylie stood to the side of the cheerleaders, wearing her huge mule head and a fuzzy brown jumpsuit. When the cheerleaders hit their final pose, she ran in, slid to a stop on one knee, and threw out her arms as if to say "Ta-da!"

One or two kids in the crowd clapped listlessly. Someone offered a thin whistle.

What's the point of having cheerleaders if no one cheers? Sophie thought unhappily. *And even if they do cheer, is it really going to make a difference?* Suddenly, she wondered what she was doing there at all. Maybe Kylie was right. Maybe she should have quit at the beginning.

Keisha yelled at the cheerleaders to get into formation again. For the next forty-five minutes, they ran through cheer after cheer. They did defense cheers when the other team had the ball and offense cheers when Meridian got it back.

Whenever Meridian did something good, the girls raised their arms and kicked their legs high.

The whole time, Sophie kept one anxious eye on Keisha. She didn't know much about football, and she was afraid she'd cheer for the wrong team if she wasn't careful.

By halftime, Sophie's voice was hoarse from shouting. Her cheeks hurt from forcing a smile she didn't really feel.

The Meridian marching band strode onto the field, playing a wobbly version of "Stars and Stripes Forever." A plump, curly-haired boy holding a pair of cymbals brought up the rear. Sophie didn't recognize him. She thought he must be a sixth-grader, new to the band. Every few steps he happily bashed the cymbals together, heedless of the music.

Watching the cymbals player, Sophie began to giggle. Suddenly, the whole situation seemed upside down. Shy Sophie had become a cheerleader. Stylie Kylie was a mule. And the cymbals player . . . well, she didn't know where he belonged, but it clearly wasn't in the band.

It was all like one big accident. The idea struck her as funny. At that moment, the cymbals crashed again, making Sophie giggle harder.

She glanced up at the stands and saw Joel laughing. He looked over and caught Sophie's eye, and she knew he'd noticed the cymbals player. They smiled, sharing the joke. Sophie surprised herself by giving him a little wave. He waved back.

Just then her eyes fell on Kylie. She was running in front of the bleachers, trying to get the crowd to do the wave. Everyone ignored her.

Sophie's smile faded. She couldn't see Kylie's face inside the mule head. But from her slumped shoulders, Sophie could tell she wasn't having a good time.

For the rest of the game, when she wasn't watching Keisha, Sophie watched Kylie. When Meridian got the ball, the mascot jumped up and down. She tried again to get the crowd to do the wave. But as the game wore on, Kylie jumped less and less. Soon her feet barely left the ground.

Meridian lost the game, 14–7. Sophie was headed over to commiserate with Kylie when she spotted her mother coming down the bleachers toward her.

"Mom!" said Sophie. "What are you doing here? I thought you weren't going to pick me up until five-thirty."

"I snuck out of work early," her mother confessed. "I left behind a whole stack of work. I didn't want to miss your first game."

Sophie's mother was a librarian at the local

college where her father worked as a dean. Both her parents took their jobs very seriously. They almost never missed work, even when they were sick.

"You were wonderful, sweetheart," her mother said, putting an arm around her. "All those high kicks. And some of those cheers were very . . . clever. Like little poems."

Sophie smiled. She had the feeling this was the first football game her mother had ever been to. Her parents weren't exactly the sports-going type.

Both her mother and father had been astonished when their shy, quiet daughter told them she'd made the cheerleading team. Astonished, and a little concerned. "Well, I always said you could do whatever you put your mind to," her father had blustered. "But it won't get in the way of your schoolwork now, will it?" "That's amazing, sweetie," her mother had said, not even bothering to hide her surprise. "Is that what you really want to do?" Sophie couldn't exactly blame them. She could hardly believe it herself.

So Sophie was surprised and pleased that her mother showed up at the game. She knew she was trying to be supportive.

"You were wonderful, too, Kylie," Sophie's mom added as Kylie walked up holding her mule head.

"Thanks, Mrs. Smith," Kylie said dispiritedly. "But I know I stank."

"Well, I don't know much about mascots, but I thought you were terrific. I'm taking you both out for ice cream to celebrate," said Sophie's mom.

Another surprise. Sophie's eyebrows shot up. Her parents hardly ever bought sweets. Their idea of a tasty dessert was fresh fruit and yogurt.

Her mother caught her look. "It's a treat," she said. "Don't tell your dad."

"Thanks, Mrs. Smith," said Kylie, "but I'm not really hungry. I think I'm just going to catch the late bus home."

"We can give you a ride, Kylie," Sophie's mom volunteered.

Kylie shook her head. "That's okay. See you, Soph."

"I'll call you later," Sophie said. She watched as Kylie shuffled away, her mascot head tucked under her arm. She knew Kylie was upset about the game, and she wanted to talk to her. But her mom seemed so excited about the treat she had planned. Sophie didn't want to leave her hanging.

"Shall we go?" said Mrs. Smith.

Sophie nodded. "Ice cream, here we come!"

CHAPTER Eight

The next two games didn't go any better for the football team — or for Kylie. Though she wore herself out running up and down in front of the crowd, trying to get them to do waves, they mostly ignored her.

Sophie could tell her friend was growing more and more discouraged. She started to dread game days, more for Kylie's sake than anything. At the same time, she worried that Kylie would quit. Sophie didn't want to be stuck going to games without her.

Then, on the afternoon of the fourth game, Kylie didn't show up.

Sophie watched for her while the cheerleaders warmed up, and through their first several cheers. When Kylie still wasn't there by the second quarter of the game, Sophie started to realize she wasn't coming.

But by then the Mules were ahead. Sophie forgot about Kylie for a moment. It looked like the football team might actually have a chance at winning a game.

The Mules scored a touchdown. The crowd cheered. Sophie kicked her leg up by her ear to show how happy she was.

Keisha gave them the signal to take their places for another cheer.

"Are. You. Ready. For. M-M-S.
Are you ready
To be challenged
By none but the best!"

They were halfway through the cheer when Sophie realized that some people in the crowd were laughing.

Are they laughing at us? she wondered.

She looked around. Kylie, wearing her mule costume, had finally arrived. She was standing behind the cheerleaders, trying to follow along with the cheer. But since she hadn't learned it, her moves were all one step behind.

The cheerleaders finished their cheer with high kicks and cartwheels. Out of the corner of her eye, Sophie saw Kylie trying to lift her leg into the air. The huge mask made it difficult. Her wobbly kick looked especially funny.

The crowd laughed again.

Encouraged, Kylie put her hands on the ground and kicked her feet in the air in one of her lopsided cartwheels.

"Go, Mules!" someone shouted.

Sophie glanced over and saw Keisha watching Kylie. She had her hands on her hips and was frowning.

For the rest of the game, Kylie cheered right alongside the cheerleaders. When she didn't know the moves, she made them up. The crowd seemed to love her. They laughed and hollered every time she started dancing.

By the end of the game, the Mules had won, 21–6.

Afterward, Sophie was collecting her pom-poms when Kylie walked up. She was holding the mascot head under one arm. Her cheeks were pink and the curls at her temples were damp with sweat. "Can you unzip me?" she asked Sophie. "This costume is crazy hot."

Sophie unzipped the back of the furry suit. "Where were you at the beginning of the game?" she asked. "I was looking for you."

"I lost my head."

"You what?"

"I lost my mule head. I accidentally left it somewhere."

"Where?"

"In the janitor's closet in the basement."

Sophie looked at her. "You mean 'accidentally' on purpose?"

Kylie gave her a sheepish smile. "Yeah. I guess I thought if I didn't have the head, I wouldn't be able to come to the games anymore. Lucky for me, the janitor found it and brought it to Ms. Charge. And Ms. Charge *made sure* I got to the game."

Sophie giggled. "I'll bet she did. I'm glad you made it, though. You were really good. Everyone was laughing."

Kylie grinned. "Yeah, they were, weren't they? It was actually pretty fun acting so goofy. I figured I already looked so dumb, I had nothing to lose."

Over the next couple of weeks, Kylie made Sophie teach her some of the cheers. Then at the games, she mixed them all up, adding her own crazy moves.

She was a hit. The crowd cheered even louder when Kylie came onto the field.

Even at school people started to say "Go, Mules!" whenever they saw Kylie. Sophie thought it was kind of embarrassing. But Kylie just laughed. Sophie could tell she liked the attention. Kylie liked most kinds of attention.

Sophie herself was actually starting to like cheerleading. At practices, Keisha and the other girls treated her as part of the group. She'd become the best flyer, nailing the stunts almost as soon as Ms. Charge taught them. The games were better, too. Sophie didn't have to keep reminding herself to smile — it had started to come naturally.

Sophie couldn't tell if all the cheering actually made a difference to the game. But something seemed to be working. By the middle of October, the Meridian Middle School football team had started to come around from their losing streak.

One afternoon, after winning another game, Sophie and the other cheerleaders were in the locker room, when Keisha walked up. "Hey, Bitsy."

"Hey, Keisha!" said Sophie. "Good game, right?"

"Yeah, it was good. So, I wanted to let you know, I'm having a party next Saturday," Keisha said. "You can come. All the cheerleaders are invited."

"Really?" Sophie's eyes widened. "Great, I'll ask my —" She stopped herself. Maybe it wasn't cool to say you had to ask your mom. "I'll be there," she finished.

Keisha nodded. "I'll e-mail you the address. By the way, Bitsy, your hair looks really good these days. See ya." With a little wave, she walked back over to where Courtney, Trisha, and Kate were waiting for her. Sophie watched as they picked up their bags and left.

A few lockers down, Alyssa was folding her uniform into a gym bag. Sophie turned to her, excited. "So you're going to Keisha's party?" she asked.

Alyssa shrugged. "Probably not. Next Saturday is Renee's parents' anniversary. She's got to babysit her little brother and sister. I told her I'd help out."

Alyssa was choosing babysitting over a party at Keisha's house? Sophie stared at her in disbelief. "Wow, too bad for Renee," she said. "But she could probably get someone else to help out, couldn't she?"

"She probably could," said Alyssa, "but I already told her I would. I don't back out on my friends just because Keisha snaps her fingers." There was an edge to her voice.

Alyssa zipped up her bag. "See you tomorrow!"

she said. Swinging her bag over her shoulder, she headed out the door.

Well, Sophie thought, *whatever Alyssa's problem with Keisha is, it has nothing to do with me.* She smiled and hugged herself. She was invited to a party at an eighth-grader's house. And not just any eighth-grader, but Keisha Reyes, the most popular girl in school!

"Serious shivers!" Sophie murmured.

"What's serious shivers?" Kylie asked, walking up behind her.

Sophie turned to her with a grin. "Guess what? We're invited to a party at Keisha's house!"

CHAPTER Nine

All week, Sophie carried the words around with her like a charm. "You are invited." They made her feel different — prettier, more interesting. It was as if she had been cast under a magic spell and transformed into someone cool.

She wasn't the only one who noticed. Lately, kids Sophie hardly knew were saying hi to her in the halls. And not just anyone, but popular kids, the ones who had hardly even looked at her last year. But last year, Sophie reminded herself, she would have blushed and ducked away. The new, cool Sophie was much more outgoing.

"Are you running for class president or something?" Kylie asked her as they walked to class on Thursday.

"What are you talking about?" said Sophie.

"You've been saying hi to practically every person we pass. It's like you're on a campaign."

Sophie frowned and shook her hair back from her eyes. "They said hi to me first," she retorted. "I'm just saying hi back."

Kylie gave her a funny look. "Right. Whatever. So, I was wondering, do you want to come over after school today? I figured since you don't have cheerleading practice you'd have time. There's some stuff I want to get ready for the game tomorrow."

The game the next day was with Northwest Middle School, Meridian's main rival. Ms. Charge had given the cheerleaders the day off, with instructions to carbo-load and get lots of rest. Sometimes Sophie thought Ms. Charge forgot that they were just cheering and not actually playing the game.

"I'd like to," Sophie told Kylie apologetically. "But I can't. My mom and I are going shopping together this afternoon."

Ever since she'd gotten the invitation to Keisha's party, Sophie had been aware of a new problem. She had nothing to wear. Normally, she took all her fashion problems straight to Kylie. But Kylie didn't really seem interested in talking about the party. Every time Sophie brought it up, she changed the subject.

Not that she'd had much chance to bring it up.

Sophie had hardly seen Kylie all week. Twice when Sophie had gone to meet her at her locker for lunch, Kylie hadn't been there. So Sophie had sat with some of the other cheerleaders instead. She'd always scooted over to make room for Kylie when she finally arrived in the cafeteria. But each time Kylie had walked right by as if she didn't see her.

Sophie knew something was wrong. But Kylie wasn't saying anything, so neither did Sophie. She didn't want to make a big deal out of it.

In the meantime, Keisha's party was in two days. Sophie was starting to realize that if she was going to find an outfit she would have to take matters into her own hands.

"You're shopping with your mom? That's cool," said Kylie. "Maybe she could drop you off at my house afterward. You could have dinner with us. My mom's trying to close a deal on a house, which means we'll probably be ordering Chinese."

"I can't," Sophie said with a sigh. "I really need to catch up on my homework. I've been so tired after practice this week, I haven't had time to get to it all."

"Oh, okay. Well, do you think you could help me after school tomorrow? I'm going to have a lot of stuff to carry."

They had arrived at Sophie's Spanish classroom. Sophie paused at the door and smiled. "Sure thing," she said to Kylie.

"How about these, sweetheart?" Sophie's mom said. She held up a pair of shorts for Sophie's inspection. Each pocket had a big calico heart stitched onto it.

Sophie cringed. They had been browsing through the store for half an hour, and so far her mother had managed to pick out twenty things that would have been absolutely perfect if Sophie were a six-year-old.

"They have rules about shorts at school," she reminded her mom. *Rules about not looking like a total dork,* she added to herself.

Sophie was starting to worry. The department store would close in an hour, and she still hadn't found the perfect outfit for Keisha's party. Plus, she had an extra errand she needed to do without her mother around.

"Actually, Mom, it might take me a little while," Sophie said. "Do you want to go to the shoe department? I can meet you there."

"Are you sure? You'll be okay here?" asked Mrs. Smith, a twinkle forming in her eye at the mention of shoes. Sophie's mom loved shoes. She owned pairs and pairs of loafers, clogs, sandals, and flats, all in unthrilling shades of brown, black, and beige. It was a great mystery to Sophie that someone could have such an enormous shoe collection and still not own a single interesting pair.

When her mom was gone, Sophie began quickly to riffle through the clothes on the racks. She considered a T-shirt with a graphic of a cat, then put it back. She looked at a denim miniskirt with a frayed hem, a jeweled camouflage tank top . . . nothing seemed right. Sophie wished Kylie were with her. Kylie could plunge her hands into the sale rack and pull out a dazzling outfit. She was a magician that way.

Then Sophie rounded a corner and saw it. A soft jade-colored sweater, as thin as tissue paper. It was paired with dark gray jeans that had a design in rhinestones on the back pocket.

"Please let them come in my size," she whispered aloud.

They did. The jeans fit like they'd been made just for her, and the sweater was the softest thing she'd ever felt against her skin. It was the perfect outfit for Keisha's party.

When she looked at the price tags her heart nearly skipped a beat. The jeans were almost a hundred dollars. The sweater, which turned out to be made of cashmere, cost even more.

Sophie had never spent that much money on anything in her life. She couldn't imagine spending it on a single outfit. And yet . . .

She didn't let herself think about it. Her mind was blank as she walked over to the cash register and took out her credit card. She watched numbly as the cashier rang up her purchases.

As soon as the clothes were in a shopping bag, Sophie felt better. It was done, and there was no going back. Now she had just one more errand.

The cosmetics counters were located on the first floor, just across from the women's shoe department. Sophie went to the counter at the far end of the store, away from the shoes. She hovered in front of the display case, waiting for the saleswoman to notice her.

"Can I help you?" the woman asked at last. She had bright red lips and silvery eye shadow.

"I'd like some mascara," Sophie told her.

"Which kind?"

Sophie was confused. "The kind that goes on eyelashes?"

The woman's red lips pinched in what Sophie took to be a smile. "What would you like it to *do*? Condition? Thicken? Lengthen?"

"Oh, lengthen," Sophie said quickly. "And thicken, maybe."

"That kind comes in six colors. Soft black, midnight black, blue black, brown —"

"Soft black is fine," Sophie interrupted. She wished the woman would hurry. Her mother could show up any minute.

The woman took a slender box from beneath the counter. "That will be seventeen dollars and twelve cents."

Sophie swallowed. She knew it would have been cheaper to buy mascara from the drugstore. But she couldn't think of a reason to give her mother for going to the drugstore. And besides, the saleswoman was already ringing up her purchase.

Sophie took out her credit card.

A few moments later, she found her mother in the shoe department, surrounded by open boxes.

"Done already?" Mrs. Smith said. She stuck out her feet for Sophie's inspection. She wore a tan loafer on one foot, a brown one on the other. "What do you think? Tan or brown?"

Sophie thought they looked equally boring. "Brown, I guess."

Mrs. Smith sighed. "I really shouldn't get anything. So what did you buy?" she asked, spotting Sophie's shopping bag.

"Not much. Just some jeans and a sweater."

"That's all?" said her mother. "You're just like

your father. So practical. I should take a lesson from you. I really don't need any more shoes." She turned her attention back to her feet, then sighed and told the salesman, "I guess I won't get anything today."

She slid her feet back into her own shoes and watched as he packed up the boxes and took them away. She gave Sophie a little regretful smile. "They were too expensive. I guess we can't buy everything we want just because we want it, can we?"

"No," said Sophie, trying to swallow around the lump of guilt in her throat. "I guess we can't."

Sophie blinked her eyes and scanned the crowd assembling on the bleachers. She was looking for Joel. He had been to every football game this season, and Sophie figured he wouldn't miss the big game against Northwest. But she hadn't seen him all afternoon.

Sophie blinked a few more times. Her eyelashes felt like they were wearing little sweaters. Just before the game she'd been in the girls' bathroom, practicing putting mascara on with Trisha and Kate. They were impressed by the brand she'd bought, and Sophie had congratulated herself on getting such a good kind. She hoped Joel would get a chance to see her with her new lengthened and thickened lashes.

I'll have to tell Kylie, Sophie thought. *Maybe she won't think mascara is so gross when she sees how good I look.*

Kylie! Sophie's heavy eyelashes flew open. She'd told Kylie she would meet her in the equipment room after school. But then she'd started talking about makeup with Trisha and Kate, and she'd forgotten all about it. It was too late to go now. The football players were lining up for the kickoff, and Keisha was already signaling the cheerleaders to get ready for their first cheer.

The game got off to a close start. In the first quarter, Northwest scored two touchdowns, and Meridian scored one. But in the second quarter, Meridian's kicker missed a field goal. The receiver fumbled two important passes. Northwest started to pull ahead.

At halftime, Northwest was winning, 24–7. The cheerleaders were pulling out all their best cheers. But as the team continued to fall behind, the crowd seemed to grow more and more discouraged.

"Where's Kylie?" a couple of the other cheerleaders asked Sophie. Each time Sophie shrugged, fighting an uneasy feeling. She wondered why Kylie had wanted her help in the equipment room. Was it her fault that Kylie wasn't at the game now?

Halftime was almost over when Sophie spotted

Joel standing at the edge of the field. She waved and started to head over to ask if he'd seen Kylie. Joel seemed to look right at her, but he didn't wave back. A second later, he turned and walked away.

Sophie stopped in her tracks. Had he not seen her?

Just then, Kylie arrived. She was wearing her mule costume and carrying what looked like a large piece of white paperboard.

She marched over until she was standing right in front of the bleachers. She turned to face the crowd and held the sign up in front of her.

Kylie's back was to the cheerleaders, so Sophie couldn't see what the sign said. But a few kids who were sitting in front read it out loud. "MULES RULES."

Kylie tossed the sign away. There was another sign underneath it.

"NUMBER ONE," the kids read. "BE COOL."

More people had started to look. Kylie tossed that sign away and held up the next one.

"NUMBER TWO: DON'T DROOL." Several kids laughed at that one.

"NUMBER THREE," they joined in reading, "CHEER LIKE FOOLS . . ."

Kylie held up another sign.

"FOR YOUR SCHOOL!"

Kylie threw that away and held up the last sign. "CUZ THE MULES RULE!" everyone in the bleachers shouted.

Kylie threw down the sign, put her hands on the ground, and bucked her feet in the air.

The crowd cheered. They made so much noise that the fans from the other team turned to see what they were yelling about.

For the rest of the game, whenever there was an important point to be scored, Kylie held up the MULES RULES sign, and the crowd roared. When the Mules made a touchdown, Kylie did a crazy dance and bucked her feet in the air, and everyone yelled, "MULES RULE!"

The only people who didn't seem to love Kylie were some of the cheerleaders. From the look on Keisha's face, Sophie could tell she was getting seriously annoyed.

The team seemed to respond to the cheers from the crowd. By the end of the game, the Mules had managed to come from behind. The final score was 24–21. Northwest won by three points.

"That was cool, Kylie," Renee said after the game as the cheerleaders collected their things. "Mules Rules. That's really clever."

Kylie was sitting on the bleachers. She had taken her mask off and was using one of the paperboard signs to fan her face. "I'm glad you think so," she said coolly. She didn't sound like she meant it.

Sophie wished for once that Kylie would try to be friendlier to the cheerleaders. Sometimes she acted like they were playing on different teams.

"No, really," Angie piped up, oblivious to Kylie's attitude. "I think you made a big difference. The team really came back with all those people cheering."

"She didn't make a difference," said Keisha, giving Angie a withering look. "We *lost* the game."

Angie seemed to shrink.

"But we didn't lose by much," pointed out Alyssa.

Just then, Ms. Charge hustled over. "Terrific, Kylie!" she boomed. "That is *just* the sort of spirit and creativity we need on this team. Well done! But next game, be on time."

"Thanks, Ms. Charge," Kylie said sweetly. "I will." She looked directly at Keisha as she spoke.

Keisha narrowed her eyes. Then she turned and stalked away. Courtney, Trisha, and Kate trailed after her.

When the group had broken up, Sophie sat

down next to Kylie. "Um, when did you make all those signs?"

"Last night, when you were shopping with your mom." Kylie gave her a steady look. "Joel came over and helped me. He also helped me carry them *today*, when you *didn't* meet me in the equipment room."

Sophie flushed. "Kye, I'm sorry about that. I . . . got busy doing something."

"Yeah, I guess you're really busy these days."

"It's just that . . ."

Sophie wanted to explain how being a cheerleader was more complicated than she'd imagined. You had to say hi to the right people in the halls and have the right clothes and nice eyelashes. And when girls like Trisha and Kate wanted to hang out, you couldn't just say no. Sometimes it was hard to keep track of everything you were supposed to do.

Instead, she said, "It's like the STAR thing Ms. Charge always talks about. You know, studies and being part of the team and training and all — I've got a lot going on."

"Did you ever notice," Kylie said slowly, "that STAR backward spells RATS?"

Sophie stared at her. Suddenly, she was angry. Why should Kylie get all bent out of shape just because once — just once — Sophie hadn't showed up? What about all the times Kylie had flaked out on Sophie, or gone back on her word, and Sophie hadn't said a thing? Well, she had something to say now.

"You're just jealous that I made the team and you didn't," she told Kylie.

Kylie drew back like she'd been slapped. Without a word, she stood up and started to collect her things.

But there were too many things to carry. When she tried to pick up the signboards, she dropped her mask. She grabbed the mask, and more signs slipped from her grip.

Sophie watched her, filled with regret. As soon as the words had left her mouth, she wanted to take them back — even if they were true.

"Let me help you," she said contritely.

"I don't need your help," Kylie snapped.

Sophie picked up the signboards anyway. With her assistance, everything was soon precariously balanced in Kylie's arms.

Kylie started to leave. A few steps away, she paused and turned. "Soph."

"What?"

"You'd better wash that stuff off your eyes

before your mom sees you. It's all down your face. You look like a raccoon."

Sophie rubbed a finger under her eye. It came off black. "Thanks," she said.

Kylie nodded and walked away. Sophie watched her go. Even angry, Kylie still had her back.

CHAPTER Ten

The large brick house was set back from the street, in the middle of a rolling green lawn. In the dim twilight, Sophie thought it looked like a great rocky island floating in an emerald sea.

She double-checked the number on the invitation: 2014 Rightside Drive. This was it.

Sophie let her father drive past it. When they reached the house next door, she said, "This is it, Dad!"

Mr. Smith steered the station wagon over to the curb. Sophie hadn't wanted him to stop right in front of Keisha's house. She was keenly aware of how dirty the Smiths' old station wagon seemed compared to the shiny SUVs and sedans parked in the driveways of the neighboring houses.

Normally, Sophie didn't pay attention to things

like cars. But somehow she had the feeling that Keisha did.

She leaned over and gave her father a peck on the cheek. "Thanks, Dad."

"Thanks, Mr. Smith," Kylie and Joel echoed from the backseat.

"Have fun," Mr. Smith said. "I'll be back at eleven to pick you up."

The kids got out of the car. Sophie waved good-bye to her dad, then turned and started up the walkway of the house in front of them.

As soon as Mr. Smith pulled away, she began to cut across the lawn toward Keisha's house.

"What are you doing?" asked Joel. "I thought you said it was this one."

"I made a mistake," Sophie said, holding up the invitation. "It's actually 2014, not 2016. It was hard to read the numbers in the dark."

It had been Kylie's idea to invite Joel to come to the party with them. After their argument the day before, Sophie had had to beg her to come. Kylie had finally agreed, but only if Joel came, too.

Not that Sophie minded. She hoped Joel noticed how nice she looked in her new clothes. She had added a silver necklace with a heart charm, and she'd worn her best sandals, the ones with the wraparound straps, even though the night was cool. Sophie had decided to forget the mascara. She didn't want to find it smeared all over her face halfway through the party.

Joel and Kylie followed Sophie across the grass. The sprinklers had been on, and Sophie could feel the cuffs of her almost-one-hundred-dollar jeans getting soaked.

When they reached the front door, Sophie rang the doorbell. A little girl with black hair like Keisha's answered the door. She stared at them without saying anything.

"Hello!" Kylie said, bending over to smile at her. "Who are you?"

The little girl stuck out her tongue and ran away. A moment later a woman came to the door.

"I'm sorry," she told Sophie and her friends. "That was Missy. She really wanted to answer the door. I'm Mrs. Reyes. Come on in." Mrs. Reyes stood aside to let them pass. "The rest of the kids are downstairs. Just go down the hall and you'll find the stairwell."

The Reyeses' entire basement had been converted into a huge rec room. On one side of the room, a group of eighth-grade boys were sprawled out on couches, watching music videos on a widescreen TV. On the other side of the room, the girls were clustered around a built-in bar. Some perched on bar stools, while others stood. They nibbled on chips and snacks from bowls that sat on the counter.

Trisha and Kate were there, of course. And so was Courtney, wearing more than her usual amount of makeup. The twins, hair plaited in matching French braids, sat on either side of Keisha. Amy, Angie, and Joy hovered together over a bowl of corn chips, looking thrilled to be there. Alyssa and Renee were the only cheerleaders missing.

The girls all looked up when Sophie, Kylie, and Joel walked in. Sophie saw Trisha lean over to Courtney and whisper something in her ear. Courtney smirked.

Keisha was sitting on a bar stool sipping a can of soda with a straw. She watched as Sophie walked over to her.

"Hey, guys," Sophie said to the cheerleaders. "Hey, Keisha."

"Hi, Bitsy," Keisha said coolly. "Glad you could make it." She glanced over Sophie's shoulder at Kylie and Joel. "I guess you brought the whole Mule train with you."

A few of the cheerleaders snickered.

Sophie hesitated. As the cheerleaders went

back to their conversation, she pulled Joel and Kylie aside. "Maybe you should go hang out with the guys," she suggested to Joel in a whisper.

Joel looked over at the boys. They were all eighth-grade football players. " I don't know any of those guys," he said.

Sophie started to feel nervous. She wanted to talk to Joel. But he wasn't exactly going to fit in with the cheerleaders. "Well, what else are you going to do?" she hissed. "You can't stand around chitchatting with the girls."

Joel gave her a funny look. Immediately, she was sorry she'd said it that way. "I think we should bail," he said.

"But we just got here!" Sophie protested.

"I'm with Joel," Kylie agreed. "I'm getting bad vibes."

"You can't leave yet, Kylie. Scott Hersh is here." Sophie pointed over to a couch where Scott was slumped, his eyes glued to the TV.

Kylie's eyes flicked toward him. "I don't like him anymore," she told Sophie. "I don't know why I ever did. He's just a dumb jock."

Sophie stared at her in surprise. Since when had Kylie stopped liking Scott? "Well, we can't leave now. It would be rude," she argued. "And besides, my dad's not coming to pick us up until eleven."

"We don't have to wait for your dad," Kylie said. "We can walk to the Esplanade and call one of our parents to pick us up." The Esplanade was an outdoor mall with upscale stores and a fancy restaurant. It was only about half a mile from Keisha's house.

Sophie didn't want to leave. She'd been waiting for this party all week. And Keisha would think she was weird for leaving five minutes after she arrived. So she said the last thing she could think of to get her friends to stay. "You guys are being lame."

Joel looked at Sophie silently. Then he said, "Come on, Kylie." A minute later, the two had disappeared up the stairs.

Sophie wandered back over to the cheerleaders.

"Where're your friends?" Keisha asked.

"They had to leave."

"Too bad," Keisha replied. "Kylie probably just left to get attention. She wants everyone to miss her."

"Boo-hoo," Courtney said sarcastically.

"So, Bitsy, are you, like, best friends with Mulegirl?" Keisha wanted to know.

"Why?" Sophie said carefully.

"Just asking. I think she looks really stupid at the games, dancing around like that and messing up the cheers. It makes everyone look bad."

"It does?" said Sophie. "But isn't that what she's supposed to do?"

"Last year the mascot just ran around and got the crowd to do the wave and things. He was a guy. I think it's kind of weird for a girl to be a mascot, don't you?"

"Maybe." Sophie couldn't see how it mattered whether there was a guy or a girl in the costume, since no one could see who it was, anyway. But she wasn't going to say so to Keisha.

Sophie nibbled on a handful of snack mix and listened halfheartedly as the other girls gossiped about boys at school. She couldn't stop thinking about the way Joel had looked at her right before he left, as if he were making some kind of decision about her. She half wished that she had left the party with him and Kylie.

But I'm here now, she told herself. *I might as well enjoy it.* She tried to tune back in to the conversation.

The girls were admiring Keisha's bracelet. "I always wanted a charm bracelet like that," Joy gushed.

Sophie nodded. "Serious shivers," she agreed.

Keisha looked at her. "What?"

"Serious shivers," Sophie said, suddenly very aware that everyone was looking at her. "You know, when something's so cool it sends chills down your spine."

"You're cute, Bitsy," said Keisha. Then she turned and looked over at the boys. "Those guys are being lame," she said.

She stood from her stool and picked up a bowl of cheese puffs. The girls watched as she walked up behind Dominick, who was slouched on a couch, and dumped the bowl over his head.

Dominick let out a whoop. He reached out, grabbed a bowl of chips from the table, and flung it backward into Keisha's face.

Suddenly, as if the invisible levee separating them had burst, the boys and the girls were all mixed up. The girls took bowls of ammunition from the bar and began to fling chips, candies, and pretzels at the boys. The boys were scooping up handfuls and throwing them back. A variety of snack foods were getting crushed into the carpet.

Sophie hovered by the bar. She couldn't imagine how to insert herself into the scene. She also didn't want to get cheese puffs squashed on her new cashmere sweater.

Jake, who was one of the biggest guys on the

team, accidentally stepped on the TV remote and broke it. To Sophie's amazement, Keisha laughed. Sophie's parents would have been furious if her friends made a mess in her house and broke things, but Keisha didn't seem to care at all.

After a while, Scott Hersh, who had been sitting silently on the couch, extracted himself from the fray. He wandered over to the bar and took a can of soda from the fridge. Then he scooped up a handful of corn chips from one of the few bowls remaining on the bar.

Sophie took a chip, too. They stood side by side, munching and watching the rest of the kids. Sophie tried to think of something to say.

"It would be good if they had some dip," Scott said after a moment.

Sophie looked at him.

"You know, for the chips."

"You should try the potato chips," Sophie told him. "They have a, um, diplike flavor."

Diplike flavor? She could have kicked herself. She sounded like some loser in a bad TV commercial.

Scott took a chip from the bowl and popped it in his mouth. "Diplike," he agreed.

Sophie finally thought of something to say. "So how's football going?" *Not brilliant,* she told herself. *But better than "diplike flavor."*

112

"'S'okay," Scott said. There was a pause. "Um, how's cheerleading?" he asked.

"It's okay. Cheerful."

He laughed. Sophie felt a tiny surge of confidence.

"So how come you're standing over here?" asked Scott

"How come *you're* standing over here?" countered Sophie.

Scott looked over at the food fight. "I dunno. Quieter, I guess."

"Yeah." It was starting to dawn on Sophie that Scott wasn't as stuck-up as she'd thought. He was just shy — like Sophie.

"I've seen you guys practicing out on the field," Scott told her. "You're pretty strong for someone so small."

"Thanks," said Sophie, "I think."

"No, really," said Scott. "I've seen you do back handsprings and stuff. Where did you learn to do all that?"

"I started taking gymnastics classes in first grade," Sophie told him. "And then I just kept on going, I guess. I only stopped last year."

"Why'd you quit?"

Sophie shrugged. "My coach told me that if I was going to keep doing it, I had to get serious. You know, practice four hours a day and go to national tournaments and all that. I decided it was too much. I just wanted to be a normal kid."

"Yeah," Scott said. "I get that. I mean, don't get me wrong. I love football and all. But sometimes when it's really hot out and Coach is making us run sprints until we want to puke, I think, *dang,* I could be inside playing video games right now."

Sophie laughed. They ate more chips and talked about sports and school. Sophie was surprised to find that Scott was funny and friendly. In fact, he was easier to talk to than Keisha and some of the other cheerleaders.

She would have to tell Kylie he wasn't a dumb jock at all. *Good thing I stayed at the party,* Sophie thought. *Otherwise, Kylie might never know.*

After a while, Courtney walked over to them. She was wearing so much lip gloss her mouth look shellacked.

"Why are you all the way over here, Scott?" Courtney asked, giving him a glossy pout. She grabbed his hands and tried to pull him off the stool he was sitting on. "You should come hang out."

"No, thanks," Scott said pleasantly. He withdrew his hands. "I'm okay here."

Courtney looked surprised for a second. She

glanced from Scott to Sophie, and her eyes narrowed. Then, with a toss of her pumpkin-colored hair, she turned and flounced back over to the rest of the kids.

Later, when Sophie was home in bed, she went over the evening in her mind. After everyone had calmed down from the cheese puffs attack, Keisha had organized a game of Truth or Dare. She'd dared Dominick to call Alison Martin, a shy, quiet girl in their class, and tell her he loved her. He'd dialed information so the Martins wouldn't see Keisha's number on caller ID, but Alison turned out not to be home. Then Dominick had dared Jake to eat a raw egg, which Keisha happily fetched from the refrigerator upstairs. When he'd completed his dare, Jake, looking a little green, had dared Trisha to kiss Scott. Trisha told everyone she couldn't because she had a cold, and even though no one believed her, they didn't make her do it. When it was her turn, Sophie had said "Truth," and when Amy asked her how many boys she'd kissed, she lied and said one.

All in all, Sophie thought it had been one of the most exciting evenings of her life. She couldn't wait to tell Kylie about it.

CHAPTER
Eleven

On Monday, Sophie sat in her sixth-period math class, struggling to concentrate. As her teacher wrote out a problem on the board, Sophie dutifully copied it into her notebook. But her mind was on Kylie and Joel.

When Sophie had called Kylie on Sunday to tell her about the party, Kylie barely seemed to listen. Even when she mentioned Scott, Kylie just said, "Hmm." Then Kylie had launched into a description of her evening with Joel.

When they got to the Esplanade, they hadn't called their parents right away, she told Sophie. Instead they'd walked around, ate ice cream, and looked in the shops. That's when they discovered the wedding party being photographed in the courtyard outside a ritzy restaurant. Kylie and Joel had spent the rest of the night lurking in the background, seeing how many wedding photos they could sneak into.

"The bride and groom were getting their picture taken," Kylie said over the phone, practically choking with laughter, "and Joel was standing in the background pretending to pick his nose."

Sophie laughed when Kylie told her about it. On Monday, when Kylie and Joel rehashed their evening over lunch, she pretended to be amused. But by Tuesday they were still talking about it, and Sophie was starting to get annoyed.

It wasn't *that* funny, she fumed as she copied history notes off the board. In fact, when you thought about it, it was pretty immature. What about the poor bride and groom who would get their pictures back from the photographer and see Joel picking his nose in the background?

But the poor bride and groom weren't really what bothered Sophie. What bugged her most was that Kylie and Joel had had so much fun without her.

Did Joel like Kylie? Did Kylie like Joel?

She didn't think so. Kylie was her best friend. She would have told Sophie if she liked Joel.

Then again, Sophie thought uneasily, *I didn't tell Kylie that I liked him.*

As she mulled this over, Sophie felt something nudge her elbow. She looked over and saw Melissa, the girl in the next seat, passing her a note. Melissa rolled her eyes toward the back of the room. Kate was giving Sophie an urgent look from the back row.

A note from Kate! Suddenly, Sophie felt better. She didn't need Kylie and Joel. She was friends with one of the most popular girls in the seventh grade.

Casting a quick glance at the teacher to make sure she wasn't looking, Sophie unfolded the note. Kate had written,

Sophie, Do you ♥ *Scott Hersh? FF, Kate*

What?! Sophie turned and looked at Kate with astonishment. Kate nodded for Sophie to write her back.

NO!!! Sophie wrote. She underlined it four times. Then she added, *Who told you that? FF, Sophie.*

She refolded the note and passed it to Melissa, who passed it to the guy behind her, who passed it to Kate.

Sophie's thoughts churned as she waited for Kate's reply. Were people talking about her and Scott? What were they saying?

A moment later the note came back.

It's so obvious. Everyone saw you flirting with him

118

at Keisha's party. Kate had drawn a bunch of little hearts around "flirting."

Sophie hesitated. Had she been flirting with Scott? She didn't think so. How could you be flirting with someone you didn't even like? Then again, Sophie didn't know anything about flirting. Was it possible she had been flirting without even knowing it?

At last she wrote, *We're just friends. I don't <u>like him</u> like him.*

Cool, Kate wrote back. *FYI, everyone is getting together at Courtney's to get ready for the Halloween dance. B there or B square.*

The Halloween dance was two weeks away. Kylie had been talking about it practically since *last* Halloween. She wouldn't tell anyone what her costume was going to be, not even Sophie.

Sophie and Kylie always got ready for Halloween together. *Then again,* Sophie thought, rereading Kate's note, *I definitely do not want to be square.*

She folded the note and put it in her pocket. She wanted to think more about it. She was going to have to figure out what to do.

It turned out she didn't have to. Every day at cheerleading practice Sophie waited for Courtney to

119

mention the party at her house before the Halloween dance. But Courtney never did.

Finally, Sophie decided the party must have been canceled. It was just as well. Now she didn't have to make up an excuse for why she couldn't go.

On the night of the dance, Sophie and Kylie got ready at Kylie's house. "What do you think?" Kylie asked, turning away from the mirror. She was wearing a ruffled skirt, red lipstick, and a giant basket of plastic fruit tied to her head with a scarf.

"You look like one of those gift baskets my dad gets from work at Christmastime," Sophie told her.

"I'm Carmen Miranda," said Kylie. Carmen Miranda was one of Kylie's favorite actresses from the old black-and-white movies.

"*I* know that," said Sophie. "I'm just not sure anyone *else* will. Carmen Miranda didn't wear a basket on her head. She just wore fruit. And besides, she was alive, like, a million years ago."

Kylie turned back to the mirror and considered herself. Going over to her closet, she rummaged around and came up with a crumpled red ribbon. She tied it to the basket handle. "Voilà. *Now* I'm a gift basket."

Sophie fiddled with her stocking cap. At the last minute, she'd decided to be a green M&M. She was wearing a green cap and a long-sleeved green shirt with the letters M&M stenciled on. It was Sophie's kind of costume. Subtle, she thought, but clever.

The dance was being held in the school cafeteria, a low-ceilinged room with small windows and a grubby gray floor. The dance committee had done their best to give it some atmosphere by hanging orange-and-black crepe paper streamers and placing smoking buckets of dry ice around the sides. Music blared from huge speakers set up in the corners.

Several kids turned to look when Sophie and Kylie walked in the door. A few of them laughed when they saw Kylie's costume. Kylie held her fruit high and smiled like a queen.

Sophie and Kylie agreed they should make a loop and look for people they knew. Halfway around the room, Sophie spotted Alyssa and Renee, dressed in disco outfits and neon-pink wigs. They were standing with a few kids from the student council. She went over to them.

"Hi!" Alyssa and Renee shouted over the music.

"Hey!" said Sophie. "Are you having fun?"

"Yeah!" said Alyssa. "The music is great!"

"Where's everyone else?" Sophie asked.

Alyssa and Renee shrugged and shook their

heads. They hadn't seen any of the other cheer-leaders.

Sophie told them she'd see them later and caught up with Kylie. They found Joel standing in a corner by the door with a few guys from the soccer team. He had Ace bandages wrapped over his clothes and around his head to look like a mummy.

"Let me guess," he said when he saw Kylie. "Carmen Miranda."

"Good guess!" said Sophie. "How do you know Carmen Miranda?"

Joel shrugged. "I like old movies."

"Good guess," Kylie agreed, "but wrong." She pointed to the bow. "Gift basket. It was Sophie's idea," she said when Joel chuckled.

"Good idea," Joel said to Sophie, who blushed. He looked at her green cap and shirt. "What are you? Green with envy?"

"A green M&M."

"Oh," said Joel. "Right." He didn't laugh.

A slow song came on. Around them boys and girls started to pair off. One of the guys from the soccer team asked Kylie to dance, and they moved out to the dance floor.

Sophie stared straight ahead. She was afraid to look at Joel. She didn't want him to think she was waiting for him to ask her to dance.

Think of something to say, she told herself. *Something funny.* The harder she tried to think, the more her mind stayed blank. The loud music seemed to mingle with the sound of blood rushing in her ears.

She was concentrating so hard she almost didn't notice when Joel turned to her and said something.

Sophie leaned in closer. "What?" she shouted over the music.

At that moment, the doors near them banged open. Joel and Sophie turned. Keisha and Courtney strode into the room, with the rest of the cheerleaders in tow. They were all dressed like cowgirls in cutoff jeans or denim skirts, plaid shirts, and boots. Written across the crowns of their cowboy hats were the words MULE DRIVERS.

Sophie stared. They had obviously gotten dressed together. So there had been a party at Courtney's after all. And she hadn't been invited. Sophie felt a pit in the bottom of her stomach.

Just then, Keisha spotted her. She swooped over and slung her arm around Sophie's neck. "Hi, Itsy-Bitsy!" she hollered. "Come join the group."

Before Sophie could say anything to Joel, Keisha pulled her away.

"Hey, Sophie!" the other cheerleaders said when they saw her.

Courtney folded her arms. She looked at Sophie from under lashes heavy with mascara. "What are you? The Jolly Green Midget?"

"I'm, um, a green M&M."

"You're so cute, Bitsy," said Keisha.

"So, you guys all got dressed together?" Sophie tried to sound casual.

"Yeah, we were over at Courtney's house," Keisha told her. "I wondered why you weren't there."

"Nobody . . . I mean, I wasn't . . . I didn't know if I should come."

"Oh?" Keisha raised her eyebrows. She turned and looked at Courtney. "Courtney didn't tell you?"

Courtney's smile reminded Sophie of a crocodile's. "I guess I forgot to mention it," she said with a shrug.

Keisha put her arm around Sophie. "Our bad, Bitsy."

She sounded genuinely sorry. Sophie looked around at the other cheerleaders. Amy and Angie gave her sympathetic looks. Maybe Courtney had really forgotten to mention it to her, Sophie thought. Maybe it had just been a mistake.

The slow song ended, and a fast one came on.

"Come on!" Keisha said. "Let's dance!" With her

arm still around Sophie's shoulders, she headed for the dance floor, dragging Sophie along.

For a second, Sophie caught a glimpse of Joel watching her. She tried to give him an apologetic look, but the rest of the cheerleaders surged around, blocking her view. They put their arms around each other's shoulders, forming a big circle.

The cheerleaders danced that way for several songs. They jumped up and down and sang along to the music. Sophie could feel the envious looks from other kids in the gym. She was certain they wished they could be on the inside of the circle, too.

After a while, another slow song came on. The circle broke up. A few football players who had been standing nearby asked some of the girls to dance. Joy, Amy, and the twins wandered out into the hall to get a drink of water. Sophie decided to look for Kylie and Joel.

She had just started to circle the cafeteria when she ran into Scott. He was wearing a sombrero and a Mexican-style poncho.

"Hey, Sophie," he said. "You're here. So, what are you?"

Sophie sighed. "A green M&M," she said unenthusiastically.

Scott laughed. "That's cool."

"What are you?"

Scott shrugged. "Uh, a guy in a sombrero? I don't know. I just found this stuff in my older brother's room. I'm not really into making costumes."

"Me, neither," said Sophie.

"So, do you want to dance?"

"Okay."

They moved onto the dance floor. Scott put his hands on Sophie's waist, and she put her hands on his shoulders. They shifted from foot to foot, revolving in time to the music.

This wasn't the first time Sophie had danced with a boy, but it was the first time she'd danced with someone as tall as Scott. She found herself staring at the middle of his chest. When he exhaled she could feel his breath on the top of her head.

Here was Sophie Smith, former nobody, dancing with the most popular guy in school. *This should be the highlight of my year*, Sophie thought. But even as she danced with Scott, she found herself thinking about Joel. Scott was cute and sweet, but, well, there was no one like Joel Leo.

But what if Joel was dancing with someone else? The thought made her stomach drop. Sophie began to surreptitiously scan the room. Before long she spotted Joel on the other side of the cafeteria. He was with Kylie, and they weren't dancing. They were both watching Sophie.

Kylie looked stunned.

She thinks I'm with Scott! Sophie thought. Sophie tried to signal with her eyes that Kylie had misunderstood. But before she could, Scott turned her, continuing his slow revolution. Sophie looked back over her shoulder at Kylie. Instead, she found herself locking eyes with Courtney. Courtney smiled in a way that sent chills down Sophie's spine.

To Sophie's relief, the song ended. Scott and Sophie moved apart. "Thanks," he said.

"Thanks," echoed Sophie distractedly. She looked around for Courtney again and saw her talking to Keisha. As she watched, both girls glanced in Sophie's direction.

Suddenly, Sophie was more anxious than ever to find Kylie. She wanted to explain that she and Scott were just friends, just in case Kylie had misunderstood. She circled the cafeteria once, scanning the crowd. She circled again. By the third loop she realized that Kylie and Joel were gone.

Sophie made her way back over to the cheerleaders. They were dancing in a circle again, arms tightly woven around one another's shoulders. Sophie bounced around outside the group for a while, waiting for them to let her in. But no one seemed to notice her. Eventually, she gave up and moved over to the wall to watch.

All over the cafeteria, groups of kids were dancing together in little knots. Sophie didn't know any of them well enough to join them. She hoped maybe Kylie and Joel had just gone outside to get some air. After half an hour, though, she had to admit that they weren't coming back.

With a sigh, Sophie dug some change out of her pocket, went to the pay phone in the hall, and called her mother to come pick her up.

CHAPTER
Twelve

Kylie wasn't speaking to Sophie.

When Sophie called Kylie's house on Saturday, Mrs. Lovett said that Kylie wasn't home. But Sophie was almost sure she'd heard Kylie's voice in the background. She'd called again Saturday afternoon and again on Sunday. By Sunday night it was clear that Kylie wasn't calling back.

Sophie didn't know why Kylie wasn't talking to her. On Monday, she caught her at her locker and confronted her. Kylie had just swished her hair and said, "Why don't you ask your cheerleader friends?"

Sophie couldn't ask her cheerleader friends, though, because they weren't talking to her, either. That Monday at practice, when Sophie asked a question about a cheer, Keisha turned to Courtney and said, "Do you hear something?" Sophie repeated her question, but no one would answer, or even look at her. For the rest of the day, whenever Sophie tried to speak, Keisha or Courtney starting talking over her, as if Sophie were nothing more than an annoying fly buzzing in the background.

The twins caught on. By Tuesday, Sophie couldn't so much as say hello without them laughing hysterically. The other cheerleaders wouldn't speak to her either. Kate and Trisha snubbed her in the halls. Amy, Angie, and Joy wouldn't make room for her at their table at lunch. When they couldn't avoid her, they ignored her.

On Wednesday, Sophie cornered Angie in the bathroom and asked her what was going on.

"Well, I'm not completely sure," said Angie, watching the door as if she feared Keisha might walk in any minute. "But the twins told Amy that they heard Courtney telling Keisha that you were all over Scott at the dance. Scott is Keisha's ex-boyfriend, you know. They went out for three weeks last year."

"I didn't know that," Sophie told her. "But I wasn't hanging on Scott. I swear I don't even like him!" Angie just shrugged and edged out the bathroom door. Sophie wondered why Kate hadn't stuck up for her. Kate knew that Sophie didn't like

Scott — Sophie had told her in the note in math class. So why was Kate being mean to her now?

And was that why Kylie was mad, too? Because she thought Sophie liked Scott?

Sophie would have liked to ask someone these questions, but there was no one to ask. Not Joel, who hadn't so much as looked at her since the night of the dance. Not Amy or Angie, who hadn't spoken to her in over a week. Their awe of Keisha seemed to outweigh their natural instinct to be friendly. After Sophie's interrogation in the bathroom, they had gone out of their way to avoid her.

Not even her parents had much to say to Sophie these days. They'd had a *lot* to say when they received the latest credit card bill, which arrived the Monday after the dance. Her father, red in the face, had delivered a very loud lecture about responsibility and bad spending habits. Her mother, who seemed mostly alarmed by how much Sophie had spent on mascara, chimed in with a few teary comments about broken trust. Their speech was so long that at the end of it her parents, unaccustomed to giving lectures, had looked as exhausted and miserable as Sophie felt. But after they'd taken away her credit card and phone privileges, they'd settled into a stony silence that made Sophie almost wish they'd go back to scolding her.

On the bright side, Sophie told herself (since there was no one else to tell), at least being grounded wasn't so bad. She didn't have anyone to hang out with, anyway.

The only person who was talking to Sophie was Scott. Every day at their lockers he greeted her with a cheerful "Hey, Sophie," seemingly oblivious to the drama that was swirling around them. And Sophie, determined not to lose what seemed to be her one friend left in the world, returned his greeting and tried to ignore the poisonous looks from any of Keisha's friends who happened to overhear.

One day, Sophie rounded a corner and almost ran into Kylie. Sophie was wearing the dragon jeans that day. Kylie, it turned out, was wearing them, too. For a moment the two girls stared at each other.

"Kye —" Sophie began.

But before she could say more, Kylie turned on her heel. When Sophie saw her later that day, Kylie had changed into the track pants she usually wore to practice.

Kylie wasn't just mad, Sophie realized with a shock. She didn't want to have anything to do with Sophie.

After two weeks of the silent treatment, Sophie felt ready to snap. Tears seemed to be constantly on the verge of spilling from her eyes. Then one day at cheerleading practice Sophie fell out of a lift and hit the ground hard, and finally the tears came.

Ms. Charge stood over Sophie, her hands on her hips, frowning with concern. "Are you hurt?" she barked.

Sophie shook her head. She was crying too hard to say anything.

"Stand up and walk it off."

Sophie wobbled to her feet, still crying.

Ms. Charge regarded her for a second. "Take a lap around the field," she told Sophie. Then she added more gently, "Walk, don't run. Just take a breather."

All the other girls were watching. Sophie heard Keisha and Courtney snicker as she set off to walk around the perimeter of the football field. "Stop crying," she whispered to herself angrily. But the tears had been building for days, and they just kept coming.

She had finally managed to get them under control when she heard feet pounding the ground behind her.

"Are you okay?"

It was Alyssa. She slowed to a walk next to Sophie.

Sophie nodded.

"I'm sorry I didn't catch you."

"It's not your fault." And it hadn't been Alyssa's fault. They had been practicing a shoulder stand. Sophie was supposed to stand with her feet on Angie's shoulders. For the stunt to work, Sophie had to keep her legs locked and her muscles tight. But Sophie had let go too soon and tumbled forward. There was no way Alyssa, who was standing behind, could have caught her.

They walked in silence for a moment.

"So, what's up?" said Alyssa.

Sophie snuffled. "What do you mean?"

"The pep assembly is next week. All the other groups on the team have their shoulder stand down. But you haven't managed to hit it yet."

The shoulder stands were going to be the finale of the cheerleaders' big routine at the pep assembly. All three flyers had to be in the shoulder stands. If Sophie couldn't get the stand down, the formation would be ruined.

"You've always been really good at stunts," Alyssa told Sophie. "But lately it's like your mind is in outer space."

134

Sophie's throat ached. She was so grateful to have someone talking to her, she was afraid she might start crying again.

But this time instead of tears, words came spilling out. Sophie told Alyssa about Keisha and Courtney's campaign against her, how none of the other cheerleaders would talk to her.

"You can't let those girls get to you," Alyssa told her.

"It's kind of hard not to."

"Let me tell you something about Keisha," said Alyssa. "She's a good cheerleader, and I respect that. But the only person she cares about is herself. She'll act like your best friend one minute, then she'll drop you like a dirty Kleenex the next, just so you'll fall all over yourself trying to get her to like you again. Haven't you ever noticed how she leads the twins around by their noses?"

Sophie nodded.

"She does it to everyone," said Alyssa. "She even tries to do it to me. I just don't go along with her."

"What about Courtney?" asked Sophie.

Alyssa snorted. "Courtney's just plain mean. I think she's always worried that Keisha is going to drop her and she takes it out on everyone else. Plus, she hates anybody she thinks is prettier than she is."

"But Courtney's pretty," Sophie pointed out.

"She's not, really. She just wears a lot of makeup. That doesn't necessarily make you pretty."

Sophie thought about that. Suddenly, she felt stupid for spending seventeen dollars on mascara. "So, you're saying that's why they turned everyone against me?" She asked Alyssa. "'Cause Courtney is jealous and Keisha is just being Keisha?"

"It might be," said Alyssa. "It probably doesn't help that you're friends with Kylie."

"*Was* friends," Sophie corrected her.

"Really?" Alyssa looked at her. "That's too bad. I think Kylie's pretty cool. I thought it was rotten what Keisha and Courtney did to her at the Halloween dance. Wearing those mule-driver outfits just to burn her."

Sophie was startled. She hadn't even thought about what mule driver meant. She'd been too worried about the fact that they hadn't invited her to get dressed with them. No wonder Kylie had been upset.

"It drives Keisha crazy when Kylie shows her up at the games. Keisha can't stand anyone upstaging her." Alyssa chuckled. "It's kind of funny watching her face, actually."

They had almost circled back around to the cheerleaders. Sophie stopped. Alyssa stopped, too.

"So, why do you do it?" Sophie asked.

"What? Why do I cheer?" Alyssa paused. "I do it 'cause I like it. All this stuff —" Alyssa flapped her hands to indicate everything they'd been talking about — "is not cheerleading." She pointed to the girls, who were still practicing shoulder stands. "*That* is cheerleading. So are you ready to cheer, or what?"

Sophie swallowed and looked over at the other girls. Slowly, she nodded.

Alyssa grinned. "Well, then. Come on!"

The more Sophie thought about what Alyssa had said, the more she felt she owed Kylie an apology. The problem was how to do it.

Sophie went through all the options. She couldn't call Kylie and say she was sorry, since she had lost her phone privileges. She couldn't talk to her at school — Kylie walked the other way whenever she saw Sophie coming. She could go over to Kylie's house, but she was afraid Mr. or Mrs. Lovett would be there, and Sophie didn't want to make a scene.

At last she decided to write Kylie a note. It took her all weekend to do it, and she went through four sheets of paper. In the end, the note read:

Stylie Kylie,

I know you're mad at me right now, and although I don't exactly know all the reasons why, you have sure given me plenty of time to think about it. The more I think about it, the more I realize I have put a lot more time into cheerleading than I have into our friendship lately. I am sorry for that. I guess I got a little carried away with all the excitement, but now I know that some of that excitement is nothing more than a bunch of drama. Also, maybe you think I like Scott Hersh, but I don't. We're just friends. But just so you know, he's not a dumb jock.

I miss you, Kylie. I hope we can still be friends.

Your friend forever,

Sophie

Now Sophie had to figure out how to give it to her. She was afraid if she handed it to Kylie, she would throw it out without even reading it. The best thing to do, she decided, was to put it in Kylie's locker.

But she never got the chance. On Monday, just as she was about to slip the note in Kylie's locker, Scott happened to pass by. He stopped to chat. When Kylie saw Sophie and Scott talking in front of *her* locker, she gave Sophie such a look of cold fury that Sophie was afraid to even pass by Kylie's locker for two whole days.

On Thursday, she worked up the nerve to try again. As she turned down the hall to Kylie's locker, she saw Kylie talking with Joel. Sophie could've sworn she heard Kylie say her name. Sophie slunk past them, the note still in her pocket.

At last, Sophie decided to wait and give Kylie the note on Friday. The pep rally was Friday morning, and she would put the note in Kylie's locker Friday afternoon, right after the rally.

On Friday morning every seat in the gymnasium was filled. The whole school was crammed into the bleachers — sixth-, seventh-, and eighth-graders. In the center of the gym, the student council performed a skit dressed as Vikings, the Northwest mascot. Meridian's second big game against Northwest was that afternoon, which was the reason for the pep assembly. Whoever won this game would go on to the district championship.

Sophie and the other cheerleaders stood on the sidelines, waiting to go on. Sophie had no idea what the student council skit was about. She was too excited and nervous to pay attention. Now was the big moment. For once, they wouldn't be cheering from the sidelines. They'd be the main attraction.

Unlike the short cheers they usually did at the games, their routine was a dance to an entire song and involved lots of stunts. At one point, Sophie and Amy, the two best tumblers on the team, did backflips. All the flyers did basket tosses, where they were thrown in the air and caught in the hands of the other girls. And then there was the shoulder stand at the end of the dance.

As soon as they hit their final formation, Kylie was supposed to run on and do her Mules Rules. Over the past few games, the Rules had become very popular. Kylie no longer even had to hold up the written signs. She'd just hold up a number and everyone would shout the corresponding rule.

The more success Kylie had with the crowd, the more frustrated Keisha became. Ever since the crowd started reacting to the mascot, the tension between Keisha and Kylie had thickened, until they could barely be in a room together. Now that Kylie wasn't talking to Sophie, she barely communicated with the squad. But on the field, you never would have known it. And the fans still adored her.

At last, the skit ended. When the audience had

finished clapping, Keisha gave them the signal. The cheerleaders took the floor, doing cartwheels and back handsprings.

They had just started the dance when Sophie realized something was wrong. There was another sound playing over the top of their music. At first she couldn't tell what it was. Then she heard it.

HEE-HAW! HEE-HAW!

Sounds of a mule braying blared from a boom box set up at the side of the gym.

Kylie, wearing her mule suit, was running up and down the bleachers, in between all the assembled kids. As she ran, she threw handfuls of hay at the crowd.

The cheerleaders continued with their dance, but no one was watching them. All eyes were on Kylie. When she ran out of hay, she loped to the middle of the gym and stood in front of the cheerleaders.

She held up a poster board sign. She was starting the Mules Rules early.

Only Sophie realized they weren't the Mules Rules, not exactly. The kids in the gymnasium hollered out the signs as she held them over her head.

"BE COOL!

OVERRULE!

DON'T CHEER

FOR *THOSE* FOOLS!"

Kylie dropped the sign, turned, and pointed at the cheerleaders.

For a moment, Sophie wasn't sure what was going on. The other cheerleaders had all stopped dancing. The entire gymnasium was in an uproar. Lots of kids were laughing. Others were yelling "Boooo!"

Sophie looked over and saw Keisha shouting something at Kylie. She was so angry, the veins in her temples were standing out. But Sophie couldn't hear what she was saying over the noises. She looked in the other direction and saw Ms. Charge. Her mouth hung open in a perfect O.

Then she understood. Kylie had burned them. She'd burned all the cheerleaders right in front of the entire school.

In the middle of the gym, Kylie danced as if she'd scored a touchdown, which just made the kids in the bleachers holler louder. Sophie could no longer even hear their dance music over all the noise.

The principal took the microphone and threatened to send everyone back to class if they didn't calm down.

Sophie didn't stick around to find out if they

calmed down. She ran from the gym straight to her locker. As soon as she got there, she tore up the note. Kylie had humiliated the whole cheerleading team. Nothing in the world would make Sophie apologize to her now!

CHAPTER
Thirteen

On Friday afternoon, Ms. Charge called an emergency meeting of the pep squad, which meant all the cheerleaders, plus Kylie. She paced up and down in front of them, hands clasped behind her back, brow furrowed like a judge. Today her T-shirt read, ATHLETES LIFT WEIGHTS, CHEERLEADERS LIFT ATHLETES, but Ms. Charge looked like she wanted to lift Kylie and throw her out the window.

First, she'd wanted to know if anyone had helped Kylie plan her cheerleader ambush. Kylie, sitting apart from the rest of the team, calmly said no, she'd thought of it all herself. Sophie had to admit Kylie had guts. The most popular girls in school were sitting three feet away staring daggers at her, and Kylie acted like she didn't have a care in the world.

After another lengthy speech about teamwork, during which even Keisha, who'd been gloating throughout the entire scene, started to wilt, Ms. Charge asked the cheerleaders what they thought should be done. "Suspend her," Keisha said at once. "Make sure she can't cheer at the games any more."

Ms. Charge raised her eyebrows. She looked around at the other cheerleaders. "Does everyone agree that Kylie should be suspended?"

The other cheerleaders nodded. A few said, "Yeah."

Sophie glanced at Kylie. She didn't want to see her suspended from the squad. But she couldn't bring herself to stand up for Kylie either. After all, Kylie certainly didn't seem to be on Sophie's side.

Sophie sat there, frozen with undecision, until it was too late to say anything.

"All right," said Ms. Charge. "It's the team's decision that Kylie should be suspended.

"That means," Ms. Charge turned to Kylie, "you cannot mascot at the game this afternoon — or any other game until the team feels you're ready to join again."

Kylie just shrugged.

Angie raised her hand. "But who will be the mascot?"

"We don't need a mascot, Angie," Keisha snapped, giving her a withering look.

But for once Keisha was overruled. The other cheerleaders agreed that, in fact, they *did* need a mascot. Northwest's mascot would surely be at the game. If the Mule wasn't there, it would look like Meridian didn't have spirit.

Several ideas for Kylie's replacement were thrown out. Angie suggested Mr. Green, the vice principal, who was a gangly, goofy man, but they quickly realized the costume wouldn't fit him. Courtney suggested calling last year's mascot, but no one could remember his name. Joy suggested Ms. Charge, and everyone, including Ms. Charge, looked at her like she was crazy. During the entire conversation, Kylie studied her nails and didn't say a word.

Finally, they decided they would ask Howard Heller. Howard was the cymbals player in the school band, the one who was always bashing the cymbals together at the wrong moment. All the cheerleaders agreed that this was a good solution. Not only would they have a mascot, but without Howard playing, the quality of the school band would be significantly improved.

That afternoon after school, Keisha and Courtney cornered Howard and told him he was going to be the mascot. Howard was so astonished that Keisha was talking to him, he would have agreed to anything she said.

At last, it was time for the game to start. As the teams lined up for the kickoff, the tension in the bleachers was thick.

For the first quarter, the score remained tied. The cheerleaders did cheer after cheer. Sophie yelled until she started to feel hoarse.

Howard, wearing the Mule mascot costume, lumbered up and down the sidelines. Occasionally, he would raise one arm and shake his fist, like someone who had just discovered he had been cheated and was vowing to get back at the person who did it.

"He's awful!" Amy said to Sophie as they watched Howard between cheers.

In the second quarter, Meridian started to fall behind.

Keisha called the pep team into a huddle. "We need to keep everyone's spirit up," she instructed. "Howard, do a wave."

When the huddle broke, Howard dutifully trotted back to the sidelines. He ran up and down in front of the bleachers, trying to get the crowd to do a wave. But at that exact moment, the Meridian kicker was lining up for a field goal. All eyes were on the game. Nobody was looking at Howard.

The kicker booted the ball. It swerved left. Everyone groaned. No one did the wave.

"He's worse at being a mascot than he is at playing cymbals," Angie said to Sophie.

Just then a shout went up from the other side of the field. The Northwest cheerleaders had all turned to face Meridian.

"We've got spirit, yes, we do!" the Northwest cheerleaders and fans shouted. "We've got spirit, how 'bout you?"

They were starting a spirit war. Sophie and the rest of the cheerleaders had no choice but to try to rally the Meridian fans.

"We've got spirit, yes, we do! We've got spirit, how 'bout you?" They yelled their loudest, but they couldn't make up for the listless crowd.

"We've got spirit, we've got more! If you don't believe us, just look at the score!" The Northwest cheerleaders swiveled and pointed to the scoreboard.

Northwest was leading by fourteen points. Meridian was losing the game, and the Meridian cheerleaders had no response. How could they get the crowd energized when they felt defeated themselves?

Keisha called another huddle. "We need to do an offense cheer," she told the cheerleaders.

"What we need is *Kylie!*" cried Sophie. The words were out of her mouth before she'd even realized she was going to say them.

Everyone turned to stare at her. "We do *not* need Kylie," said Keisha, giving Sophie a murderous look.

"Yes, we do!" Sophie couldn't believe she was standing up to Keisha, but she was. Her heart beat faster with a mixture of fear and elation. She knew what was right, and she'd finally found the nerve to say it. "We need her, and we need the Mules Rules. That's the only thing that will get the crowd's spirit back up."

"But Kylie is suspended," Amy said, wide-eyed. "She can't cheer at the game."

Sophie replied, "Amy, remember after the last game with Northwest? You said Kylie's cheering rallied the team. You were right. We were behind by fifteen points —"

"Seventeen," corrected Kate, who always kept track of the scores.

"We were behind by *seventeen* points," Sophie amended. "And when Kylie came on the field the fans got psyched up and the team came back."

Around the circle, heads began to nod — Renee, Amy, Angie, Joy, even the twins agreed. They all remembered the effect the Mules Rules had had at that game.

"I can't believe you guys are even considering this," said Keisha, "after what she did to us at the pep rally."

The girls stopped nodding. Keisha had a point.

"That was messed up," Sophie agreed. "And I'm mad at her, too. But you have to admit she has a way with the crowd."

Alyssa suddenly spoke up. "I think we can consider this a cheer emergency. You know, drastic times call for drastic measures." She gave Sophie a smile. Sophie grinned, relieved to have someone back her up.

Keisha looked around furiously. She could sense she was losing control. "Well, what will Ms. Charge say?"

"Let's ask her!" Sophie cried. She turned to go get Ms. Charge. But she didn't have to. The coach was already charging down the sidelines toward them.

"Why are you all standing around?" she demanded. "The team's drowning out there! The *fans* are drowning."

"Ms. Charge," Alyssa said somberly, "we believe this is a cheer emergency. We'd like to bring Kylie back."

"Howard's not cutting it," Joy added bluntly.

Ms. Charge glanced over at Howard. He was trying to do the tail shake, but he looked like he was doubled over with gas pains. "He's terrible," she agreed. She turned back to the team. "Is this what you all want?" she asked.

"No!" said Keisha. "It's not what we *all* want."

Ms. Charge folded her arms. "I may act like a dictator," she said, "but I can run a democracy. Let's vote. All those who want Kylie back on the field — just for this game — put your hands up."

Sophie raised her hand. So did Alyssa, Renee, Joy, Amy, and Angie. Keisha, Courtney, Trisha, and Kate kept their hands down. The twins glanced at Keisha and tentatively raised their hands. She scowled. Quickly, they lowered them again.

It was tied, six and six. Then, to Sophie's astonishment, Kate's hand crept into the air.

"Kate!" Keisha and Courtney shrieked in outrage.

"What?" said Kate. She tossed her hair. "I think it's a good idea."

"That's it, then. We bring Kylie back," said Ms. Charge.

"But I'm head cheerleader," Keisha burst out. "Shouldn't my vote count twice?"

Ms. Charge gave her a tired look. "Keisha, your mouth might be big enough for two people. But you only get one vote."

Keisha's mouth fell open. Sophie hid her smile behind her hand.

151

"Now that we've got that solved," said Ms. Charge, "does anyone know if Kylie is even here?"

"I'll bet she is!" said Sophie. She broke away from the group and began to run along the foot of the bleachers, scanning the crowd.

She saw Joel first. Kylie was sitting right next to him. She wore dark glasses and a hat, her golden curls cascading down around her shoulders, as conspicuously inconspicuous as she possibly could be.

Sophie took the steps two at a time. "Sorry, Joel," she said when she reached them. "I have to borrow Kylie for a minute."

Before Kylie could protest, Sophie grabbed her wrist and dragged her down the stairs.

"We need you," Sophie said when they were standing to the side of the bleachers. "You have to do the Mules Rules."

"I can't," Kylie said coolly. "I'm suspended, remember?"

"Ms. Charge said you can come back for this game." Sophie pointed to the sidelines, where Ms. Charge and the rest of the team were watching them.

"Well, maybe I don't want to," said Kylie. "I'm not exactly welcome out there."

"We voted," Sophie told her. "Almost everyone wants you to come back. The team is losing. The crowd is fading. We need someone to get the spirit back up. And Howard is not the one."

"He's the worst," agreed Kylie.

"So, will you do it? Please?" Sophie paused, then added, "I'll be your best friend."

Kylie looked at Sophie for a long moment. "Okay," she said at last.

Quickly, they located Howard. Sophie told him to take off the suit and give it to Kylie. Howard didn't mind. He was just glad to have cheerleaders paying attention to him.

As soon as Kylie was on the field, Alyssa said, "We're running out of time. We need to do the Mules Rules now, before the second half."

Kylie mumbled something from inside the mask.

"What?" said Alyssa.

Kylie repeated it.

"She said she doesn't have her signs with numbers on them," said Amy, who was standing closest to her. "So, she doesn't have any way to signal the crowd."

Sophie smiled. "I have an idea," she said.

A moment later, the cheerleaders and Kylie were back out in front of the crowd. The cheerleaders waved their pom-poms and kicked their legs high in the air.

Kylie kicked her legs, too. She did her goofy cartwheels. She danced around. She did everything she could to let the fans know she was back.

They noticed. The crowd seemed to perk up a little. "Go, Mules!" a few people shouted.

The cheerleaders got into position. "MULES RULES!" they shouted in unison.

Behind Sophie, Alyssa quietly counted, "One, two, hit!" A second later, Sophie was standing straight and tall on Angie's shoulders.

Next to her, Keisha was on Courtney's shoulders. And to the other side of Keisha, Renee stood on Amie's shoulders. They were finally getting a chance to do their shoulder stands. And everyone had hit them perfectly.

High in the air, Sophie and Renee raised their right arms in a number one sign.

In the center, Keisha kept her hands on her hips and her lips pressed tight together. She was boycotting the Mules Rules. But it didn't matter. The crowd got it, anyway.

"RULE NUMBER ONE!" the cheerleaders yelled.

"HAVE FUN!" the crowd yelled back.

"RULE NUMBER TWO!" called the cheerleaders.

"DON'T DROOL!" the crowd responded. A few people whistled. On the ground in front of the cheerleaders, Kylie danced like crazy.

154

"RULE NUMBER THREE!"

"CHEER LIKE FOOLS FOR YOUR SCHOOL! CUZ THE MULES . . . RULE!"

Right before "Rule!" the flyers all dropped and were caught by their spotters. All the girls raised their arms in a V for Victory sign. Kylie bucked her feet in the air. The crowd whooped and hollered.

For the second half of the game, Kylie cheered right alongside the cheerleaders, acting goofier than ever.

Meridian came back. In the end, they won, 31–28.

As players trotted off the field, the cheerleaders lifted Kylie onto their shoulders. The band played an off-key version of "We Are the Champions." Howard was back on cymbals, blissfully bashing them together at all the wrong moments.

Sophie grinned. Everything was as it should be. Kylie was a mule. Howard was a cymbals player. The eighth-grade football team would go on to the district championships.

And she finally had her proof that the cheering made a difference.

Later that afternoon, Sophie and Kylie walked down the school's main hallway. Kylie was still wearing the fuzzy brown mule suit, though she was carrying the mask.

"Thanks for coming through," Sophie told Kylie.

"It was actually fun," she replied. "I guess I'm better at being a mule than I ever wanted to be."

They stopped in front of the counselor's office. "Well," said Kylie, "this is where I get off." Ms. Charge had said she wanted to meet with Kylie in the counselor's office.

"I'll wait for you here," Sophie told her.

"You don't have to."

"I know that. I want to."

Kylie smiled. "Well, here goes." She took a deep breath and walked into the office.

Suddenly, Sophie felt exhausted. She leaned against the wall and let her body slide down until she was sitting on the floor. Today felt like the longest day of her life.

Still, it had all been worth it. And it *definitely* had been worth it to see Keisha's face when Kylie was lifted into the air, Sophie thought. She knew now why Alyssa enjoyed it so much.

She wondered what Ms. Charge and the counselor were saying to Kylie on the other side of the door. Considering that Ms. Charge was in there, it was strangely quiet.

A door to the outside opened at the end of the hallway, and a figure appeared, silhouetted against the daylight. As it came closer, Sophie saw that it was Joel.

"Hi," she said as he walked up to the office.

"Hey," Joel replied. He seemed surprised to see her sitting on the floor. "I was just looking for Kylie. The other girls said she'd be here."

"She's inside," Sophie told him. She sounded calmer than she felt. It was the first time she and Joel had spoken since the Halloween dance, and her insides were jumping like grasshoppers.

Joel nodded. "So . . . good game."

Sophie smiled. "Yeah, Kylie was good."

"You were all good," Joel said quickly. He brushed a lock of hair back behind his ear. "I mean, you looked really good, too. Those stunts and everything."

"Thanks." Sophie blushed.

"Do you want to wait for Kylie with me?" she asked.

"Nah," said Joel. "I have to get home. But I'll see you around?"

"Okay," said Sophie. She watched him as he walked back down the hall.

Finally, the office door opened. Kylie came out.

"Well?" said Sophie.

Kylie sat down next to her. She hesitated a moment, then said, "I'm finished."

"No!" said Sophie. "That is so unfair. You saved

157

the game today! Maybe we can get a petition together. We can get the cheerleaders to sign it. And the football players, and —"

"Wait." Kylie held up a hand. "It's okay. Ms. Charge told me I could stay on the team. But I quit."

Sophie stared at her. "Why?"

Kylie shrugged. "I don't know. It's like Ms. Charge said. I'm not really a team player."

It's true, Sophie thought. *Kylie definitely marches to the beat of her own drum.*

"But what about the Mules Rules?" Sophie asked. "You made them up. They're yours."

"They don't need me just for the Mules Rules. Someone else can do them."

"But no one will do them as well as you."

Kylie nodded. "That's true."

Sophie looked at Kylie's fuzzy brown suit. "I'm going to miss you in that outfit," she said.

"Me, too," said Kylie. *"Not!"*

They both laughed. Then their chuckles faded into silence. They sat quietly for a moment. Sophie knew what she had to say.

But Kylie spoke first. "I'm sorry about dissing you guys at the pep assembly. I guess that wasn't very cool. Some of those girls are okay."

"Yeah, some of them are," agreed Sophie. "And some of them aren't. I'm sorry about what happened at the Halloween dance. About ditching you to hang out with the cheerleaders, I mean."

"That was pretty lousy," Kylie admitted. "I mostly felt bad for Joel, though."

"For Joel?"

"When you wouldn't dance with him."

Sophie frowned, confused. "I would have danced with him if he'd asked me."

"He *did* ask you, but you walked away."

Sophie's mind whirled. She remembered Joel turning to her to say something just as the cheerleaders walked in. Joel had wanted to dance. With her.

"I shouldn't tell you this," Kylie confessed, "but he likes you. Or he did, anyway."

"I thought he liked *you*," said Sophie, dumbfounded. "I mean, you've been hanging out all the time, so I thought you guys . . ."

"What? Me and Joel?" Kylie squawked. "Ew! No way."

"Do you think . . . he might like me again?" Sophie asked hesitantly.

Kylie smiled. "Maybe. That is, if he can get over you being a cheerleader."

Sophie turned pink all the way to her ear tips.

"But what about you and Scott?" said Kylie. "'Cause I've been hearing rumors —"

"None of which are true," Sophie said quickly. "I've been trying to tell you, we're just friends. I would never step in on someone you like. Or even *used* to like."

"I guess I still like him. I don't think he'll ever get over that attack by his locker though."

"You never know," said Sophie.

"Hmm," said Kylie, thinking about that. She turned her back to Sophie. "I think I'm ready to get out of this costume. Would you unzip me?"

Sophie undid the zipper and Kylie wriggled out of the furry suit.

She held it up. "What should I do with it?"

"Turn it into a fur coat?" suggested Sophie.

"It would make a nice rug," said Kylie.

"Or boots!"

"How about a fabulous set of furry pom-poms?" Kylie joked. "I can wave them at the games. You can show me some cool moves."

Sophie shook her head. "Sorry. Can't do it. I'm sworn to cheerleader secrecy."

"C'mon." Kylie poked her in the side. "Give 'em up. I'll be your best friend."

Sophie swatted away her hand. Then she put an arm around Kylie's shoulders.

"Okay," she said, laughing. "It's a deal."

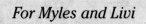

For Myles and Livi

Chapter 1

✿✿✿ TARYN ✿✿✿

I Guess It's a Boy Thing

"Jeff Rasmussen, I'm going to get you for this!" I scream at the top of my lungs.

My head pounds and I reach up to make sure there's no bump. Meanwhile, Jeff zips across my lawn into his own backyard, taunting me the whole time.

"You can run," I scream even louder, "but you can't hide!"

I can't believe Jeff would do this. Sure, he's been teasing me for eleven summers straight. There have been times over the years when he's even dared to pinch or poke me, but he usually keeps his distance. And he never actually *hit* me with anything before, especially not a flying object. Mostly he just calls me obnoxious names like "stinky" and "bones. " He sure knows how to make me squirm, the rat.

Of course, I've plotted my own kind of revenge. It drives Jeff crazy when I tease him right back about the two extra-long toes on his left foot. And I got him once with a mean triple-knuckled noogie. The main difference between my teasing and his, however, are the aftershocks.

A single harsh word from Jeff and I'm bawling for five minutes.

But Jeff's different. He never ever cries. He just laughs out loud.

I guess it's a boy thing.

Jeff's family and my family have been friends forever. His mom and my mom always remind us that Jeff and I were born on the exact same week-end at the same hospital in Rochester, New York. We both weighed exactly seven pounds and four ounces, and measured twenty inches. Sometimes I wonder if Jeff is actually my secret twin brother, except that I don't really need (or want) another brother. I already have three of those: Tim, Tom, and Todd. Three Taylor brothers is more than enough for anyone.

I guess the worst part about Jeff's sneak attack

today was that he didn't hit me with a Wiffle ball or anything accidental. No, he hit me with a sneaker aimed directly at my head — a smelly, brown, disgusting sneaker with a rubber sole that's peeling off.

How gross is that?

"Jeff, where are you?" I growl, climbing over the break in the fence between our houses. I scramble through the thicket, trying hard not to scratch up my legs. I'm already covered from head to toe with mosquito bites.

It's too warm out today. The air feels like mashed potatoes and I can't find Jeff anywhere. He's not in the small shed behind his house. He's not under his front porch. I've checked all of his usual hiding spots.

I'm getting thirsty.

"Jeff, come out!" I cry. "Come on, it's too hot. Truce? Please?"

Jeff appears from around the side of his blue-shingled house. He's whistling and carrying two Popsicles. I take a cherry one. He keeps the lime. We sit on the porch steps. I realize that he's still only wearing one sneaker, the one he didn't hurl at my head.

"That really, really hurt, you know," I grumble, biting the end of my Popsicle.

He looks right through me. "Yeah, sorry, Taryn," he says. I want to believe him, but he's smirking.

"You're sorry?" I repeat, my eyes widening.

"Yeah, sorry. Truly."

"You mean it?" I ask, twisting the ends of my long, brown hair.

"Yeah," Jeff replies. "I didn't really mean to hit you. I just got carried away. And I know how gross my sneakers are."

He sounds genuine this time. As if.

But somehow, despite all the teasing over the years, Jeff always finds the right thing to say or do to make things better. Somehow, a word or even just a smile is like a Band-Aid, and I can instantly forgive Jeff for whatever he's done.

That's how it works with best friends.

Jeff leaves me on the porch with his Popsicle peace offering and races across the lawn, back to my yard. He's gone to find his other stinky shoe. He returns with both sneakers laced up and a yellow dandelion tight in his fist.

"Here," Jeff grunts, pushing the little flower toward me.

Now it's my turn to laugh. "Thanks," I say with a smile, taking the flower. It's peace offering number two. I'm secretly glad that he's feeling so guilty.

The sun beats down hard on the steps, so we

move up to the wicker rocking chairs on his porch. We've spent more afternoons than I can count rocking in those chairs together. Sometimes we play Scrabble or cards out there. Sometimes his mom makes us peanut-butter-and-marshmallow sandwiches. Sometimes his Maltese, Toots, sits on my lap, while my cat, Zsa-Zsa, sits on his lap. We tickle their ears and sing dumb songs.

Today, all we can think or talk about is sixth grade. It's already late August and school is right around the corner. We're moving to Westcott Middle School from the elementary school down the street. That means that I'll be taking a bus to school every morning instead of walking with Jeff.

Mom got a letter from school the other day that listed the different sixth-grade homerooms. I'm in 10A. Jeff is in 11B. I hate the fact that Jeff and I won't be in the same room. It will be the first time in all of our years in school together that we'll start each day in a different class with a different teacher. My best girlfriends, Leslie and Cristina, are in my homeroom, so I guess I'll survive.

But it won't be the same.

"Westcott has an awesome soccer team," Jeff mumbles, taking a final lick of his drippy Popsicle.

"Yeah, everyone knows that," I say.

Jeff likes soccer more than almost anything

else — even more than Toots. And that's saying something. He's been dreaming about winning a World Cup title since he was little. Fifth-grade soccer camp, and fourth-grade camp before that, just didn't cut the mustard. He has at least three pairs of cleats in his closet. Late this summer, Jeff was a part of this youth soccer league in our town. The kids told him that even though he was going into sixth grade, sometimes really good players were allowed to join the seventh and eighth grade middle school team. Now that's all he can talk about. He wants to be the exception to the rule.

"What are *you* going to do at Westcott?" Jeff asks with the usual daydream-y look in his eye that he always gets when thinking about soccer.

"What do you mean? Like after school?"

Jeff nods. "Yeah."

"I haven't really thought about it. I guess I'll try out for the school play, or maybe the school paper," I reply, licking my sticky, cherry fingers.

"Yeah," Jeff grunts. "You would."

"What is that supposed to mean?"

"*Nada.*"

I stand up and readjust my shorts, leaning back just a little so the sun isn't in my eyes. "Don't be a toad," I caution him, wagging my index finger in his face.

Jeff laughs and pinches me on the arm.

"Ribbit," he croaks, dancing off the porch steps.

Ow! I can almost feel the imaginary steam escaping out of my ears as I chase him around a tree, circle his shed, and speed back up the porch steps.

"Tag, you're it!" I shout, leaning in for the touch. But just as I brush his arm, I catch my toe on a step and go flying.

Splat.

Jeff gets this stunned look for a split second. Then he bursts into a fit of hyena laughter. Here I am, sprawled on the steps, and he doesn't even try to help me up.

Instead, he *tags* me.

"You're it again!" Jeff hollers.

Just then, two boys appear at the fence gate near the side of Jeff's house. It's Jeff's best guy friends, Peter and Anthony. They're starting sixth grade at Westcott in a few weeks, too.

"Hey, Taryn, nice fall," Peter calls out to me.

I want to laugh, but my knee is killing me.

Jeff shoots me an abrupt look that says, "Okay, see you later. I have to hang out with the guys now." He's been giving me that look all summer long. We used to hang out together, the four of us, but lately they don't seem to want a girl around. I'm not sure why.

I wish I could pull off my own shoe and hit Jeff on the head with it, right there in front of his friends, so he would know how it feels. But somehow I don't think a flimsy pink flip-flop will have quite the same effect as his smelly sneaker. And I don't really want to hurt anyone, especially not him.

So I slink away from the boys, taking the hint, waving and hiking back through the break in Jeff's just-painted gray fence. In a few minutes, I'm back in my own yard, sidestepping my mother's purple daisies.

My brother Tim is lying in a lawn chair with his sunglasses on. He's as ginger-brown as an almond. He's spent the whole summer perfecting his tan. His girlfriend, Amy, works at a tanning parlor. The two of them look like an unnatural color to me, but I'm no tanning expert.

"Yo, Taryn, you got a phone call," Tim calls out to me.

"From who?" I ask.

"Dr. Wexler," Tim says, giving me a dramatic, low whistle and peering over the tops of his dark shades. "He wanted to schedule your eye exam. Man, are you in trouble, sis. That guy's Dr. Dread if you ask me."

"Ha, ha, ha . . . No one asked you," I groan, rolling my eyes and trying to act cool. I skip up the steps up to our house and push open the screen door.

The last person in the world I want to think about right now is Dr. Wexler.

Ever since I found out that I my eyes don't work right, Tim's been trying to scare me about the optometrist. I hate to admit it, but his big-brother tactics are beginning to work. I'm trying hard not to be scared about the whole experience, but how am I supposed to feel about wearing glasses for the rest of my life? I know Tim's right about Dr. Wexler, too. Everyone says that guy has cold hands and death breath when he leans in to check your vision.

It all started at school last year, when I couldn't see the board. I didn't say anything at first, but then my grades started to slip. Then I found myself getting eye aches and sitting really close to the TV. And then I failed that stupid eye test the nurse gave me. The only reason I'm getting glasses at all is because Mom and Dad didn't give me a choice. Otherwise, I'd be perfectly content to walk around in a blurry haze for the rest of my life.

When I wander into the kitchen, I'm not surprised to find Mom there, chopping carrots.

"Are you in or out?" she asks me. "I'm trying a new recipe and I need all the taste buds I can find."

Mom's always experimenting in the kitchen. I think she dreams of being on Iron Chef one day, making weird dishes with rutabaga and octopus. I prefer grilled cheese myself.

"I'm in," I say, and take a seat at the table. My other brothers are, of course, nowhere to be found. "What's on the menu today, Mom?"

Her face lights up and she pushes some kind of salad in front of me. It smells like vinegar and onions. Cautiously, I lift a forkful into my mouth.

"So? So?" Mom hops up and down in front of me, looking for some kind of reaction.

Of course, I know what to say.

"Deeeee-licious," I mumble, choking down the salad. Mom beams.

Dad says Mom's sick of predictable dinners, so she's always looking for new recipes to try. And all summer I've been trying, really trying to deal. But it's hard.

And it's not just about the food.

School starts in exactly two weeks and I want to know one thing: Isn't there some way to make sure that, in sixth grade, things can just stay the way they've always been?

Chapter 2

• • • Jeff • • •

Call Me Worm King

"I dare you to eat one of those," Peter says, pointing to a brown, crusty leaf on a burned-out bush.

"No prob," I say, grabbing the dead leaf and shoving it into my mouth. It crunches loudly as my friends laugh.

We're always playing games like this. Peter and my other buddy Anthony are pretty good with doing certain dares. They'll walk on rickety fences, climb jagged rocks, and jump into cold lakes. But they won't eat half the stuff I will. This summer alone, I've swallowed a ladybug, twelve pebbles, a dish of dirt, and a long list of other things, including half of a moldy cheese sandwich. They wouldn't even take a single bite.

"Okay," Anthony pipes up after I've swallowed the leaf. "Now you need to . . ."

"Wait a minute," I interrupt him. "It's *your* turn."

Anthony makes a face. "All right," he says begrudgingly. "Bring it on."

Peter has an idea right away. He's spotted something in the grass. He leans down and holds it up. It's a fat, wet earthworm.

"Gross me out," Anthony says, tightening his lips. "You want me to eat that? Uhh, no way, man."

I cluck like a chicken.

"If you're so brave, you do it," Anthony says, glaring at Peter.

Peter looks momentarily stunned by the reverse dare.

"I-I-" Peter stammers. "I don't think so."

I step in and reach for the worm. It's cold.

"You guys are wimps," I declare, throwing the wriggling thing into my mouth and taking one quick gulp.

The only thing is: I don't really eat the worm. I toss it over my shoulder. It's a trick I've been practicing for years. But Peter and Anthony don't see.

Suckers.

"No way!" Anthony screams.

"You didn't!" Peter joins in.

"It's so salty," I say, gagging and pretending to chomp on the worm. "Mmmm. Mud and guts . . ."

By now my friends are both frowning *and* cracking up at the same time.

"That's just way too gross, dude," Anthony says, making a face. "I can't believe you —"

"Hold on!" Peter screams. "What's that?"

He points to my shoulder. *Oops*. The worm never made it into the grass at all. Now it's inching toward my neck.

"You faked us out?" Anthony says, slapping me on my arm.

My cheeks get hot. I shrug.

"Excellent!" Peter says, giving me a high five in appreciation of my prank.

I fling the worm off my shoulder, and the three of us double over with laughter. As far as they're concerned, I'm the funniest thing they've ever seen. A sense of pride takes over.

"You might as well just crown me now," I announce. "From now on you can call me Worm King."

That only makes Anthony laugh harder.

We quit the dares and play a few innings of Wiffle ball until Peter grand slams the ball over our neighbor's fence. Then the guys get on their bikes and head home. I head for our porch steps.

I lean back, feet crossed in front, counting a trail of bruises from my ankle to my knee. As clouds drift by, the sun begins to dip down until I can't see it anymore. It won't be dark for an hour or more, but the sky fades from blue to white to pink. Leaves rustle.

I can't wait to call Taryn and tell her about the great worm fake out. The last time I ate anything that crawled, she practically threw up. She loves my bug stories. I can tell.

Maybe I should have asked her over to play Xbox with me tonight. I thought about it, but then she seemed annoyed at me about the sneaker incident. I still have no idea why I threw my shoe at her head. It seemed so funny at the time.

"Jeffrey!" Mom shouts from behind the screen door. "Get inside, will you?"

My stomach does a massive roller-coaster flop. I feel like Mom's been on my case in a major way all summer long.

In June she made me cut my hair really short. I looked like I'd been attacked by a lawn mower.

In July, she started ironing my T-shirts. All she talked about was all the wrinkles in my clothes.

This month, for some reason, she's freaking out about sixth grade. Since I nearly flunked fifth-grade math, Mom wants to make sure that I take math more seriously this year. I tried explaining to her that I *do* take school seriously, and she bought it; at least for a little while. Then she made me this killer deal. In middle school, if I get a B or higher in math, she'll buy me tickets to a pro baseball or hockey game.

I can't blow that bargain.

"Coming!" I scream at the top of my lungs, even though Mom's only a few yards away.

As I leap up and fling open the screen door, Mom's standing there with her hands wrapped in a tight knot at her waist.

"Is it really necessary to yell?" Mom asks, smirking.

"You always tell me to speak up for myself."

"Jeffrey . . ."

"Sorry," I say.

Mom grabs my earlobe and smiles. "You're a beast," she teases, pretending to yank me inside. She's not pulling very hard, but I yelp in fake pain. Then she hugs me. It's just this thing we do.

"I need to get supper in the oven. Your step-father has to stay late at work again," Mom explains as we stroll into the kitchen together. She picks up a handful of untrimmed green beans from a bowl on the table.

"Care to snip?" she asks.

I take a pair of scissors from the drawer and park myself in front of the bowl.

Rowwwf!

My half sister, Blair, races into the kitchen chasing our dog, Toots. The dog is wearing a pink doll's dress with two snaps shut, a polka-dotted bow looped around his collar, and these teeny purple glitter barrettes by his ears. As he scampers up into my lap, his little pink tongue flaps. In no time, my shirt is covered in drool.

"What's wrong with Toots?" Blair whines. "He won't sit still. And I haven't finished fixing his fur."

Blair whines all the time, especially when she doesn't get her way. She's only eight, but she has something to say about everything.

"Nothing is wrong with Toots," I snap at my sister. "And in case you hadn't noticed, he's a *boy* dog. . . ."

"Jeffrey," Mom says in a stern voice, cutting me right off. She knows I am about to say that the problem is not Toots, but Blair. But Mom also knows that if I say this, Blair will throw one of her princess fits.

"Jeffy, give me back the doggy," Blair demands.

Groaning, I kiss the top of Toots's head and place him gently onto the floor. "Good luck, buddy," I whisper.

Toots takes off for the living room. Blair zooms after him.

Five minutes later, the bowl of beans is perfectly snipped. I dump them into our microwavable steamer and ask Mom what else she needs. She kisses me on my head and says, "Nothing." That's exactly what I hoped she'd say.

It's still warm and the sky is light, so I head back out to the porch again, plopping into one of the wicker rockers. From where I sit, I can see up into the windows of Taryn's house. She's walking around . . . now she's petting Zsa-Zsa . . . no, she's reading a book.

Ever since we were kids, Taryn and I have played spies, inventing secret ways to communicate between our two houses. We hold up notes in our windows with short messages, sometimes even coded ones. Other times we try to disguise our voices on the telephone. One time, we tried to string a couple of cans across the yard from window to window, like old-fashioned walkie-talkies.

It was a great experiment until the wind blew. That's when the string wrapped itself around a row of cables. My stepdad, J.D., still busts on me for that one. I don't know how it happened, but that lousy string knocked out our cable TV for two days, just before one of his big football games.

And J.D.'s like an elephant. He never forgets.

The screen door to the front porch opens with a loud squeak.

"Jeffy, Mom wants you again," Blair says.

I ignore her, as usual.

"Jeffy, Mom wants you NOW," Blair says again, louder this time.

I keep looking the other way.

"Move your butt, bro!"

"Watch your mouth, sis," I shoot back, knowing that if Mom hears Blair talking like that, the only person who will get into trouble is me.

I amble inside to find out what Mom wants now. It's a phone call for me. She stands there, arm extended with the portable. I can hear breathing on the other end.

"Guess who?" Mom asks.

I know who. I take the phone.

"Hey, Taryn," I say into the receiver.

"How did you know it was me?" Taryn asks. Her voice sounds muffled.

"Where are you?" I ask. "It sounds like you're in a tunnel." I wonder if she's pulling one of our old secret agent tricks.

"Duh, I'm in my room," Taryn says matter-of-factly. "But you know that already, don't you? I saw you on the porch, Jeff."

180

"You saw me?" I can't help but laugh out loud. "Spying, right?"

Taryn laughs right back. "Hey, are you guys having dinner soon?" she asks.

"Nah. Sounds like J.D.'s going to be late again. What about you?"

"Mom's cooking. Want to meet up later for flashlight tag?" Taryn asks. "Maybe Peter and Anthony can come over, too? I think that kid Mike from down the street is back from camp. Your sister could even play."

"My sister? You're kidding, right?" I grunt.

"Whatever. Just meet me when it gets dark," Taryn says.

"Okay," I say. I'll do almost anything for a good game of flashlight tag. So far this summer I'm undefeated in our neighborhood. Not that anyone really keeps score except for me.

"Meet you by the shed," Taryn says.

As I hang up the phone, I wonder just how many good games of flashlight tag we'll play for the rest of August and then September.

I miss summer already.

Chapter 3

❀ ❀ ❀ TARYN ❀ ❀ ❀

A Very Big Biggie

It was all Cristina's idea in fourth grade. She decided to take the letters of each of our first names and make up a new name for the three of us. And so we became TLC, for Taryn, Leslie, and Cristina, otherwise known as Tender Loving Care.

I admit it was kind of dumb, calling ourselves something like the name of an old singing group, but after a short time the name grew on me. And then it just stuck like Elmer's.

Today, I'm hanging with L and C down at the town pool. I wish this weather lasted all year long. I hate knowing that summer has to end. Sometimes I fantasize that we live in Hawaii and not New York. Then we'd have our own surf club.

We'd know how to do the hula. I'm sure my brother Tim wouldn't mind being tanned and eating pineapple all year long.

The only yucky thing this summer was my bathing suit. I've been wearing the same-style one-piece, tank suit forever. This summer L and C got these cute new flower bikinis with little ties on the side. Leslie's hair got really blond so she looks like a swimsuit model. Cristina started wearing makeup, even when it's ninety degrees or hotter.

I wonder if anyone notices this stuff besides me.

Next year it's definitely my turn to get a bikini.

Bathing suits aside, swimming at the town pool is just the best. The pool has three different diving levels, and this summer I finally made the monster leap off the high board. There is no better feeling than jumping off a diving board into cold water when it's scorching hot out. Even a belly flop feels okay as long as it cools me off.

The three of us have spent a lot of time together at the pool for the past few summers, but this summer was by far the busiest — and the most interesting. Leslie declared a mega-crush on a lifeguard named Rick, and he's in ninth grade. He's so old, he has facial hair. I don't get it. What's the big deal about this guy?

Cristina's cousin came up from Puerto Rico for

a few weeks, too. She was super-duper nice and her name was Ellen, so Cristina briefly changed our name from TLC to TLCE, or, Tender Loving Care Etcetera. Cristina is always so good with words. She's won the school spelling bee three years in a row.

Now it's the last week before sixth grade, and I haven't seen much of Jeff around the pool lately. He's busy with a math tutor or something. He won't say. I think he's embarrassed. His mother is worried about school already, not that it's any big surprise. She worries about everything. I am so glad my mom's not a worrywart, bugging me about grades and report cards before school even starts.

"So did you decide on your first-day outfit?" Leslie asks Cristina and me.

Cristina breaks into a wide smile. "Of course!" she chirps. "Black pants and tank top. Perfect."

"Black?" Leslie moans.

"What's wrong with black? It's in all the magazines," Cristina says.

"Black isn't even a real color," Leslie gripes. "We should give you a makeover."

Cristina lets out one of her little snort-laughs. "Yeah, right!" she says.

Leslie laughs right back. "It could be fun. . . ." she says in a singsongy voice. "Remember when we dyed your hair with blue Kool-Aid on your birth-day last year?"

"Yeah, and I remember my mom having a fit when the color didn't wash out for a month," Cristina says.

"What are you wearing, Leslie?" I ask. I'm always tempted still — after all these years — to call her Les, but I know she'd hate me for that. Leslie doesn't believe in nicknames anymore.

"I got this incredible new shirt and these tur-quoise Capri pants that fit me perfectly," Leslie says. "Plus, I'm getting my hair cut the day before school starts."

"What about you, Taryn?" Cristina asks me.

I say something incomprehensible about jeans and a T-shirt. The truth is, I don't have a clue about what to wear on the first day of sixth grade. I hadn't really thought about it before now. Jeff and I never talk about things like outfits. He wears the same kind of clothes every day.

"Oh, look. Check *her* out," Leslie says, nudging me and Cristina.

She's staring at Emma Wallace, one of our class-mates and my neighbor. As usual, Emma's decked out in a perfect watermelon-pink two piece bathing suit. She's even wearing matching pink sunglasses. Everything complements her shoulder-length, chestnut brown curls, long legs, and white teeth. She has these pouty lips like movie stars have — but hers are the real deal. And I'm pretty sure she's never, ever had a pimple.

Worst of all, she's nice.

"Does she think she's a supermodel or what?" Cristina groans.

I have to giggle. Sometimes I feel like Zsa-Zsa, claws out, when we're talking about other people this way. I wonder what people say about me when I'm not around.

"Forget Miss Perfect. Look who's over *there*," Cristina whispers, indicating the deep end of the pool. "It's Danny Bogart. I haven't seen him all summer. He's grown, like, ten inches taller. Wow."

"He is cute, isn't he?" Leslie giggles.

"You both think everyone is cute," I say.

I stare off to catch a glimpse of Danny for myself. He's playing Marco Polo with a bunch of other guys we know from elementary school. It looks like all of them went through summer growth spurts. I hadn't noticed until now.

"I wish someone would ask me out on a date," Cristina declares.

I look at her like she has six heads. "What?" Mom has already told me I can't date until high school, so I don't even think about it.

"Now that we're in sixth grade," Cristina continues, "we all need to find someone to like."

"What are you guys talking about?" I ask.

"I already like someone." Leslie giggles, covering her face with her hands. Her cheeks look more sunburned than usual when she says that.

"Who?" I ask, surprised. She hasn't said anything about this before now.

Leslie moves her hands away long enough to mumble, "Charlie."

Right away, Cristina and I know she means Charlie West, this guy from last year's homeroom. He and Jeff play basketball sometimes.

"Charlie?" I say, rolling my eyes. "Why him?"

Leslie giggles some more, which gets Cristina giggling, too. I don't get it.

"Isn't there someone that *you* like, Taryn?" Leslie asks.

"No," I say matter-of-factly.

"I think you should go out with Jeff," Cristina declares.

My eyes bug out wide. "Jeff?" I cough. "Have you totally lost your mind?"

"Why not? He's nice," Leslie says. "And he's way cuter this year than he was last year."

"Wait. You've always told me he was a dork," I say, confused.

"Nah. He just acts that way sometimes," Cristina says.

"But all boys do," Leslie adds.

This whole conversation freaks me out. "I do not like Jeff or any boy that way," I say in a firm voice.

This sends L and C into convulsive laughter. They don't believe me, no matter how many times I deny it. It's time to change the subject — fast.

Lucky for me, the conversation is cut off because Rick comes over and tells us to move. The pool is getting ready to shut down for the afternoon. There's a camp swim meet today, so free swim is over. Briefly, the three of us consider staying up in the bleachers to cheer on some of our other friends from school. But in the end, we all pick up our stuff and head to the locker room to change back into our regular clothes.

In the locker room, no one talks about boys anymore and I am totally relieved. I walk outside with Leslie and Cristina. They're getting a ride home together with Leslie's dad. After they leave, I wait on the curb for my brother Todd to show up. He just got his driver's license last year so Mom always sends him out on errands, which include picking me up.

On the way home, Todd doesn't say very much.

He's chomping on a piece of gum and listening to one of his heavy metal CDs. Ugh.

When we get inside the house, I climb up the stairs to my bedroom and grab the portable phone. Naturally, Tom's on the other line with his friends. They always play around with the three-way-calling feature. They can stay on the phone for hours, literally. It drives Mom batty. It drives me battier.

Outside my window, our giant willow tree is dancing. I see its branches sway back and forth even though the air outside was so still and hot earlier today. I wonder when autumn will show up for real. The weather forecaster said we're supposed to have another heat wave before the season changes.

Across the yard, I can see right into Jeff's bedroom window. He's there, sitting on his bed with his Game Boy. Toots is there, too, wagging his tail. I think about what Cristina and Leslie said, about Jeff being cuter this year.

He doesn't look any different to me.

I check the phone again. Tom is finally off the line so I dial Jeff's house. His little sister, Blair, answers. I'm still looking out my window into his room when I see Blair walk in carrying the phone. She hands it to him.

"Hello?" Jeff asks in a deep voice.

"Hey," I answer.

His head bobs up, and he shoots a look right out his window. Now we're on the phone, talking, but we can see each other, too.

"Missed you at the pool today," I say.

I see Jeff shrug. "I had to help J.D. clean the garage. Man, it stunk."

"Are you listening to that Lame Brain CD right now?" I ask.

Jeff nods. "Want to listen? This band totally rocks."

I nod right back, knowing he can see me, and give him a dramatic thumbs-up. He races over to his stereo to turn up the music. It blares into the phone. I wonder if it's making his windows rattle.

When we were smaller, we used to play this DJ game together. I'd be in my room, playing the announcer, and Jeff would be in his room, spinning music like a real radio disc jockey.

The Lame Brain guitarist lets his instrument wail and then the song is done. I stand right up at the window and start clapping. I can see Jeff laugh as he picks up his phone.

"So who else was at the pool?" Jeff asks.

"L and C," I say.

"Any other kids from school?"

"Jacob, Danny, Miles, Emma . . ."

I list off the names of a few other kids and that gets us blabbing about sixth grade all over again. I let it slip (again) that I'm worried about the first day of school. It's only three days away now.

"Quit obsessing, Taryn," Jeff says.

"I don't obsess," I say.

"Yes, you do," Jeff counters.

"No, I don't."

"Yes, you do."

I let out a huge sigh. "Well, I think it's perfectly normal to worry."

"Whatever."

"Hey, can we take the bus together on the first day?"

"Of course," Jeff says matter-of-factly. "What else were we going to do?"

"I don't know," I reply, feeling silly for asking the question.

"Sixth grade will be no biggie, Taryn. Trust me." Now Jeff sounds a little annoyed.

I really want to believe my best friend. I want to believe that getting used to a new school and new teachers will be a piece of chocolate cake. But something tells me that Jeff is way wrong. Something tells me that sixth grade at Westcott is going to be a *very big* biggie.

And I still have no idea what I'm going to wear.

Chapter 4

••• Jeff •••

The Bus Stops Here

Here comes Mom again. She's got that red-in-the-face expression, even though she's smiling at the same time.

"Jeffrey, dear, why is everything from your closet now on the floor?" she asks, still smiling.

"Um . . . er . . ."

I don't know what to say. Even worse, I don't know what to wear for the first day of sixth grade.

"Do we have a fashion emergency?" Mom jokes.

"Naw," I bark defensively. "I've got everything under control. *Everything*."

Quickly, I grab the first pair of pants and polo shirt I see. The pants are corduroy and I can't remember the last time they were washed. The shirt is clean (I think), but it's been in a ball in the back of my closet for as long as I can remember. It's a little bit — okay, *a lot* — wrinkled.

"Oh, Jeffrey, take those off!" Mom wails, sounding mad. "Those are winter pants."

Mom makes me exchange the cords for a freshly washed pair of Levis. Then she takes the shirt from me and disappears into the next room. I push and shove the remainder of the scattered clothing into one large pile and nudge it toward my closet. This is my patented "pile" technique. I've been cleaning my room this way for years.

Half an hour later, I'm dressed, cool, and wrinkle-free (thanks to Mom), and headed next door to Taryn's. Ever since I was little, Taryn and I have walked to school together. Elementary school was a breeze. It was right up the street.

But this year it's different.

This year we have to walk three blocks to catch a bus and then head all the way across town. Our new middle school is across the railroad tracks, down by this multi-level shopping area in town. We couldn't walk there even if we wanted to.

On my way out of the house, I catch my reflection in the hall mirror. I look like J.D., all starched and pressed. Too bad there's no time to change out of this geeky shirt into a t-shirt. At least Mom got me a new backpack with my initials on the pocket. That adds some cool to the outfit.

Just as I'm leaving, my half sister, Blair, appears. She's wearing this yellow-striped dress I hate with these brown Mary Jane shoes I hate even more. Even worse, this morning she's actually skipping around the house and singing way off-key. Peter, Anthony, and I always joke that she was cloned from a bad episode of Barney the dinosaur.

"Shake a leg, Jeffrey," Mom says. "Taryn's on her front steps. She's waiting. I can see her from here. You have everything? Did you put your soccer cleats in your bag? I know you said you might —"

"Got 'em," I say impatiently, grabbing the new backpack.

"You look very handsome, dear," Mom says, brushing something off my shoulder. Mom is always plucking some kind of imaginary lint off my clothes.

"Mom," I groan. "Good-bye. Okay?"

"Okay," she says in a soothing voice. "Have a great first day of school."

Blair yells, "Good-bye, Jeffy!" at the top of her lungs, and Mom tells me to say good-bye, but I don't. I just wave without turning around. It is bad enough that I have to tolerate a mutant half sister. I shouldn't have to give her a big good-bye, too.

Outside, the air still smells like hot dogs and

194

honeysuckle and everything else that's summertime to me, but I know the truth: Summer is long gone. Memories of pools and sunburns and games of flashlight tag flood my brain. Then a voice jolts me from my thoughts.

"Move it, Jeff, or we'll be late!"

It's Taryn. She waves as I jump between two bushes and jog up to her house.

"You look different," she says. Is she snickering?

"My mom made me wear this," I say. "So just shut up."

"Do you like *my* outfit?" Taryn asks me, pointing at her pink shirt and jeans.

I have no idea what to say, especially after she just insulted me.

"Yeah, sure, Taryn, it's fine," I grunt.

"Thanks," Taryn says, looking pleased by my response.

Together we head to the bus stop.

The temperature feels sauna-like, or at least what I imagine a sauna would feel like if I'd actually ever been in one. By the time we've walked two of the three blocks, I'm sweating — a lot. I really wish I was wearing a T-shirt.

"I'm nervous. Are you?" Taryn asks me.

I don't know what to say to that, either. After all, I'm the one who's sweating, right?

"I just think it's so weird, being nervous about school," Taryn says.

"Everything you think is weird," I joke.

Taryn fakes a laugh and pushes me so hard I stumble off the curb.

"Hey," I growl, jumping back onto the sidewalk.

"Sorry," Taryn says, stifling a giggle. "I guess I don't know my own strength."

"Yes, you do," I say. "You're Wonder Woman, right?"

"Very funny, Aquaman."

We both chuckle and approach the bus stop slowly. A crowd has gathered there; not just kids but mothers, fathers, and even a dalmatian, a dog that belongs to Emma Wallace. She went to elementary school with us.

"Hey, Jeff. Hey, Taryn," Emma calls out as we get closer. "How are you guys? Can you believe school is really here?"

I nod and smile but Taryn doesn't say anything. Whenever we see Emma around the neighborhood, Taryn always clams up.

"Middle school seems so . . . well . . . *major*. Doesn't it?" Emma says, smiling.

"Nah," I say.

"Nah," Taryn says, just like me. I could punch her for doing that.

I can see that Emma's dalmatian wants to jump up on me — bad. He must smell Toots all over me.

"Mom was going to drive me to school," Emma explains. "But I told her no way. I wanted to come to the bus stop so I could go to school with everyone else in our neighborhood and our class and not miss out on the whole first day of school thing, you know what I mean?"

I have no idea what she means. Still, I nod.

Taryn turns to the side and makes a face at me. Hopefully, Emma didn't catch that.

Finally, from around a corner, the yellow school bus — *our* yellow school bus — appears. A hum rises from the small crowd. The bus rolls to a stop.

"Hey, want to sit together?" Emma asks Taryn.

"That's okay," Taryn says quickly. "I'm already sitting with Jeff."

"Maybe tomorrow then," Emma says, kissing her mom and her dog good-bye and climbing up the bus steps.

Taryn and I hang back a little. I'm looking for my friends Peter and Anthony. They said they'd be here, too, but I can't see Anthony's spike haircut anywhere.

"What was *that* about?" Taryn whispers to me as soon as Emma steps away. "I had no idea she was going to ask me that."

197

"Yeah, weird," I mumble. I'm focused on the people ahead of us. They move like snails.

I see this seventh grader Mike who lives a few houses away from me. He has a cast on his arm and it's covered in magic marker. I wish I could read what it says. Next to him are the giraffe twins: Brittany and Bethany. They live nearby, too. I think they're starting eighth grade this year. Everyone knows them because they've been the tallest kids in our neighborhood and at school for years — taller than all the boys, even. Off to the side is Duck. His real name is Edgar, but no one ever calls him that. Duck never goes anywhere without his asthma inhaler. He got the nickname because it sounds like he quacks when he talks.

"What's the holdup?" I ask under my breath.

Taryn laughs. "Maybe it's a sign."

"Of what?"

"Maybe it's a sign that sixth grade isn't really meant to start today," Taryn says.

I roll my eyes. "Oh yeah, that's it."

Taryn's way into omens and karma and all that creepy stuff. I tried playing that Ouija game with her once, where you ask the game board a question and it "magically" spells out an answer. She thought there was some secret power guiding our fingers across the board. I half expected ghostly organ music to start playing. Get real.

When the snails move and we finally do get on the bus, I'm relieved to spot Peter and Anthony waving from the back. They must have gotten on at the last stop.

Taryn doesn't look quite as glad to see them. "I hope they saved a seat for me, too."

"Of course they did," I insist.

On our way down the bus aisle, we pass Emma and some of the other sixth graders we know from the area, plus a whole bunch of seventh and eighth graders who live nearby. Some kids grunt hello; some are too busy talking. Everyone's jabbering like crazy and the sound in the bus is so loud that I feel an instant headache coming on.

As I get closer, Peter and Anthony give me high fives. Then I sit down on the edge of the sticky, fake leather seat across from them. Meanwhile, Taryn looms right over me with this goofy look on her face.

"Move over," she commands.

I'm about to get up to let her in when the bus jerks forward. I feel myself lift up off the seat. Peter and Anthony yell out like we're on The Scream Machine.

"Wheeee!"

And then Taryn, who isn't holding on to anything, loses her footing. I reach out and grab for her backpack, but can't catch her before she hits the bus floor.

Thud.

Peter lets out a snort, then Anthony. Soon, everyone is laughing in the rows around us. Taryn tells them all to zip their lips.

It sounds like something my grandmother would say.

"Are you okay?" I lean down and whisper. I'm trying so hard not to burst out laughing myself. She's still half on the floor. Truth is, she's lucky she didn't fly out a window or slam into a seat. The bus driver glances back and asks what's up, but keeps driving. Everything's okay.

Luckily, there are no tears. Taryn gets up and pretends like nothing happened.

"That was interesting," she says, brushing off her pants.

"Break anything?" Anthony jeers, grinning.

Peter's about to say something, too, but I shoot him my insane-asylum look.

When we finally get to school, everyone's nerves are still all tingly, and not just because of Taryn's big dive. It's the realization that sixth grade is finally here — for real.

We all pile off the bus. Westcott Middle School rises up from the ground in front of us like a huge temple with columns out front. It's one of those buildings that's brand new but made to look old. The school's name is carved next to sculpted birds at the top of each column, like buildings I've seen in my history textbooks. I've been here before, once with my stepfather and once for orientation when we were still in fifth grade. But today this place looms up like some kind of monster.

That girl Emma was right. There is something so major about all of this. Sixth grade is the big-time. I should have had an extra waffle for breakfast.

As I walk toward the front doors of my new school, Taryn grabs my elbow.

"Wait up," she says.

"What?" I sigh deliberately.

"What?" Taryn repeats. Her eyebrows crinkle at the top. For the first time, I notice that the pink shirt she's wearing has a teeny black mark on the side, probably from when she fell down. I point it out.

Bad move.

In an instant, Taryn's cheeks swell out like one of those puffer fish I've seen at the aquarium.

"Taryn, you have to chill," I warn her, lying through my teeth. "The shirt looks totally fine."

"Whatever," she moans, pushing ahead of me, way ahead until she disappears in the crowd.

I let her go. I'd rather walk into school with my guy friends, anyway. Briefly, I poke my head above the crowd to see if I can spot her, but I can't see much of anything. I can't hear much of anything, either. As we move in a clump toward the school building, everyone is screaming. It's all hellos and good-byes up the steps and into the building. Then a loudspeaker blares.

"Good morning, students," the principal's voice booms. At least I think it's the principal. He sounds like somebody important.

Peter, Anthony, and I huddle together and make our way to room 11B. As we stroll inside our homeroom, a teacher with a bald head the shape of a cantaloupe hands me a stack of papers.

"Good morning," the teacher says. "Welcome to sixth grade."

I glance down at the top sheet of paper. It has a schedule grid with a bunch of strange names and subjects. How will I remember all these teacher names? How will I know where to go every day — and how to get there? How will I survive taking math and reading diagnostic tests during the first week of school? I don't even know what diagnostic means.

On the chalkboard, the teacher has written out

a short version of the day's activities. First, we have to take attendance. Then we have to fill out all these dumb forms. Then we get a tour and go to some "meet the teacher" buffet lunch. All afternoon, we'll be filling out even more forms. I'm going to need more pencils.

This seems totally unfair to me. It's the first day! Can't we have a pizza party or something? Man, this is rough. I'd much rather be tossing a ball to Toots in the backyard.

When I glance over at my friends, they look as freaked out as me about the day's activities. Peter gives me and Anthony a double thumbs-down.

I nod. It feels like the day has lasted forever — and it's only just begun.

I grab a pencil and fill in all the little boxes and lines on the page in front of me while Mr. Melon Head paces around the room. Every time I glance up at the clock on the wall, it feels like the hands haven't moved at all. Time really is standing still.

After all the first-day forms are completed, we take a break and then we get our lockers. I have locker number 235. It's so narrow. I liked my fat fifth-grade locker way better. Plus, I can't seem to memorize this new locker combination. I keep getting it mixed up with my online password numbers and my bike lock.

By the time the final bell of the school day rings, I'm spent. Melon Head lines us up to get our new textbooks and then sends us on our way. After dropping off the books in my new locker, I spot Taryn coming out of the east stairwell. She's walking with Leslie and Cristina. As usual, the three girls laugh when they see me. They always laugh when they see me. I should have a complex, but I don't.

"Hey!" Taryn yells to me. "Way to ditch me this morning!"

I almost blurt, "Hey, loser, I did not ditch you!" Instead I shove my hands into my pockets. "Let's just get out of here," I say. "Sixth grade. Day one is over and out. Just like me."

I'm glad I didn't start a fight. After that, Taryn giggles and waves good-bye to her friends. Then we leave Leslie and Cristina standing there and walk down to the lobby of the new building. There are two buses back to our neighborhood each day. I want to be on the first one.

"Sorry about this morning," I mumble as we walk along. I feel extra bad when I see that the skid mark is still visible on her pink shirt.

"Thanks," Taryn mumbles back. "How was your first day at Westcott?"

"Wack," I say. "What about you?"

She grins. "Excellent," she says proudly.

Taryn starts to tell me all about her day. I expect to hear some outrageous story. She's good at making up stories. But her day doesn't sound that much different than mine. Same forms, same grind.

As we're walking along, I spy a huge poster on the wall.

"Look at that!" I cry, stopping in my tracks.

The poster has a list of sports team tryouts. There's the word SOCCER in bright blue letters at the very top of the list. I pump my fist in the air and let out a loud hoot.

"Wow," Taryn says. "Jeff, you will *so* make the team. I know it."

I pull out my notebook and pencil and jot down the soccer team tryout times I need to know.

"Maybe I should play soccer this year, too," Taryn says.

I chuckle. "You're kidding, right?"

When I say that, Taryn pokes me in the arm — hard. Then she keeps right on poking and talking, giving me a dozen reasons why she can too play soccer, and how I'm some kind of super-ogre to say that she can't.

Of course I didn't mean that at all. I was just kidding around.

Sometimes that girl can talk and talk and talk

and rather than try to keep up, it's so much better to just keep my mouth shut.

Kids rush past us on all sides, racing to their buses or to cars idling in the parking lot. Another bell rings as we push through the main doors into the real world. What do all these bells mean, anyway? It's like some kind of foreign language. I hope I learn it fast. A few yards away, over at our bus stop, I see Peter and Anthony. We race over, and the four of us (including Taryn) decide to sit at the back of the bus on the way home, just like we did that morning.

I make sure Taryn is sitting before the bus moves so she doesn't fall again.

The bus lurches toward home and I peer out the window. Rows of green trees flash by. There's a lot of traffic this afternoon. A warm breeze blows in. It smells like a combination of mowed grass and car exhaust.

All around me, everyone's talking at the same time, buzzing about the first day of school. I really want to join in the conversation, but my brain stalls. All I can think about is the soccer tryouts. If I get on the soccer team, everything about sixth grade will just fall into place.

At least I hope it will.

Fingers crossed.

Chapter 5

❀ ❀ ❀ TARYN ❀ ❀ ❀

Love Note

I dig my purple-painted toes into my plush, swirly bedroom carpet and just streeeeeetch.

Good morning, sunshine.

I'm so ready for day two of sixth grade. I'm even looking forward to getting some real homework. Jeff would laugh if he heard me say that one. He complained nonstop yesterday about those diagnostic tests we all have to take this week. Ever since we were teeny he's hated tests.

The only bad part about today happens after four o'clock. That's when Mom drives me over to Dr. Wexler's office, where he'll torture me and make me read E's, R's, and Z's from some chart. Today's YIGG-Day, as in "Yikes! I'm Getting Glasses!" Day.

It's the day Dr. Wexler confirms my worst suspicions about my bad eyes and tells me what kind of glasses I need. My brother Tim says I'll have to get thick ones that look like the bottom of a soda bottle. Of course, Tim's just trying to scare me. I think.

Mew, mew, meeeeew.

My cat, Zsa-Zsa, purrs and presses her back against my legs. She does figure eights, and her tail flashes in and out between the crooks of my knees. Of course it's nearly impossible to pull on a skirt when she's doing this, but I try anyway. I'm always up for a challenge. Besides, I selected the best possible day-two outfit, and I'm dying to try it on right now.

L and C helped me choose outfit number two. Last night after school ended and we all took our different buses home, the three of us talked on the phone with three-way calling.

Cristina told me today that she wants to be my fashion advisor. She didn't witness my fall on the bus, but she did see me in school wearing a shirt with this HUGE black mark on it, and she said it was a *faux pas*. That's French for "embarrassing mess," I think. Truthfully, I didn't look like I fell on a bus. I looked like I was *run over* by a bus. Jeff even told me how awful I looked. He and his friends laughed for hours. Well, for a few minutes, anyway.

Apparently, Cristina says I need an outfit that will make everyone forget yesterday's skid mark. So I decided on something girly for today: my peasant skirt, teal tee, and these brown sandals with the little gold buckles that I got at an end-of-summer sale. Plus, I'm wearing a new ponytail holder, too, with the ribbons that flow down the back. Cristina begged me to wear my hair down, but I just cringed. I am happy to change my skirt. I am happy to change my top. But when it comes to my hair, there are some things that will never, ever change.

I break my own record getting ready for school. I'm dressed, combed, and cherry-vanilla lip-glossed in only fifteen minutes. Dad is there, sitting in the kitchen reading his morning paper. I kiss him, Mom, and Zsa-Zsa good-bye. Then it's off to Jeff's house so we can hightail it to the bus stop. We alternate pickup days. Yesterday he came here; today, I'm going there.

When I knock on the Rasmussens' door, I hear Toots bark. Then the lock clicks open.

"Hello!" Jeff's mother greets me warmly.

I grin. "Hey," I say. "Can you tell Jeff I'm here?"

Mrs. Rasmussen puts a finger up to her chin, like she's thinking extra-hard.

"Oh," she says. "Jeff isn't here, Taryn. Didn't he tell you?"

Inside my new sandals, I feel my toes curl.

Tell me what? That he's an undercover agent on special assignment and he's been transferred to Siberia? That he's decided to drop out of sixth grade after only one day? What?

"Jeff got a ride with his stepfather this morning," Mrs. Rasmussen said. "Mr. Rasmussen brought him over to school early so Jeff could meet the soccer coach. You know Jeff — eager beaver!"

"Oh, yeah," I say, backing away from the door just a little bit. "He said something. . . ." But I just trail off.

Just then, Toots crosses the threshold, tail wagging like a windshield wiper, back and forth, forth and back. He recognizes me and sniffs my ankles.

"Thanks, anyway," I say, bending down to pet Toots. I back down the front porch steps and head for the bus stop — alone.

For some reason, the bus stop is way less crowded today than it was yesterday. Then I realize why: I'm ten minutes early. Everything about today started off in order but now I'm getting nervous. Something is off. I glance down at my shirt and sandals to make sure that at least my outfit is still in good shape. I need to count on that.

Before long, the usual suspects show up, one-by-one. Then the bus rolls up.

Peter and Anthony wave to me from the back of the bus like yesterday, but I don't want to sit there without Jeff. Emma says hello, too, but I just force a smile and keep walking. I spot an empty row in the middle of the bus and park my peasant skirt there. No one sits next to me, but I'm right behind the eighth-grade twins. They're laughing during the whole ride and I can't help wondering if they're laughing at me — or my skirt — or my sandals — or *worse*?

When I stare out the bus window, everything looks fuzzy, which reminds me of my eye doctor appointment. My stomach churns at the thought of Dr. Wexler's icy fingertips as he clicks the levers on the testing equipment.

Lucky for me, I forget about all that the moment the bus pulls into the cul-de-sac at school. L and C are standing right there, waiting for me.

I love my best friends.

"Taryn!" Leslie yells. Her yellow-blond hair is pulled up on top of her head and she's wearing this off-white, striped sundress that accentuates her tan. I guess she really meant it when she said she wanted to get a boyfriend this year. As I race over toward her, I notice a group of seventh grade boys staring her way.

"That outfit looks A-plus, awesome," Cristina says, as if she had not only counseled me on what to wear, but had actually come into my closet and dressed me that morning.

I beam proudly. "Thanks for your help," I say. I'm so grateful not to have a skid mark anywhere on my clothes today.

Cristina throws her arm around my shoulder and the row of bangles on her arm makes a clanking noise. She's wearing a pale green, long-sleeved T-shirt and flared jeans (black, of course) with zigzag stitching on the leg. We all have such different styles, but we look good walking along together as a threesome.

"So where's Jeff?" Leslie asks, looking around.

"He's already here, somewhere in the gym, I think," I answer. "Something about soccer. He got a ride to school early."

"If Jeff makes the middle-school team," Cristina says, "he'll be a part of the popular pack with all the older kids."

"Oh, get real!" I say. It's hard to imagine Jeff being in any kind of pack, let alone the *popular* kind.

"Knowing Jeff, that'll give him a really big head," Leslie adds.

"Speaking of which . . ." Cristina lowers her voice to a whisper. "Did you see Emma Wallace yesterday? She has a *huge* head, doesn't she?"

"It's just a different hairstyle," I say. "She's wearing barrettes, so you can see more of her face."

I don't mean to defend Emma, but that's the way it comes out.

"Yeah, well, I think she looks like one of those bobblehead dolls," Leslie says.

We all crack up at the word *bobblehead*.

"She takes my bus, you know," I add.

"I forgot," Leslie says. "She lives near you. That's such a drag."

It's really not a big deal, but I play along. "Yeah," I say. "It's hard living near Little Miss Perfect."

I can't really remember when the three of us decided to hate Emma Wallace, but we definitely made a calculated decision to do it. It would be easy to explain — and understand — if Emma were some kind of super-witch with flaming tornado hair and a flying broomstick. But she doesn't *have* any of those things.

Nope, Emma never has messy hair. Her perfectly placed, silver flower hair clips never change position, as opposed to my clips, which move around and get tangled in every possible strand of hair. She also has perfect nails, painted a different shade of pink each week, usually to match her socks. In addition to the perfect hair, nails, and clothes, Emma walks like she's on some kind of runway. It's more of a strut, really. I think she looks like a model when she does that, but Leslie always compares Emma to a rooster or some other kind of farm bird.

I know the bird comparison is unfair. And it's not like we *want* to be mean or nasty about Emma. We know she's one of the sweetest kids in our class, not to mention the smartest. She's always the teacher's first pick. She's always the one getting straight A's, even in gym class. And she pretends like work doesn't matter, but then she always asks for extra credit. No one person should be so pretty and so *perfect*. TLC vs. Emma is just the way it's always been; I guess it's the way it will always be.

Since Leslie, Cristina, and I are all in the same homeroom, we were assigned lockers near each other. As we enter school, the three of us shuffle through the crowd of kids toward our yellow locker bank.

"Hey, Taryn," Leslie says, squeezing my arm. "What's *that*?"

I spot a piece of paper poking out from the slat in my locker.

Cristina plucks it out before I can. She starts to unfold it.

"Ooooh!" Cristina coos. "Is it a love note?"

I roll my eyes. "It is not," I say, snatching the note from her fingers. Without even looking at it, I shove it into my bag.

"You're not going to open it?" Leslie asks. "Who is it from?"

I shake my head. "How should I know?" I reply.

"You have to open it!" Cristina says, reaching for my bag. She tugs and I tug back. My bag swings into a group of kids walking by.

"Watch it!" a tall boy growls. He says something else but I can't hear what it is.

"Moron," Leslie says, but he's already out of earshot when she says it.

A bell rings and we all flash one another a look. L and C open their own lockers fast. None of us have much in our lockers yet, since it's only the second day of school, but we each go through the motions: turning the dials, pretending to forget our combinations, doing it all over again, and then clicking the metal doors shut. In my bag, I have a dozen photos, postcards, and other stuff to decorate the inside of my locker. I know what I'm going to hang front and center: a photo strip of TLC from the beach this summer. We're all wearing movie-star sunglasses and posing with kissy-faces, like something from some magazine.

Before heading into homeroom, I get permission to go to the girls' bathroom. I head into one of the stalls with my bag. That's when I pull out the mystery note.

I'm surprised to see that it's Jeff's scrawl inside. I told Jeff my locker number yesterday, but I'm amazed he remembered it. He probably can't even remember his *own* locker number.

Hey T,

Sorry I forgot to tell u about soccer. See u in class or meet me after school for the tryouts!!! It's on Field B. Bring L & C if you want. LOL.

Bye, Jeff

A grin spreads across my face. I knew Jeff hadn't blown me off. Good friends never, ever, *ever* do that.

Quickly, I stuff the note back into the pocket of my bag, zip it, and duck out of the stall. Homeroom is starting and I don't want to be late.

As I head into the now-empty middle school hallway, I breathe a sigh of relief.

Somehow, I'll figure out how to finish up the school day, get to Jeff's soccer tryout, *and* still make it to Dr. Wexler's.

And somehow day two of sixth grade won't be so bad after all.

Chapter 6

• • • Jeff • • •

Beyond a Reasonable Doubt

I feel like someone just handed me a bazillion bucks. I'm standing in the middle of the field, cleats on, with the rest of the soccer team wannabes. Westcott takes soccer very seriously. This district has produced more champions than any other school district. And I could be a part of all that.

If that isn't the biggest *whoa* of all time, then what is?

I wish the air wasn't so sticky right now. Summer is supposed to be over, but today is another scorcher. Of course, Coach Byrnes also made us do ten laps before tryouts, so that could explain some of the heat.

Coach has assembled us on the field, awaiting further instructions. That sounds like secret agent talk to me. I know it isn't, but my imagination is going crazy.

At least waiting gives me a solid minute to catch my breath.

My pulse thumps.

While we're waiting, I scan the bleacher seats for a familiar face. I see lots of kids, but only a few from my new class. Peter decided not to try out for the team this year, but he still came to root for me. And Anthony doesn't even like soccer, but he also came. I see some girls I know, too, like Emma Wallace and Leslie Smart and this other girl with red hair who I met in homeroom this morning.

The one person I don't see is Taryn. She'd better get here soon to cheer me on. I left a note in her locker. What's her problem?

Coach Byrnes toots his whistle and lines us up in front of this orange-cone obstacle course. I can ace this drill. I know it.

The whistle blows and we're off, passing and receiving. I trap the ball perfectly and set up for a return pass.

"Fine job!" Coach Byrnes says with a smile as I trot around him and back to the line. I clap my hands together and glance back out at the bleachers.

Peter and Anthony spot my look.

"Go, man, go!" they clap. I throw my arm into the air, wishing they could be out here with me. Right now, no one else on the field wants to talk to me. It's a weird feeling.

Why can't I see Taryn? Is she sitting down somewhere, out of sight?

"Rasmussen!"

I hear my last name and dart over toward Coach Byrnes and his assistant. For my next test, they're setting me up for a one-on-one with this huge eighth grader named Walt. I'll play offense. Walt is defense.

I catch my breath again. This is my big chance to make a goal and prove myself.

With one swift move, I take possession of the soccer ball, dribble it to the side, and step into a wide kick. There's a loud *plock* as the ball explodes right off the side of my foot and fires directly into the goal.

Walt stands there, stunned. No one can believe I made such an easy goal, least of all me. Coach Byrnes asks me to "hang back" while he chats with Walt. Then the coach has me line up again. I can't believe it. Now he wants to match me up with this other older kid named Will. Since I'm just a lowly sixth grader, I have to prove myself and my soccer abilities beyond a reasonable doubt.

So I line up, take more deep breaths, and prepare for another goal. That's when Coach Byrnes pulls a bait and switch. He makes me play defense instead.

I race over in front of the net, bouncing on my toes. I'm expecting a shot to the right or left or way over my head. Will looks like one of those cartoon bulls, digging one foot into the ground, head down, eyes glued on me. I half expect him to start snorting.

Coach Byrnes blows the whistle, and Will charges.

I take a hop to the left. Of course, Will kicks to the right.

Swoosh.

I can practically feel the air as the ball flies past my head, right into the goal.

The bleachers erupt in applause. I hang my head down, figuring that I blew my chance. But I'm wrong. Coach Byrnes comes up to me and slaps me on the back.

"You've got a lot of potential," he says.

I'm waiting for the bad news, but it doesn't come.

"I think you'd make a great addition to the team."

Did I hear him correctly? Did he just say what I think he said?

"Of course," Coach continued, "I need to mull things over. I'll be posting the team list later this week, but I'm very glad you came to tryouts, Jeff. You know, we don't usually take sixth graders on this team. That's what the sixth-grade team was formed for, but I think you may be one of the exceptions. . . ."

Coach Byrnes wags his finger at me and walks away. With all the attention, I feel like I'm on some kind of imaginary trampoline, totally airborne. My head swings around toward the bleachers again, searching for Taryn. I don't know why it matters so much to me to know she's out there. But it does.

Finally, I spot her. She waves to me from the end of a row where she's standing with Leslie and Cristina. I wave back.

After we finish a few additional drills for Coach Byrnes and company, we're dismissed. I jog off the field.

"Way to go!" Taryn cheers from the sidelines. "I'm so sorry I was late, but I was finishing something after class and then I had to call my mom and —"

"It's okay," I say, interrupting her.

"Did you make the team?" Cristina asks, flipping her dark hair. I don't know why that girl always dresses so weird. Who wears black all the time?

Peter and Anthony have come over by now, too. Anthony puts me in a choke hold and plants a noogie on my head. It's just something we do.

The girls back off a little, but then I spot Peter staring at Leslie. I know he thinks she's cute, but he's way too shy to admit it. He said once this summer that he likes her blond hair. We made fun of him, so he hasn't mentioned it since.

"So what are you guys doing now?" Leslie asks.

"Celebrating," I say, giving each of the guys a double high five.

"My mom isn't picking me up for a half hour," Cristina says.

"Mine, neither. Let's go down to the park for a while," Anthony suggests.

In fifth grade, we always hung out together. Now that we're in a different school, there are more places to hang. Just down the street is a town park with old trees, built-in chessboards, and swings.

"I don't know," I mutter. "I'm feeling kind of tired. I got up at five this morning. But I can take the late bus, I guess."

"Forget the bus, Jeff. My mom will give you a ride. Let's all go," Peter says.

"Um . . ." Cristina crosses her arms. "I don't exactly feel like going to the *playground*," she says sarcastically.

Anthony rolls his eyes. "Then don't."

"I wish I could go," Taryn says. "But I have an appointment this afternoon at four."

Taryn's been talking about this big appointment for weeks. She has to go to the eye doctor. Last year she started getting these eye aches. Sometimes she can't even see the TV.

As we're standing there, Taryn pulls out her turquoise cell phone case and dials her mother's number to make sure she's on the way.

While Taryn's talking to her mom, no one says much, and no one moves. An eternity passes before we make any move toward the parking lot — or the park. As we're standing there, I'm starting to suspect that maybe Leslie thinks Peter is cute in the same way he thinks she's cute. She keeps staring at him. Peter is acting even goofier than usual.

"What are we doing here?" Anthony finally blurts.

"Yeah, let's motor," I say to everyone. "Let me just get my bag and change."

I head into the locker room to switch into a non-sweaty shirt and take off my soccer cleats. By the time I come out, Taryn's mother has pulled up in her SUV.

"Yo, guys," I call out, making a snap decision when I see the free ride. "I think I'm just going to hitch with Taryn."

"Hitch?" Anthony says. "I thought you said you wanted to hang."

"Naw, I'm too beat," I say.

"Okay," Peter says, "I guess it's just the four of us, then."

"Whatever," I nod. "Call me later, gators."

The girls say their good-byes and I bid my buddies so long, too. Then I follow Taryn over to her mother's car and take a seat in the back.

The floor is covered with crunched-up paper cups, crumpled notepaper, Kleenex, and other junk. If there's one absolute in the universe, it's this: The Taylor car is always a mess. Taryn's mother usually blames Tim, Tom, or Todd. I think there's still dirt on the floor from five years ago.

"Buckle up, kids," Mrs. Taylor announces after saying hello. She's such a stickler for rules.

"Mom, did you know that Jeff probably just made the soccer team and it is SUCH a big deal? Sixth graders never make it," Taryn says.

"Well, congratulations, Jeff," Mrs. Taylor says to me.

I happily accept the compliment — and I know she means it, too. Taryn's mom has watched me play soccer in our backyards since I could walk.

"I'll drive you home before I take Taryn to the doctor, Jeff," Mrs. Taylor says.

"Thanks," I say.

The SUV tires squeal as we pull out of the parking area.

"I just knew you'd make the team," Taryn says to me. She pokes me in the arm, but this time it's friendlier than usual. For once, she's not trying to inflict a bruise.

"Anything good happen at school today?" I ask her, trying to make polite conversation. After all, we are in the car with her mom.

"Nothing major," Taryn says. "Took that reading test, put some pictures up in my locker . . ."

"Whoop-dee-doo."

"What's wrong with a little interior decorating?" Taryn asks.

"I tried out for soccer. What did you try out for?" I ask.

Taryn makes a face. "Nothing. Yet."

"You said you would. What about photography club, or maybe the newspaper? Did you see the school carnival sign-up sheet?" I ask. "It was posted outside every classroom."

"Yes, I saw it," Taryn says. "But . . ."

Her voice trails off.

"But *what*?" I say.

"But . . . I don't know . . . I just didn't sign up. End of story."

"You would make the best carnival leader, T. And they need some people from every grade," I say. "Maybe *I'll* sign you up."

She thinks I'm serious and overreacts. It's such a Taryn thing to do.

"Don't you dare sign me up, Jeff!" she wails.

"Why not?" I say, still teasing her a little. "If I do soccer and you do the carnival, then we'd both be a part of something."

"Just not the same thing," Taryn says.

We're quiet for a minute, and I can see Taryn's face gets pale. She goes from jabbering to nothing in ten seconds. She's definitely thinking about the eye doctor now.

"Taryn," I say. "Don't freak. It's just the eye guy. How bad can it be?"

"Jeff, you have no idea. Dr. Wexler's breath reeks. I'll bet he's going to make me blink a hundred times or dislodge my eyeball or pluck out my eyelashes or make me read something that is just too far away

227

and then he's going to tell me that I need to wear awful, ugly glasses for the rest of my life!"

Taryn's mom glances at us in the rearview mirror.

"Taryn?" she says. "We're not even there yet. Could you please cut the dramatics?"

It's hard not to chuckle at that, especially when Taryn is acting like a true drama queen.

Taryn doesn't say anything else. She just glares.

All I can think about now is what Taryn said. I visualize Dr. Wexler plucking eyelashes or ripping out eyeballs like in some kind of bad horror movie. I can't help but laugh out loud. Lucky for me, Mrs. Taylor doesn't hear. And Taryn is too worried to pay attention to me now. Within a few minutes, we've pulled into my driveway.

Unlucky for me, my half sister, Blair, is on our porch with Toots — and she's got the sparkly barrettes on his ears again. "Good luck," I say to Taryn, climbing out of the car.

"Good-*bye,*" Taryn replies, sticking out her tongue.

Chapter 7

❀❀❀ TARYN ❀❀❀

Bizarre

I can't believe it.

Yesterday confirmed a sad fact: I really do need glasses! When I could barely identify the enormous, fuzzy E at the top of the eye chart, Dr. Wexler wrote me a prescription right there on the spot. He claims I have something called astigmatism. It sounds painful, but it isn't. At least not yet.

But I can't think about that right now. It's time for my first school carnival meeting. The sky-blue sheet of paper taped to the door of room 12C reads School Carnival Meeting, here, 2:45 p.m., so I know I'm in the right place.

Of course I have to stand on my tiptoes to read it.

It's already 2:35 and there's a line up and down the hallway, but the teacher hasn't even unlocked the door yet. I recognize a few other kids from my English and social studies classes, but none of my good friends are here. Leslie is more into drama club, and today is Cristina's first day of tennis. There are some older kids from my neighborhood here, but I don't recognize anyone else. I notice this one girl, leaning up against the wall. She has long brown hair like me, but it's down, flowing around her shoulders. She's reading a book. Then she looks up and sees me.

"Hey, are you here for the carnival sign-up?" she asks me.

I nod and smile, not knowing what to say. My brother Todd always says, "When in doubt, smile." Todd's a huge dork, but he's really smart about some things.

"This is my third year doing this," the girl says.

"Wow," I reply. I could have come up with something better than that, couldn't I?

"I'm Valerie, but you can call me Val. Who are you?"

"Taryn," I manage to say.

"Cool name," Val says. "So, what — are you a sixer?"

I assume she means sixth grader. I just nod

again. And smile. My cheeks ache from smiling so much these first three days of school.

Everything about Val screams "cool" without trying too hard, and about six different people say hello and wave to her. When Val looks at me, I notice how her eyes are this crystal green color, a lot like my cat Zsa-Zsa's eyes. Val's one-hundred-percent color-coordinated, too. She's even carrying a notebook marked "Carnival" that matches the trim on her T-shirt.

As we're standing there, a teacher shows up, waddling to the door. The way he has his sleeves rolled up makes his arms look like little, hairy sausages. Beads of sweat drip from his forehead. He opens the lock with a grimace and a groan, like he's lifting something heavy.

"I'm so sorry to be late, kids. Please file in and take a seat," he says, mopping his brow with a handkerchief. "I'm Mr. Wood."

Something about the harried expression on Mr. Wood's face says to me, "Do NOT mess around, or you'll be sorry." I shuffle my sandals inside and smile (of course), even though, at the same time, I'm desperately trying *not* to make eye contact. Not that it would matter with my lousy eyes.

"Don't get freaked out by Mr. Wood," Val whispers to me. "He's a total sweetie."

Although I have a hard time believing that any teacher can be classified as "sweetie," I believe Val. She seems to know everyone — and everything — at Westcott. I can tell. Although I'd like more than anything to sit with her, Val disappears off to one side. I head for the back of the room.

It's lonely in the back by the radiator, all by myself.

What am I doing here? Have I made a terrible mistake? I'm just about to get up and slip right back out into the hall when I see Val. She gives me this smile and for some reason, it keeps me glued to my seat.

I have to give this whole carnival thing a chance. After all, I promised myself I would. I promised Jeff, too.

I am happy to see that as soon as Mr. Wood drops his large canvas bag onto the teacher's desk his frown melts and he actually cracks a few jokes. Then he's writing something up on the board.

I squint to read the bold purple letters: BEACH PARTY.

"What can I say? I am very, very, VERY excited about this year's carnival," Mr. Wood announces. He's not so out of breath anymore; clapping his hands together like a little kid. I glance around the room and realize that everyone else seems genuinely excited, just like Mr. Wood. Even Val is clapping her hands together.

Maybe this *will* be fun?

Fun. Fun. Fun. I repeat the word, as if saying something a hundred times can make it true.

"Parents, teachers, and our entire community have gotten behind this carnival," Mr. Wood explains. He goes on to tell us that any money earned during the carnival will be used to purchase special things for Westcott *and* for a local organization that helps orphans.

I had no idea that this was all for such a good — no, *great* — cause.

Mr. Wood tells us how we'll be renting a dunk tank for the carnival (to dunk the teachers, we all hope!), and that the local newspaper will be covering the event. Everyone who participates will get their name mentioned in the Lifestyle section.

Okay. That settles it.

Now I'm totally in.

Even though most of the planning for the carnival has already taken place, including equipment rental, food purchasing, ticket mailings, and more, they still need students to volunteer their time. The school needs as many kids as possible to help out once the carnival begins. And Mr. Wood wants to find a few good carnival leaders, too. That's where we come in.

When he asks for leader wannabes, my hand shoots right up like a rocket. Jeff would probably say that's because I like to be in charge. He's always telling me that I'm too bossy. He's wrong. Across the room, I see Val's got her hand high in the air, too.

"Goodness!" Mr. Wood cries as he looks out at the roomful of volunteers. Then he asks us each to jot down our names and a few sentences about why we'd like to be a leader. I wish I had more time, but I scribble the first things that come to mind — that I'm organized, responsible, full of energy, and really want to be involved in a good cause. By the time Mr. Wood collects our pages and reads them over, I realize that I've been holding my breath.

Breathe, Taryn, breathe.

I hope I don't pass out.

Finally, Mr. Wood starts calling out names. He picks Valerie — of course. Then he says the two words I am dying to hear most: Taryn Taylor. He's called on *me* to be a carnival team leader. I get to oversee the "activity zone," an area of the carnival devoted to games like ring toss and the fake fishing pond. I'm in charge of the whole cluster of sixth-grade volunteers chosen to run those games.

That can't be too hard, can it?

Taryn Taylor, Team Leader.

I love the sound of that.

Mr. Wood starts talking about the different activities that are planned, and we all throw out ideas to make them even better. There are going to be balloons made in the shape of ocean animals, and a sand-covered obstacle course. Val suggests a spinning Wheel of Fortune with beachy prizes, like sunglasses and Frisbees. Wow. She has some great ideas. I'm impressed. Then I see Val has her notebook open; she's writing down all these notes.

Following Val's lead, I pull out a piece of yellow-lined paper from my backpack and scribble a long to-do list. I've barely begun, but I'm already behind.

1. Balloon animals? Who can make them?
2. Bean bag throw (waves) — how many bags?
3. Obstacle course — do we need extra sand?
4. Soda bottle toss — get 20 rings from ... someone?
5. Make a bizarre to sell arts & crafts for extra $$$

At some point, I glance up at the clock on the wall and realize that while we've been talking and brainstorming an hour has gone by.

It is now 4:06.

Just then, Mr. Wood realizes the time, too.

"Oh, dear!" he cries. "How did it get so late?"

"Don't worry, Mr. Wood," Val calls out. "We're cool."

"Thanks, Valerie. It just goes to show you . . . what a great big undertaking this all is . . . and how enthusiastic we all are and . . ."

By now, everyone is hauling their backpacks onto shoulders and making a beeline for the door. That's when Mr. Wood hollers, "HOLD ON RIGHT THERE, KIDS!"

Val, me, and the others kids stop dead in our tracks. Flailing his arms, Mr. Wood jumps in front of the door before anyone can leave.

"Just one more thing before you go, volunteers," he shouts. "Our next meeting will take place here in room twelve C on Monday after school, so bring all of your best beach party ideas with you then. Have a nice weekend!"

Finally, he releases the door latch. We're free.

Despite the weirdness of Mr. Wood's acrobatic act, I feel this jolt of positive energy about the whole carnival experience. Jeff was right. Being a carnival team leader is good for me. I can't wait to tell — and thank — him.

On the way out, Val bumps into me. "See you Monday," she blurts as she rushes past. I see her link arms with another friend a few feet away and then she's gone.

I head to my locker to grab my stuff and wait for Cristina. Her dad is giving us a ride home since she had to stay late for tennis practice.

When Cristina doesn't show up right away, I head for the basement gym area, but she's not there, either. Although I'm getting used to Westcott, I still feel a little bit lost. Where *is* everyone? It doesn't help matters that everything I see is a blur, so as I'm walking around panic sets in and I feel increasingly, totally *alone.* Maybe I should call Tim or Tom to pick me up. They're annoying, but at least they're reliably annoying. If they weren't, Mom would yell at them.

I take a seat on one of the locker room benches and then, magically, Cristina appears from behind a bank of red lockers.

"I've been searching for you everywhere, T!" C cries as soon as she spots me. "I've been all over the building, which is pretty tough because I don't know where anything is and tennis got out a half hour ago —"

"Wait! I was looking for you, too," I say, interrupting. "The carnival meeting ran a little long and I couldn't find you, but I —"

"Hold up, hold up," Cristina says, poking her arms into the air with a *clinkety-clank.*

I notice she's wearing white shorts and a T-shirt that says WESTCOTT TENNIS on this tiny pocket, but she still wears her favorite (and noisy) bangles and dangly earrings. Cristina always says that the clothes are the worst part of playing tennis. She'd prefer cool, black Nike outfits like Serena Williams, rather than the boring tennis whites everyone expects. Leslie and I figure that Cristina will end up being some edgy fashion designer one day.

I secretly hope that wish comes true. Then I could get free, cool clothes for life.

"I'm sorry, Cris," I say at least ten times in a row without taking a breath.

"Okay, okay, I forgive you," Cristina says, grabbing me in a bear hug. "I literally just called Dad, and he's on his way over now, so it's cool, *plus* it's Friday. . . ."

We grab our bags and head for the front doors. There's a pickup and drop-off area at the edge of the parking lot. Outside, it isn't chilly at all. I stuff my jacket into my bag.

When Cristina's dad finally arrives, my stomach is rumbling like a volcano. I should have eaten more at lunch.

I wonder what culinary surprise Mom will have waiting when I get home. Cristina knows all about Mom's kitchen experiments. One time when she visited this summer, Mom made shrimp toast. At least that was what Mom called it. It tasted more like fish cardboard. Gross. We each had to drink at least twelve glasses of lemonade to get that taste out of our mouths.

"So, was tennis fun?" I ask Cristina as we both climb into the back seat.

She grins at me so widely that I can see the edges of her retainer.

"I think I might even get a top spot on the team," Cristina says, nodding. "A couple of the older kids are good, but I'm just as good. I'm psyched."

"Wow," I mumble, impressed.

"What about you? Does the school carnival sound good?" Cristina asks.

"Really good," I say with a nod. "I'm sooooo glad I signed up. The theme is Beach Party."

"Too hot!" Cristina says. "You should have a tanning booth."

"You wish," I reply. "My brother would love that, too."

"I can't believe that the first week of sixth grade is over already," Cristina says.

"Yeah." I sigh. "What do you think is the most different thing about this year so far?"

Cristina laughs and covers her mouth. "Cute boys," she whispers.

Now I know she's officially boy-crazy.

When her dad drops me off in front of our house, Cristina yells, "Shotgun!" and hops into the front seat of his car. "Call me later!" she yells through the window.

Her dad honks and she waves as they drive off.

I walk up to my front door.

"I didn't think you'd ever get home," a voice calls out from behind our bushes. Then a familiar head pops up. It's Jeff. "I've been on my porch forever, T. So what's up?"

He stands there with his baseball glove on one hand, and a baseball in the other.

"What's up with you?" I ask.

"You know what I mean. How was the carnival meeting?" Jeff asks, stepping closer to me. "Was I right or was I right? Cool after-school thing for you, right?"

I give him a familiar grin. "Cool — as ice," I say. "You were right."

"Of course, I'm always right!" Jeff shouts. He

240

bursts into some kind of maniacal laughter that projects him across the lawn and back onto the sidewalk. I look up the street to make sure no one is watching.

"Shhhh," I say. "You're embarrassing yourself."

"Nah, I'm embarrassing *you*," Jeff says, laughing even louder.

I chase after him. We end up at my front steps again and plop down, still laughing.

"So what happened in your classes today?" I ask.

"You saw me like ten times in the hall at school," Jeff says.

"I know, but that was this morning."

"Classes were fine. Whatever. Math is going to be tough. You saw the list, right?"

"What list?"

"It's official. I made the soccer team. Coach Byrnes posted it at lunchtime."

I feel like lunging at Jeff to give him a great big bear hug. But of course I don't. He'd freak.

"Congratulations!" I cry. "You deserve it, Jeff."

"I know," Jeff says, slapping his knees. "I rock!"

Of course I'm proud of him, even though he's acting a little braggy. But I guess I would be braggy, too. Making the team in sixth grade is a very big deal, after all.

241

"Hey, what's that?" Jeff asks me out of the blue. He points to my chin. "Eww. Disgust-o!"

"What?" I ask nervously, reaching up to wipe my face. But there's nothing there.

"Gotcha!" Jeff says with one of his satisfied smirks.

"Very funny," I grumble.

"I know!" Jeff exclaims. Then he moves to get up and head back to his house.

"Wait!" I cry. "I almost forgot to tell you about something I saw in the newspaper this morning. Something huge."

"Since when do you read the newspaper?" Jeff says.

"Since forever," I reply, not mentioning that I usually just read the entertainment section. "Don't you want to hear what it was?"

"Okay. What?"

I make a loud drumroll sound, getting down on my knee for dramatic effect.

"Next week, Floyd Flannigan is coming to the bookstore downtown," I say.

Jeff's jaw nearly hits the steps.

"No way!" he exclaims. But I see anticipation bubble up inside of him like soda fizz. He stands up. "I don't believe it!"

"Believe it," I say. "He'll be there next Wednesday."

Ever since we could read, Jeff and I declared ourselves mega-fans of a fantasy writer named Floyd Flannigan. He's a hundred-year-old Irish guy who writes these incredible, amazing, fantastical books called the Outer Space Chronicles. Jeff and I have each read the entire collection of his books at least three times. On his Web site, fans of his books are called Floyd Fanatics.

That's me and Jeff all the way.

"He's coming HERE?!" Jeff screams. "That's INCREDIBLE!"

It's quiet outside, so everything we say echoes up and down the street. My brother Todd steps out onto our porch to check out the racket.

"Yo, Taryn, Jeff," Todd says in his I'm-the-older-brother-and-I-know-so-much-better-than-you-do voice. "Someone's gonna call the police if you guys don't quiet down."

"No one's going to call the police," I bark back. "Give me a break."

"Mom's the one who sent me out here," Todd says. "So why don't you just keep it down?"

"Fine," I snap.

"Uh . . . sorry, Todd," Jeff gulps, throwing his

hands into the air in surrender. As soon as Todd goes back inside, Jeff turns to me and whispers, "Floyd Fanatics unite! We totally have to go."

"Totally," I agree. "Let's make a plan. I can get one of my *other* brothers to take us."

Jeff nods. Then he ducks back toward his house. I know the Todd incident scared him off. For whatever reason, Jeff always gets intimidated by my older brothers.

As soon as I step inside my house, Todd walks by and makes this crinkly face.

"That kid is a bozo," he says.

"He's my friend," I say.

"Yeah, well you're a bozo, too."

"Moooooom!" I call.

"What is it now?" Mom asks, appearing from around the corner. "I heard you and Jeff outside. How was day three? Tell me everything. Everything!"

I expect her to yank me all the way into the kitchen for further interrogation and maybe some late afternoon food experimentation, too, but no, she just wants to relax. We collapse together onto the sofa in our living room.

By now I've forgotten all about tattling on Todd. Instead, I tell Mom about the new teachers I met today, the book report I have to do for English class, and then I talk about volunteering for the school carnival. She looks excited about all of my news. I even show her my to-do list from the meeting.

"What a big job! This all looks very cool," Mom says as she reads the list. "Wait. What's that?" She points to the last item. "Bizarre? Like . . . *strange*?"

"No, no," I insist. "It's bizarre like a flea market. You know. *Bizarre*."

"Oh, Taryn!" Mom's eyes glisten and she smiles. "You mean the word 'bazaar,' don't you? With three A's."

"Oh, yeah. Whoops."

I quickly scratch off the misspelled word and rewrite it the way Mom says to.

As I do, Mom laughs and tousles my hair. Sometimes when she does that I feel like a baby all over again. And right now, for some reason, I don't mind so much. I inhale a whiff of her perfume, and everything seems just right in the world.

"Bazaar," I say the word slowly, a little embarrassed, trying to emphasize the A's so I don't get it wrong ever again.

I may be starting off sixth grade with a bang, but my spelling still needs some serious help.

Maybe I should spend the weekend locked in my bedroom with a dictionary?

Like *that's* ever going to happen.

Chapter 8

● ● ● Jeff ● ● ●

The Soccer Table

"How was your weekend?" Anthony asks as we stroll into the cafeteria with Peter.

"Boring," I groan. "But J.D. got me a new portable goal for soccer. We set it up in the backyard."

"Nice!" Peter says. "Your old net had all those holes."

We stop at the lunchroom bulletin board and check out the specials for the day.

"What do you think they really put in Browned Meat Loaf Surprise?" I wonder out loud.

"Meat," Anthony says.

"And loaf," Peter adds.

I grab my stomach and pretend to laugh at their

dumb joke. Then I motor inside the lunchroom and grab a bright blue, jet-washed tray.

"Have one of these," Anthony teases, dangling a blackened banana in my face. Nasty.

"No, thanks very much," I say, grabbing a container of chocolate milk, a brownie, and a toasted bagel with cheese instead. I figure that as long as I get one or two food groups at lunch, I'm doing okay. I might have to start bringing my lunch from home.

We're headed toward a side table in the main area of the cafeteria when someone grabs my elbow. It's Walt from soccer tryouts last week.

"Congrats, Jeff," Walt says, extending his hand for a shake.

Both of my hands are busy holding my tray, so I grunt in his direction. "Thanks."

"Coach Byrnes thinks you're an ace," Walt goes on. "But you know that already."

"Yeah?" I ask, trying to act super-modest.

"Yeah. All the guys on the team are impressed. Why don't you come over and sit with us?"

I shoot a glance at the table where Walt's pointing. The entire soccer team is sitting there, shoulder to shoulder.

Peter pushes me from behind. "Go ahead," he whispers.

"Nah," I stutter. "What about you guys? We always eat together."

I look back at Anthony. He nods that I should go, too. Then I turn back to Walt.

Maybe I'll try out the soccer table — just this once.

I leave my friends behind and follow Walt to the table. He tells everyone to shove over and I nod hello. Then I sit on the corner edge of the table bench and rip open my milk carton for a slurp.

"That's your lunch?" some beefy-looking kid asks me. I see a plate of the surprise meat loaf on his tray, half-eaten.

He must be an eighth grader. He must be really brave, too, to eat that.

"Um, I'm not that hungry," I explain, severely grossed-out by the black crust on his slab of loaf. *That* must be the surprise part.

The soccer table guys talk about one thing at lunch: soccer. They tell stories about Coach Byrnes and share secrets about crazy things that have happened at Westcott soccer games in the past. They talk about shopping for cleats. They talk about backfield, midfield, and goals. I listen quietly in the corner. In some ways, it's like my dream cafeteria experience, only I don't really have much to add. Not yet, anyway.

"So how do you like Westcott so far?" a seventh grader named Blake asks me. He's skinny and chews his nails.

"It's good," I say. "I hope classes aren't too tough."

"Nah, sixth grade is a breeze," Blake says, still chewing his thumb.

"You played soccer long?" Will asks. I immediately have a flashback to tryouts when Will's sharp kick breezed past my head.

"Since I was a kid," I say, realizing as I say it that I still *am* a kid.

"I want to play in the World Cup one day," Will declares.

"Me, too," I admit sheepishly. All these guys at the table have the exact same fantasy as me. I guess that means I fit in.

"What position do you think Coach Byrnes will start you at?" Walt asks.

I think for a minute. "Maybe fullback?"

Someone further down the table fakes a gasp. "That's Clark's position," he says.

"Yeah," a guy that I can only assume is Clark says, standing up like he's going to get mad all over the place.

"Well, I don't really know what position. . . . I guess whatever Coach thinks . . ." I stammer nervously. The guys are all acting pretty nice to me, but I'm still having trouble figuring out when they're joking and when they're being serious. And I want — no, I *need* — them to like me.

Midway through my first official soccer lunch, I spot Taryn across the cafeteria. She sees me, too. Her hand flies up and she smiles.

I look the other way. What will the soccer guys think if I wave to some girl?

Even though I'm pretending to ignore her, I can still see Taryn out of the corner of my eye. She's *still* waving. A part of me wants to hold up a sign that says HEY, STOP, CAN'T YOU SEE I'M HANGING WITH THE GUYS?

But then there's another part of me that feels this twang of guilt. After all, she is my friend, right? So what's the big deal?

Before I have a chance to do anything else, Taryn walks right up to the soccer table. There's no ignoring her now.

"Hey," she says.

"Hey," I mutter, hoping none of the guys notice. I shoot her a fake smile.

"Didn't you see me?" she asks.

"Where?"

"There," Taryn says, pointing toward the table where she had been sitting.

250

I hang my head down and stare at my bagel. "Nope, didn't see you," I say. If I have to lie, I can't look right at her while I'm doing it.

"So where were you all weekend?" Taryn asks.

"Around."

"We went up to my aunt's house for an overnight," she says.

"Oh." I'm trying to keep the conversation short and sweet, but she keeps asking all these questions.

"Um . . . why are you sitting over here today?" she asks.

"Soccer," I say, hoping no one else is listening. "The team."

A few seats down, I see Walt staring. What am I supposed to do now? My eyes flicker between Walt, my tray, and Taryn.

Instead of walking away and getting the hint, she crouches down and whispers, "Okay, well. I just wanted to talk to you about going to the bookstore —"

"Wednesday, right?"

"Right." She hands me a slip of paper with the name of the bookstore, the day (Wednesday), the time (five o'clock), and the words FLOYD FANATICS UNITE! written in purple pen. Great.

"Fine," I say, shoving the paper into my pocket. "I'll meet you there."

Taryn steps back just a little. I can see she's getting annoyed. She's on to me.

"You don't have to be a jerk. . . ." Taryn says.

Guys down the other end of the soccer table snicker. Their eyes target me like lasers.

"Jeff," Taryn continues. "I thought you *wanted* to go to the book signing."

I shrug but don't say anything.

"So?" she asks, poking me in the arm.

I still say nothing.

"So . . . I guess I'll talk to you later then," Taryn finally says, exasperated. She turns and heads back to her lunch table with Leslie and Cristina. Of course, they start to whisper the moment Taryn sits down.

Girls.

The soccer guys don't say anything about my little encounter, but I know what they're thinking. Then Walt stands up.

"Let's bail," he says.

"Like a whale," another guy says, flicking Walt's ear.

Just then, the cafeteria bell rings loudly. Class periods are about to start all over again. After the bells, everyone bolts: the team, Peter and Anthony, and even TLC take off. Even though I was still sitting

252

at a table packed with guys a minute ago, I end up standing all by myself.

I walk back toward the nearly deserted kitchen and clear my dirty tray. Then I grab two granola bars, pay, and shove them in my pockets. I'll try to eat them before my math diagnostic test next period. I'm going to need a major dose of brain food if I'm going to test into the right math class. After all, when I get home, Mom is *definitely* going to grill me about everything math-related.

If only I could get graded on my soccer playing.

Then I'd be at the top of the class.

Chapter 9

✿✿✿ TARYN ✿✿✿

Four Eyes

It's Tuesday and I'm standing in front of the mirror with my mouth stretched open, about to let out the biggest, loudest screech I can.

Only no noise comes out.

I don't know what to say or how to feel or even what to think right now.

Hello, my name is Taryn Taylor, and I wear glasses.

Mom helped me choose these frames yesterday afternoon. They're not so bad, really: wire-rimmed, copper-colored, with anti-scratch, nonreflective lenses. Since I already had my prescription from Dr. Wexler, we went to one of those places where they have all these display cases packed with frames and where they make new glasses for you in an hour. I thought instant photo places and Pizza Huts were the only places that promised service in such a short period of time. Apparently, that's not true. Eyeglass places fit into that category, too.

I just can't get used to having something on the bridge of my nose like this, no matter how light the frames are. They make my face itch. And why are my eyes magnified to twice their size? That's what I see looking back at me, anyway. Big, dark green saucer eyes. Ugh.

Mom comes into the bathroom to see how I'm doing with my new look. She rubs my shoulders and kisses the top of my head, which makes me feel better for exactly thirty seconds. After that, my nose starts to itch again and I get cold feet about showing my face in public. Even though Mom has been trying to encourage me all morning long (I've been up since 5:46 A.M.), nothing about my glasses seems to look right.

Eventually, I have to race out the front door to catch the school bus. I'm still wearing the glasses, but my head is bent so far over that no one can tell I have them on.

At the bus stop, though, Emma Wallace notices my new look right away.

"Nice glasses," she says as soon as she sees me.

"Thanks," I mumble, staring at the ground. I hope she means it.

"You know, my sister wears glasses to see things that are far away," she goes on. "She likes her tortoiseshell frames, but says glasses always make her nose itch."

"Yeah," I say. "Mine itch, too."

"Those frames go great with your hair and shirt," Emma says, laying on the compliments like buttercream frosting.

Sometimes she's just *too* nice. Why does she have to try so hard?

I look from side to side, scoping the crowd for Jeff. But he's not here yet. I didn't have time to go by his house this morning. Besides, I haven't actually talked to Jeff since yesterday at lunch when he was hanging with his soccer buddies, acting like some kind of VIP. He tried to blow me off. Ha! No one blows off Taryn Taylor. I'll get him back later — for sure.

Hopefully, L and C were wrong when they said that being the youngest kid on the team will give Jeff a big head. I say his head is already plenty big enough.

Emma asks me to sit with her again. But I say "No, thanks," as usual. Instead, I sit in one of the middle rows. As we drive off, staring out of the bus window becomes this totally different experience for me. It's the glasses. All at once, fuzzy trees sharpen so I can see the smooth outline of leaves and jagged bark and squirrels, with their tails flicking across the branches. For once I can actually read street signs and shop signs, and even the cottonball clouds in the sky seem clearer. I can see anything and everything — even a zit on the back of this eighth grader's neck right in front of me.

Blecch.

I look around and notice other kids on the bus who wear glasses like me. There's one kid with big, huge, black frames that dwarf his round face. There's another girl with cat's-eye, pointy-corner glasses, who looks like she's trying too hard to look hip. It's funny how I never really noticed these particular kids before. Now that I have glasses, I can physically *see* my classmates close-up, as opposed to seeing big blurs that just look like middle-schoolers.

So I guess I'm glad to have the glasses. I just need to get the hang of them.

The ride to school seems to take longer than usual today since I don't have Jeff there to keep me company, but I'm really enjoying the view. Soon enough, I'm out of the bus, up the school steps, searching for L and C. I head for my locker near homeroom 10A and wonder if Jeff got a ride to school again today.

"Look at YOU!" Leslie cries as soon as I walk up to the lockers.

"Wow! You look great!" Cristina says.

My cheeks blush. "Thanks," I whisper, grinning.

"You look like a model in those glasses," Leslie gushes. Sometimes she likes to overstate stuff. But I don't mind overstatement this morning — at least not from her. My glasses and I are happy to accept kind words from a best friend. I guess it's just Emma's compliments that bug me.

"Let's get your hair out of that ponytail," Cristina, my fashion advisor, says.

"Not a chance," I snap back.

The tallest kid in sixth grade, Danny Bogart, strolls by and Cristina elbows me in the side. She has sharp elbows.

"What did you do that for?" I moan.

"Did you see Danny? Oh, wow, he's so dreamy. His eyes are dreamy. His shirt is dreamy. Even his freckles are dreamy." Cristina makes these googly eyes and flutters her eyelashes.

"Oh, brother," I say to Leslie. "Cristina's gone nuts."

"Yeah," Leslie says. "No one should get *that* bugged about some boy."

I laugh out loud. "Ha! What about you and Charlie West?" I say to Leslie. "You've got a radar detector for that guy. You just said yesterday that he was cuter than anyone you'd ever met."

"Tarrrrryn," Cristina groans.

"Yeah," Leslie says. "Well, just because you're afraid to admit how much you secretly love Jeff. . . ."

"Stop saying that!" I howl. "That is so not true."

"Oh, come on. You must have a crush on *some-one*," Cristina insists. "You just don't want to admit it. Jeff is the obvious choice."

"I don't have a crush, I don't," I reply, rolling my eyes. "Can we change the subject, *please*? Someone might hear."

Right then, I recognize familiar voices, getting closer. Then I spot Jeff, Peter, and Anthony scuffling down the hall in our direction. They walk three-across, shoulder-to-shoulder, stopping next to an orange locker. Anthony breaks formation and opens the locker, reaching for a book. Then Peter leans down to tie his shoe. It's weird, I notice that Jeff's all decked out in a checkered shirt and Levis.

"I can't believe I'm saying this," Cristina says. "But Jeff looks nice."

"No, he doesn't," I scoff, checking him out again.

What's the big deal?

As they're standing there, a cluster of girls passes in the hallway. And who's at the front of the pack? Emma Wallace.

Of course.

I watch as Emma and her friends stop to say hello to the boys. She's standing really close to Jeff and he's grinning nonstop, like some kind of smile robot. He keeps nodding his head up and down, up and down, up and down. Is there someone behind him pulling the strings? I've never seen him act like this. What could he and Emma possibly be talking — and smiling — about? And why do I even care?

"Check her out," Leslie snipes. "See what I mean about Emma's head? It's humongous."

I cross my arms in front. "I know," I say. "She really thinks she's all that, doesn't she?"

"All that and then some," Leslie adds.

"Miss Perfection," Cristina says.

"That is so weird, seeing them flirt with each other," Leslie says.

I think about what she says. My new glasses give me a better look. Is Jeff *flirting*? The whole concept of Jeff and Emma making googly eyes at each other causes my stomach to do flips.

"Obviously Emma likes his outfit," Cristina says.

"So?" I ask.

"So . . ." Leslie jumps in. "You know how that works."

No, I don't. I don't know anything, it seems.

As I'm staring right at the group of them, Jeff looks up. He catches my eye and just like that, he stops talking to Emma and comes over. The boys follow Jeff to where we're standing. Emma and her pals follow, too.

"What's up, Taryn?" Jeff says. Everyone else exchanges hellos.

I wait patiently for Jeff to say something about my glasses.

Does he even notice that I have them on?

Emma is as polite as ever, which totally makes my skin crawl.

Leslie sighs and I can see the look in Cristina's eyes that says, "I am SO out of here."

I'm still waiting for Jeff to say something nice.

Waiting . . .

Waiting . . .

Then he finally clears his throat and grins.

"So . . . how do you like your new glasses, *Four Eyes*?"

There is dead silence. At least there's dead silence inside my head. Jeff looks at me with this dumb smile on his face. Then he looks back at Peter and Anthony. And then everyone, *everyone* except L and C, bursts into laughter.

My knees turn to jelly.

Then Cristina steps right over to Jeff. "I can't believe you said that," she huffs.

Jeff pretends to look stunned by Cristina's angry reaction. But I can tell he still thinks it's funny.

"What's your problem?" Jeff asks.

"You know what the problem is?" Cristina says. "Y-O-U."

"W-H-A-T?" Jeff spells back, like he's trying to be cute or something. This makes Peter and Anthony laugh even harder. But I know what's up. He's just showing off for Emma and everybody else.

Now it's Leslie's turn to get him back.

"L-O-S-E-R," she says, wagging an index finger in his face.

"I know how to spell, *Les*," Jeff grunts.

When he calls her that nickname, Leslie's whole face scrunches up like a geyser ready to burst. Without another word, she and Cristina each take one of my arms and spin me around so we're walking away from Jeff.

"What's the matter, Four Eyes?" Anthony calls out after us.

Peter joins in. "Got a problem, Four Eyes?" he asks.

I can hear Jeff and the other boys laughing — and I want to disappear, right there, right in the middle of the hallway.

Plus, I want to rip my glasses off — NOW.

Jeff always calls me names. He's been making up mean names for me ever since we were little. They have never bugged me. But he's never, EVER called me a name in public, especially not in school. Especially not in front of Emma and other girls like her. And now his friends are calling me the same name, too!

Talk about a nightmare — with a capital *N*.

Jeff knows how hard it was for me to get used to the idea of glasses. He heard me worrying about it all last week. He even said Tim was mean for teasing me about Dr. Wexler. And now *this*?

"Ignore that jerk," Leslie crows as we walk fast.

"He's acting so un-Jeff these days," Cristina says.

"It must be sixth grade, or soccer," Leslie says.

"Yeah," I say, realizing *just* how weird Jeff has been acting since the school year started. Whatever the reason for his attitude, I'm feeling insecure all over again.

"Do you guys think the glasses make me look bad?" I ask my friends. "Be honest."

"No!" Leslie cries. "And if they did, we'd totally tell you."

Dozens of kids race past, searching for their classrooms. We've been back in school a few days now, but there's still a mass of confusion about where, when, and how to get to different places in the building. They should teach a class in figuring out where you're going.

All at once, Cristina stops short. "I have a brilliant idea," she says.

"What?" I ask, hoping that it really is brilliant.

"A makeover!" Cristina declares.

I stare at her. "Huh?"

"That's a great idea!" Leslie says.

"Isn't it?" Cristina says, looking pleased with herself. "We can find a trendy outfit in one of those celebrity magazines and you can raid our closets and wear your hair down for a change —"

"I told you, I don't want to change my hair," I say. My breath feels shallow. I know there are tears in there somewhere. I just don't want them to come out in school. Please don't let them come out in school.

"Why do I need a makeover?" I ask quietly. "It's the glasses, isn't it?"

"No, of course not," Cristina says, putting her arm around me. "The makeover is just to make *you* feel better. Everyone needs a makeover now and then — even *moi*."

"Cristina's right," Leslie says. "We'll show Jeff and Emma and everyone 'Four Eyes.' Ha!"

I cringe when she says the words "Four Eyes," but somehow I'm feeling cheerier. My friends usually do know best. The last time we did anything like this was over the summer. We painted each others' toenails with little palm trees and yellow moons. Cristina stuck on mini-crystals for stars. Everyone at the pool was totally impressed.

"Let's do the makeover next week, right before the carnival," Leslie says.

"Awesome!" Cristina says. "That way you'll look like a princess the next day."

"Maybe," I mutter, feeling slightly self-conscious. "I just need to check with my mom."

"Let's do it Thursday, right after school. I can throw some ideas together before then," Cristina says, slipping into full fashion-advisor mode.

At once, the class bell rings. Now we have to hurry. In a flash, Cristina's already halfway down the hall.

"Taryn, wait," Leslie says, taking my arm before I dash off, too. "Just because we want to give you a makeover doesn't mean you aren't beautiful already. Because you are. You know that, right?"

I look at Leslie's yellow-blond hair, cute Hello Kitty! T-shirt; and fitted-at-the-waist, flared-at-the-

265

cuff white pants. I guess she must know what she's talking about. After all, *she's* beautiful. What else can I say?

"Right," I reply.

Leslie looks happy to hear my positive response. As we walk on, I catch my reflection in the window of a science lab room. I wonder what I would look like without the ponytail.

For the first time, I consider the possibility that maybe change doesn't have to be so scary or awful like I've always thought. Maybe it's like Mom's far-out dinners.

A little octopus or rutabaga never *really* hurt anyone. Right?

Chapter 10

••• Jeff •••

Miss Understanding

I haven't seen Taryn since this morning in the hall. I know she's avoiding me. It's the whole Four Eyes thing. L and C act like some kind of army of two, protecting Taryn from the enemy who is so obviously me. Why can't everyone just lighten up? Okay, so I shouldn't have called T that name, but somehow it just slipped out.

The glasses didn't even look that bad.

I have to stop thinking about this. First of all, I've got a full day of classes. I only skim-read my first English assignment and my new science teacher gives me the creeps. Then we have soccer practice today after school and I need to be in A-plus form. All eyes are on the new kid, after all.

That's what Walt and Will tell me. There's a scrimmage tomorrow and scrimmages count.

The team meets up in the locker room after school to change. Then we jog over to the field together. When we get there, Coach Byrnes gives us a pre-season pep talk. He carries around this clipboard and whistle and talks really, really fast.

"Passtheballovertherenowturnaroundandkick-itintothegoalrightnow!"

Sometimes I have no idea what he's talking about. I thought I knew everything there was to know about soccer. Boy, was I wrong.

The sky is gray and overcast. I'm on my back with the rest of the team, doing sit-ups, staring at the thick clouds. I can hear all the guys around me huffing and puffing as they do their warm-ups. It doesn't take me long to make friends with this one seventh grader named Jake. I remember him from tryouts and lunch the other day, and he's a total crack-up. We compare notes about games and practical jokes. I realize he's the only other person I've ever met who actually ate rocks on a dare, just like me. Together, we hatch an instant plot to apply to one of those reality shows like *Fear Factor*. We'd be an awesome team.

Just before practice, Jake told me what it was like to be one of the lucky sixth-grade soccer recruits *last* year. He tells me that I shouldn't get my hopes up too high about playing in a real game.

"Coach'll keep you on the bench mostly," Jake says. "But you can't bum out, no matter what."

"I won't," I say, laughing it off.

Bench? Ha! We'll see about that.

Of course, a half hour later, I'm beginning to believe what Jake says. Coach Byrnes benches me and doesn't even assign me a real position. I have no idea where I'm slotted on the team, so I watch the other guys kicking the ball around and pick at a scab on my knee.

Some of these guys aren't that great, but some are amazing. Walt jumps way off the ground and heads the ball into the goal. I wish I had a chance to get out there and prove my stuff, too. Lots of people come to watch our practices and scrimmages, and I want to show them all what I'm made of.

There are only ten minutes left of "official" practice when Coach finally calls me and a few of the other benched guys onto the field. We all look at each other, eager to have a chance to shine. When the soccer ball finally drifts my way, I dribble it all the way down the field, only to have it kicked away by a mysterious cleat. I'm so focused on the ball that I don't even see the foot coming.

The whistle blows and practice ends. I feel like a flat tire, but Jake tells me not to worry so much. Then we hustle back to the locker room.

Once we're all changed, the team splits up and heads home. I grab my backpack and head into the school hallway. I'm thinking that maybe I can still catch Taryn when she gets out of her carnival planning meeting.

Yeah, I owe her.

I casually walk up to the door of 12C where the meetings are usually held, only the room is empty. There's no sign on the door, either. No alternate location. Maybe I should scout around the rest of the floor? Put out an all-points bulletin?

Nah, I don't have time. And the more I think about it, the more I realize that I am a little afraid to see T in person right now. Maybe a note is better? I tear off the corner of a page from my math notebook and start to write.

Dear T — I looked 4 u but ur gone. Sorry about what happened & I really shouldn't have said that. Hey, I'd be SOO psyched if u came 2 my soccer scrimmage Wed. (2morrow). It's field B as always, right after school gets out. C U THERE! Don't 4get. Bye, J

When I'm done writing, I fold the note into quarters and slide it into the slat of Taryn's locker.

Hopefully the paper won't fall out.

Hopefully she'll be Miss Understanding.

Hopefully, she'll accept my apology *and* my invitation to come to soccer. I could really use the moral support. If I even get to play, that is.

There are lots of kids still milling around outside the school. I notice Taryn's pal Cristina, standing with a whole bunch of girls dressed in white shorts. I forgot she plays tennis. I give Cristina a wave but she ignores me — big-time — even though I know for a fact that she saw me. I guess I deserve it.

Everyone else is standing around waiting for their parents or somebody to pick them up. It's like a middle school people jam out here. There's a long line of cars in the cul-de-sac, too. I never saw so many minivans in one place.

Finally, I spot Peter sitting on a low wall next to the school. He waves me over. We walk a block or two to the local park. Anthony is waiting there with his bike. He's already been home and back again.

We play catch for about a half hour. Then Anthony takes off on his bike. He needs to get home to walk his dog. Peter has to split, too. He has relatives coming in from out of town and his mom's making a Greek feast. That just reminds me how hungry I am.

Peter flips open his cell phone to call his sister, Marisa. All the way home in Marisa's huge boat of a car, Peter won't shut up. He and Marisa fight over the CD player. I get a little nervous when he wrestles her arm off the remote. After all, she *is* driving.

Meanwhile, way, way, *way* back in the big backseat, I'm dreaming of spaghetti. That's what's on the table every Tuesday at the Rasmussen house, and I'm starved.

If I can't count on playing first string on the soccer team, and I can't count on Taryn giving me a break, at least there are some things I can count on these days.

Even if they are just garlic bread and meatballs.

Chapter 11

✿ ✿ ✿ TARYN ✿ ✿ ✿

Talking Boycott

I woke up this morning and decided that maybe I really *do* need a makeover.

I also decided that Jeff is, categorically, a big fat jerk. Those are really Leslie and Cristina's words, but I agree with them.

After all, best friends know best, don't they?

Here's my plan: I am executing a talking boycott today, at least as far as Jeff is concerned. Maybe this will get him to apologize for what he said and how he's been acting these past few days. A little cold shoulder will definitely freeze that boy out.

At least I hope it will. Sometimes it's hard to follow through on these things.

The bus ride to school is Test One. Jeff is at the

bus stop for the first time in a couple of days, and he's joking around with some other guys. Emma's there, too, standing near them and smiling.

I merge into the crowd of kids, decked out in my embroidered jean jacket, purple cotton pants, and lace-up flats. Cristina called me last night to help pick my outfit over the telephone, so I'm feeling fashion friendly this morning.

I haven't been standing there for more than a blink when Jeff sees me and waves.

My stomach grinds. I don't acknowledge him, even though it's way harder to ignore my former best friend than I thought it would be.

Jeff waves again, but when I don't respond a second time, he gives up.

He doesn't even walk over to me.

That's weird.

The bus driver opens the squeaky bus door and we all pile inside. I wait until the very last minute to climb on. The middle rows, where I've been sitting happily for the past few days, are full, so I squeeze into the front part of the bus.

"Hey, aren't you on the carnival committee?" some boy asks. He's wearing glasses just like me, but I don't recognize him from sixth-grade home-room or anywhere else at Westcott so far.

"Yeah, I am," I say.

274

"I thought I remembered you from the meeting last week," he says. "I'm Alex."

"I'm Taryn."

"Are you in sixth grade?"

"Yeah, are you?"

He shakes his head. "Nah, I'm in seventh."

The bus is getting noisier by the second, so I can hardly hear myself think, let alone hear what Alex is saying to me. I wonder why I've never noticed him before now.

He leans a little closer to the edge of his seat and I can hear him better. "I was on the carnival committee last year," he says. "Mr. Wood is the best."

"He seemed kind of . . . well . . . nervous at first," I stammer, sounding kind of nervous myself, although I have no idea why.

"He sweats a lot," Alex says plainly. "But the truth is: He keeps his cool. Trust me. Carnival is one of the best experiences I've had at Westcott. Last year, the money we made helped to pay for the new climbing wall in the gym. This year, they're trying to add a special multimedia area in the library. And most of the other money is given to charity."

"Those are all the reasons I signed up," I explain.

"Me, too."

"So what else do you do at school?" I ask.

"Chess club, math Olympiad, and debate."

"Oh," I say, and the word "brainiac" pops into my head.

In no time, we pull into the school parking lot. I get off the bus first, and Alex follows right behind me. A few seconds later, I hear my name. It's not L or C calling me.

It's Jeff.

"Wait up, Taryn!" Jeff hollers. I pause and think about turning around, breaking my boycott, and saying good morning. But then I decide to keep right on walking. Alex is talking to me the whole time. He's the perfect alibi.

There are so many kids squeezing inside the school doors that Jeff can't catch up to me. Once we're inside, Alex dashes off to his homeroom. I'll see him later at the carnival meeting.

When I reach my locker, I dial the combination and stuff my bag inside. It's only been a week of school and already my small locker is crammed with a pair of shoes, books, and some random paper scraps. I can't deal with any of it right now, I think as I push everything to the back and click the lock. Maybe I'll clean it out later.

Across the hall, through the crowd, I see Leslie

and Cristina at their lockers, too. I approach them quickly with the 4-1-1 on the Jeff situation.

My friends don't look surprised by my talking boycott; in fact, Cristina gives me a cheer for the whole plan. They don't mind my complaining a little more than usual about Jeff this morning, either. In no time, the conversation has shifted from chatting about our weekends to boy talk. L and C pipe up about their latest Charlie West and Danny Bogart sightings. For a split second, I think about mentioning Alex from the bus. After all, he's a boy, and Leslie told me she wants to be informed of any boy–girl contact I may have. But she's so insistent about the fact that I have a secret crush that I don't want her to get the wrong idea and think that crush is *Alex*.

So I keep my lips zipped.

We all slip into Homeroom 10A just as the bell rings.

During my first two classes, reading and math, I don't see any sign of Jeff. By third period, social studies, I run into him in the hallway. He's bound and determined to stop me in my tracks.

"Taryn," Jeff says, putting his hand out to stop me.

"Jeff," I snap, biting my tongue. So much for the talking boycott.

"I've been looking for you, T. What's your problem? Didn't you hear me call you this morning at the bus stop? And before homeroom?"

"Um . . . no," I say with a shrug.

"Well, I saw you," Jeff says emphatically. "And I thought you saw me."

"You mean like how I thought I saw you in the cafeteria the other day?" I ask.

"Uhh . . . not exactly . . ."

Jeff rocks from foot to foot. A quiet moment passes. We're still standing there in the hallway not saying much.

"Okay then, if that's it," I say, breaking the silence first, "I have to go."

"Go where?"

"To social studies. Duh. Don't you have class?"

"Yeah, but what about later today? I'm going to see you, right? After school, I mean. We have a plan."

"A plan?" I repeat.

My head spins. Of course! I'd almost forgotten. Later today is the book signing with our favorite author in the whole wide world, Floyd Flannigan. With all of the angry back and forth between Jeff and I over the past few days, it nearly slipped my mind. But Jeff remembered?

278

"We do have a plan," I say to him with a small smile.

"Cool," Jeff says. "So I'll see you there?"

"Yeah, I'll see you there," I reply. "Unless you see me first. Ha, ha."

Jeff chuckles at my lame joke attempt. It feels — for a second — like everything is back to normal between us. Then we walk off in opposite directions. I have Social Studies this period and we're getting another textbook.

As the day goes on, I begin to feel better and better about Jeff and the fact that I didn't have to cut off all conversation for the entire day. Tonight, when we Floyd Fanatics unite, everything will be patched up for good.

But L and C still think I should be giving Jeff the silent treatment.

"Are you saying that Jeff still hasn't apologized for the whole Four-Eyes thing?" Leslie asks me at the end of the school day. "Like, he didn't say those exact words, 'I'm sorry?'"

"Not exactly," I reply.

"And after everything that happened, you're still going to the book signing with him?" Cristina asks.

I nod. "What's the big deal?"

"Taryn!" Leslie snaps. "*You're* the big deal. He owes you a real apology."

"You guys don't understand. I know Jeff. He's been my best friend since forever. He's probably just waiting to apologize until later when we're at the bookstore. I know he'll do the right thing."

"Yeah, sure," Cristina says, looking in the opposite direction.

I'm not sure what to say now. Maybe friends don't always know best about some things.

Like the boy next door.

After classes end for the day, my life becomes a little bit of a drag race. I take the steps two at a time up to the carnival meeting. The room is packed. As soon as I spot Alex near the windowsill with an open seat next to him, I sit nearer to the door. For some reason, I don't feel like talking to him right now. I have another boy on my mind.

Mr. Wood passes out more lists of things to do. He hands me a bright yellow team leader folder, and I am floored. On top it reads: TARYN TAYLOR, TEAM LEADER in all capital letters. That makes me sound so important.

Across the room, Alex holds up a two-finger-split sign for peace. Or is it some kind of Star Trek code? I'm not sure. I wonder what Jeff would think of him. I *know* what L and C would think.

280

Inside the folder, I find all sorts of papers about how to organize and play the different carnival games like Bottle Toss, Cake Walk, and Wheel of Fortune. A small group of us talk about how we'll organize materials for those games, and who will man the booths once everything has been set up. I take a bunch of notes. Mr. Wood tells me that the difference between a regular Carnival volunteer and a team leader is simple: INITIATIVE. To be honest, I had to look up that word. But now I know it means being the *first* one to get to the meetings, to collect information, and to get everyone pumped up.

Today's meeting lasts exactly fifty minutes. I'm amazed that when I share my ideas and notes kids listen to me. Me! Even with all the work I do, I'm out the door before four, just in time to catch the late bus that makes stops in our neighborhood. For some reason, Alex isn't right behind me so he misses the bus.

Whew. No distractions.

After a bumpy bus ride home, I walk inside the door of our house. Right away my brother Tom gives me grief about driving me to the bookstore signing. I had said he could drop me off at four-thirty, but now it's four thirty-eight and he says, "I really have somewhere *else* to go."

Tom and I yell at each other for exactly two minutes. This makes Mom crazy. She throws her hands into the air and Tom stomps out of the room — just like that. Exasperated, Mom volunteers to drive me to the bookstore herself.

"I'm really sorry," I tell Mom later as the two of us climb into the car.

"That brother of yours . . ." Mom says, gritting her teeth. "But this works out better. I was curious about this book signing. You've been reading those outer space books for a long time, haven't you?"

Mom quickly shifts the car into gear and drives downtown. I stare out the window as we go, pressing my nose to the pane, only my glasses get in the way and I bonk my forehead.

I'm still having trouble getting used to these things. At least they don't look so terrible.

When we arrive at the bookstore, I'm glad to have Mom along for company. There's a long line already forming inside the store by the signing area, and I can see signs with Floyd Flannigan's photograph. The oversized author picture is the same one that's on the flap of all his book covers. In the photo, he's dressed in some kind of tweed jacket and tie. His face has all the nooks and crannies of an English muffin. He has a long, unkempt gray beard, a crooked grin, and squinty eyes that look like they've been glued shut. He's my hero.

I scan the room for Jeff's baseball cap while Mom takes a place in line. They're handing out numbers, so everyone who gets one is guaranteed a signed copy of his latest title in the Outer Space Chronicles, "Madman from Mars: Return of the One-Armed Alien."

As I move around the bookstore from one pack of fans to the next, my pulse quickens. It's one of those moments when everything comes together in just the right way. I can't wait to talk to Jeff. He's the only person I know who understands just what it means to be a true Floyd Fanatic.

This is a once-in-a-lifetime moment, for sure.

Mom gets our numbers (49, 50, and 51) and manages to find two folding chairs where we can watch the reading part of the event. By now, it's a little bit after five o'clock. Jeff isn't here yet. Luckily, neither is Floyd. There's still time.

By quarter after five, Mom actually looks a little worried about Jeff's no-show.

"Should we call his house?" she asks me.

"Not yet," I say, stalling. "He's just late."

I stand up and search the crowd again, but it's no use. Jeff isn't in there. And for the first time, I begin to suspect that he isn't coming.

Someone behind me starts to clap and then the whole room bursts into applause. I see Floyd Flannigan enter the room. He's at least six feet tall, way taller than the bookstore employees who escort him to the front of the room. I clap along with everyone else. Then Mom leans into me again.

"Taryn," she whispers. "Maybe Jeff just forgot. There's still time for him to get here. Let me call . . ."

Unfortunately, by the time Mom begins to dial Jeff's house, a clerk tells her to turn off her cell phone. The reading begins and everyone has to hush up.

Floyd starts to read the first chapter of his latest saga in his thick brogue. I feel quite speechless myself, and not in a good way. As exciting as all of this is, the signing just doesn't feel the same without Jeff.

I close my eyes and try to focus on Floyd's words to block out my surging feelings of disappointment.

But it's no use.

Somehow, I fear that there's a *second* talking boycott in my cards.

Starting. Right. Now.

Chapter 12

• • • JEFF • • •

Pants on Fire

So I'm lying in bed after my alarm clock goes off this morning, Thursday, staring at the piles on my shelves. My eyes move across the room, and I see all this stuff I know I don't need but can't (or won't) throw out. But I know the time to toss is coming fast. I reached critical mass a long time ago.

J.D. told me that we're having a yard sale. He's already picked a good weekend next month to do it. Meanwhile, Mom just wants to give everything away. I can just see her heaving my clothes and books into one of those enormous black trash bags. She'll cart it over to the Salvation Army faster than

I can say, "Hold up, I really need my second-grade Transformers lunch box!"

Okay, I admit there's a lot up there: maybe two hundred Matchbox cars, shoeboxes of baseball and Yu-Gi-Oh trading cards, a stuffed alligator with the eyes chewed off (I've had that since I was born), marbles, and way too many books to count. In fact, I have an entire shelf devoted to my favorite author, Floyd Flannigan.

Gulp.

That's when it hits me.

I forgot about the book signing.

I leap up from my bed and race over to a wall calendar tacked on the door. Is the bookstore signing today? Tomorrow? Then I remember the piece of crumpled paper in the pocket of my jeans. Taryn handed me that note at lunch the other day. I'd forgotten all about it — and the signing — until just now.

I fish through the pile of dirty laundry on my closet floor. The jeans in question are right there. And there, too, in the right pocket, along with a chipped Wint-O-Green Life-Saver, is one crumpled slip of paper with the name of the bookstore and time. The words, FLOYD FANATICS UNITE are written in capital letters alongside, WEDNESDAY.

Oh, no. That was yesterday.

My stomach lurches. I definitely missed the signing.

I collapse back onto my bed, rubbing my eyes hard. I can't believe I missed it.

How did things get so messed up?

My first instinct is to call Taryn, of course. But it's too early. She's probably in the shower or eating breakfast. I'll see her later on the bus. I can explain then.

I just can't believe it. There I was yesterday, kicking the ball around the soccer field in our very first scrimmage, looking for encouragement. All I've been able to think about for the past week or so has been soccer. Of course, my sister, Blair, would say that all I *ever* think about is soccer. But who listens to her — except for poor Toots? And he doesn't have much of a choice.

Yesterday, I wondered why Taryn didn't show up at my scrimmage. I wanted her to see me play, but then she wasn't in the stands. We had talked about it, too. When I saw her in the hallway, Taryn told me she would be there. She said those exact words. "See you there." I said them, too. But her "there" and my "there" were two different places!

Peter and Anthony told me she was a bad friend to be a no-show. And I believed them. Does that make me the lamest friend in the history of the universe?

A half hour later, the digital clock reads 7:33 and I contemplate dialing the Taylor house. But still, I don't. I can't see Taryn in her room. So I convince myself that she's busy and can't talk. I think I'm probably just freaked out about what she'll say if I call.

Instead, I pull on my khakis, a blue-striped polo shirt, navy-blue sweatshirt, and my sneakers. Then I run a wet comb through my hair. I have this cowlick that pokes up sometimes in the morning. It's like someone's playing a bad trick on my hair. Today, no matter how hard I try to keep it down, the hair stays poked up.

I yank on a baseball cap, hoping that will help.

After a fast bowl of Honey-Nut O's, I'm off to the bus stop. I cross my fingers and hope to see Taryn leave her house at the same time as me. I have to talk to her, to explain — even if I don't want to. Outside, I pause and wait for nearly five minutes in front of her fence. Wait and hope.

But she's left already. No one comes out. She's gone.

Quickly, I hustle toward the bus stop. There are fewer people than usual but I see all of the regulars, including Emma Wallace. She says hello.

Every day when she does that, Anthony says how much she likes me. That cracks me up. Everyone knows that Emma is just being nice. She does *not* like me.

Taryn never shows up at the bus stop.

Where is she?

I don't say much to my buddies on the ride to school. Peter's blabbing in my face the whole time. Still, I say nada.

When we finally get to Westcott, a few guys from the soccer team are hanging out outside the main school doors. Walt holds up his hand as I walk toward them.

"Good scrimmage yesterday," Walt says. "Coach might put you in a real game now."

"Thanks," I respond. But for the first time since school began, my mind is anywhere *but* soccer. I just want to find Taryn and tell her I'm sorry.

It isn't until the hallway at lunchtime that I see Taryn face-to-face.

Her face is red.

I know I'm in for it.

"Taryn," I say, going close to talk. I try to keep my voice at a whisper so no one around us hears.

"I'm not talking to you," she snaps. But I know she will. She always does.

In the hallway outside the cafeteria, kids stream by. No one seems to pay much attention. I like it that way.

"We need to talk," I say.

"I waited for you," Taryn replies in a low voice.

"The bookstore. I know. I forgot. I swear! I feel terrible, T."

"How could you forget something so important?" she asks.

"Soccer," I say. It sounds lame. But it's the truth.

"It's *always* soccer," Taryn says.

"Was the signing good?" I ask, trying to hit a positive note.

Taryn shoots me a hard look. "Uh-huh. You missed the best-ever book signing ever in the history of book signings. So there."

She has me feeling like I'm only an inch tall by now.

"Taryn," I continue to plead my case. "Why didn't you remind me? Didn't you get my note about the scrimmage?"

"Your note? What note?" Taryn snaps.

"The one I left in your locker."

"You did not leave me a note."

"Yes, I did."

"No, you didn't."

"Yes, I did."

"Liar."

"Whoa." I cough, surprised. She's called me names before, but never anything that mean.

"Pants on fire," Taryn adds, for emphasis.

"I swear. I left you a note the other day. It said I was sorry."

"For what?" Taryn snarls.

"For what I said."

"You mean the whole Four Eyes thing?" Taryn asks pointedly.

I'm glad she said those words and not me.

Now what?

I wait for Taryn to accept my late apology, give me one of her pokes in the shoulder, and tell me to buzz off in that fun way that she does. That would be the happy sitcom ending. But I'm in for a big surprise.

"You know what, Jeff? It's too late to say sorry. First you embarrassed me in front of all those people. Then I waited for you at the bookstore forever. You blew me off and I'm mad at you, and I'm not just going to stop being mad at you for no reason."

"What? No reason? Wait a minute. . . ."

Slowly, over the course of this conversation, our voices have gotten a teeny bit louder. Now I realize we've attracted the attention of some kids and a hall monitor.

This is not a good thing.

"Um . . . can we just start over?" I ask very quietly, trying to lighten up the situation.

"I don't THINK so," Taryn declares in a big voice. What a drama queen.

"This is stupid," I say. "Don't be stupid, Taryn."

"Now you're telling me I'm stupid?" Taryn exclaims.

"No, that's not what I —"

"*You're* stupid, Jeff Rasmussen. And you're obviously not my friend!"

"Hey! What did you say that for?"

"Because you've been acting weirder and weirder these last few weeks, but especially weird toward me. I thought I knew you better than that. I really and truly thought we were best friends."

"We were." I shrug. "I mean, we *are*."

"Liar."

We stand there, eye to eye and toe to toe. This is the biggest fight we've ever had, by a long shot. I can't believe we're having it at school. We're minutes away from getting reeled in by some teacher passing by.

And I'm not sure what else to say that won't make Taryn madder than an electric eel.

I decide the best thing to do is just walk away.

Taryn calls out after me, but I am so out of there. I'd do anything for a soccer ball right about now. I could kick away all my frustration. Hard.

I head toward the other cafeteria entrance. But first I glance back to see if Taryn's still there.

She is. And she's staring.

By now L and C are there, too, staring just as hard.

And I *really* feel like road kill.

There has to be some way to fix this. I just wish I knew what it was.

Chapter 13

❀ ❀ ❀ TARYN ❀ ❀ ❀

Carnival Shmarnival

Mom made one of her one-of-a-kind, experimental feasts on Sunday.

I have never eaten so much food in my life. I tried everything Mom put in front of me, including these strange, international dishes like Cornish hen with pomegranate sauce, sautéed Swiss chard, and French profiteroles for dessert. Everything was yummy, especially the little vanilla ice-cream puffs with chocolate sauce. Lucky for me, there was no shrimp toast on this menu.

"It's hard to bounce back from a big friend fight," Mom kept telling me.

I know she's right.

When Jeff and I had our big blowout last

Thursday, I thought the universe folded in on itself. I've been thinking a lot about how Jeff and I used to play those secret-agent games. All weekend, I wished for super-binoculars to spy on his every move. I feel like I need to gather evidence and try to figure out why we aren't friends anymore.

Why didn't I see all this coming?

Now that it's Monday, chances are at least fifty-fifty that I'll see Jeff on the bus ride to school this morning. But what am I supposed to say when I see him? Maybe I need to apologize, too? Leslie and Cristina say no way. But I wonder if maybe I over-reacted just a little bit. Mom's always telling me to cut the dramatics. Should I have called, "Cut!" on Thursday or Friday? Should I have left *him* a note?

No, that's how half this mess got started — his stupid note. When I finally pulled it out of the bottom of my locker, I understood our miscommunication, but it didn't make the hurt feelings go away. It was too late for that.

The one I really feel bad for in all this is Zsa-Zsa. My poor kitty has been listening to me talk about Jeff nonstop. The way she mews at me sometimes makes me feel like she understands every word. I don't know what I'd do without her. She purrs and rubs herself against my leg and lets me scratch between her ears and I know everything will be just fine.

Isn't that what a friend is supposed to do, too? Well, except for the purring and rubbing and scratching part, of course.

As early morning passes and it gets closer and closer to the start of the school day, I get cold feet. I'm second-guessing the whole meet-Jeff-on-the-bus thing. Instead, I beg Mom to drive me to school.

The ride over to Westcott turns out to be just what the doctor ordered. I just sit there and Mom drives. We don't even try to have a conversation. I'm so glad she isn't bugging me about Jeff. Not now.

Mom pulls into the school parking lot, and right away I see L and C on the steps. I hug Mom goodbye, hop out of the car, and make a beeline for my two pals.

Cristina has this horrified look on her face.

"Taryn! What are you wearing?" she asks.

"Clothes," I say meekly.

"Taryn, have you let all this Jeff stuff affect your fashion sense? Why didn't you call me this weekend for advice?" Cristina asks. Right now she sounds like one of those obnoxious, know-it-all makeover experts I always see on cable TV.

"I don't need you to pick out my clothes every day, do I?" I ask back, although when I look down at my outfit, I realize she may have a point. Today I'm wearing baggy, striped pants and a flowered shirt with boots and a pilly old sweater that my grandmother sent me about five years ago. The sleeves are a little short. Okay, the sleeves are more than a little short. They go up to my elbows. It's like something I probably shouldn't have worn after second grade.

"Don't forget. Thursday, after school, at my house," Cristina announces as we enter Westcott. "I'm turning my room into makeover central."

Leslie leans in close to me. "It'll be so much fun," she promises in that sweet voice she always uses to make me feel better.

I'm still not one hundred percent convinced. I have a lot on my mind.

"I'm not sure I can do Thursday," I protest. "I may have to do last-minute carnival work that day and there's just so much —"

"Carnival shmarnival," Cristina says. "We made a date."

"Cristina is right." Leslie smiles.

"Okay, okay," I concede. "You win. I'll do it."

"You won't be sorry," Cristina squeals. "I promise."

All week long, thoughts of my pending make-over hang in the back of my mind. But I turn most of my daily attention to one thing: the carnival. All over school, bright posters scream BEACH PARTY! with enormous, orange suns and sailboats dancing in the background. It's like getting the best parts of summer back again.

There are a million and one things to do before Friday comes. Thankfully, my carnival volunteer team is in great shape. As carnival leader, it's my job to keep everyone motivated. All week long we work together after school to paint waves, sandcastles, and seagulls on homemade signs and backdrops. We invented this quicksand pit stop for the beach obstacle course, which is really just a plastic kiddie pool filled with those Styrofoam packing peanuts, but everyone says it's the best. I can't wait to see the kids and teachers trying to wade through that. On our "Wheel of Fortune" game spinner, we added funny categories like "Feeling Crabby," "Something's Fishy," and "Catch the Wave." I think they're a little cheesy, but Mr. Wood loves those sayings.

The volunteers aren't the only ones with carnival fever. Everyone else in school has it, too. The swim team instructors added a last-minute kickboard and diving contest in the school pool. The newspaper staff decided to issue a special Friday edition of the school paper with the headline, BEACHED! And most teachers volunteered time in the dunk tank. Even Principal Simms is jumping on the bandwagon. Every day during morning announcements he has the school secretary play "Surf City" and "Beach Baby" beach tunes over the loudspeaker. Someone says Principal Simms is planning to show up to the carnival in swim trunks. Ha! People would pay to see that, I bet. Plus, he decided to formally dismiss school for a half day on Friday. That way, everyone can enjoy the carnival before the weekend.

If all this isn't reason to celebrate, then what is?

By late Thursday afternoon, everything is ready to go. During our last meeting, a very sweaty Mr. Wood runs around checking displays and games. Then he gathers us together for a final pep talk, hands us each a name tag, and offers a huge round of applause for all our hard work.

"Let's face it, kids. This is the best beach party I've ever seen," he tells us, clapping all the while. "I can practically smell the suntan lotion."

I'm standing right next to Valerie. She flips her hair and looks right at me with those eyes.

"Didn't I tell you? Isn't this the best of the best?" Val asks.

"You said that," I reply. Somehow, when I'm around Val, I get a little tongue-tied. But Val doesn't seem to notice, or care.

"I can tell Mr. Wood likes you," Val says, smiling.

She starts to say some other nice things, too, but then I realize I'm not really listening to the words. I'm just staring at her hair. Val's long, whirly curls fall perfectly onto her shoulders. In that moment, I want to be *just* like her — hair and all.

Then it dawns on me: My hair *can* look the same. It's Thursday afternoon and my makeover is today! In fact, Leslie and Cristina are waiting for me in the school lobby right now.

As soon as Mr. Wood dismisses us, I gather up my team of carnival volunteers to make sure that everyone knows where and when to meet tomorrow. Then my feet can't carry me to the lobby fast enough. I'm bursting with excitement. L and C look even more excited than me. We head over to Cristina's house, which is only a ten-minute walk away — tops.

Since the last time I visited her house, Cristina painted her bedroom lavender and put up framed posters all over her walls. Her walk-in closet is concealed by these cool curtains that she pulls back so I can see her entire wardrobe. The place looks like something I'd see in a magazine, with brightly colored bean-bag chairs, a rainbow lamp, and shelves of books and magazines.

I wish my room looked like this. Zsa-Zsa would love to nap on a bean bag.

Once we get comfortable, Cristina turns up the radio and tosses a pile of magazines in front of me.

"What do you want to look like?" she asks.

The three of us pore over the pages together, picking out our favorite hairstyles. I find one pic I love of a fancy updo held in place with sparkly clips. But I think L and C have something different in mind.

I'm a size smaller than Cristina, so when she and Leslie hand me clothes to try on, nothing fits quite right. We decide to stick with makeup and hair — as if I've ever used any makeup before now. The only thing I use is lip gloss and I have *that* in about ten different flavors. My favorite is banana split. Jeff made fun of me once for wearing it. He said I smelled like a fruit bowl.

But I am *not* going to think about Jeff right now.

Cristina applies mascara and eye shadow to my eyes and it's all I can do not to wiggle or sneeze.

301

Then she powders my forehead and dusts blush on my cheeks.

"Not too much," I warn her, worried that I'll come out looking like I've been over-painted.

Cristina grins. "I know, I know," she says. "We're just experimenting. You can redo it yourself in the morning."

"This is SO exciting," Leslie coos, rubbing her hands together.

I want to be excited, too, but not until I see results.

It's nearly six o'clock when Leslie finally hands me a mirror to show me the major makeover. I can't believe how different my face looks with makeup on it, although Cristina overdid it just a little. But I don't have to use all this purple eye shadow when I put it on myself.

My hair, on the other hand, is perfect. I don't even recognize myself. And it's not piled on top of my head — not by a long shot. My brown hair cascades down onto my shoulders, loose and free, just like Valerie's hair. I think it looks even more perfect than Emma's hair, which is saying a lot. I always thought wearing my hair down was flat, straight, and *boring*, but this is something else. And Leslie stuck in these fabulous glitter bobby-pins. . . .

I loooooove it.

Dad picks me up in time for dinner and on the ride home, he keeps asking me, "What's different about you tonight, kiddo?"

I just sit there, beaming, with my new 'do and my painted fingernails and funky eyeglasses. "Oh, nothing much," I say with a big grin on my face. Then he realizes what he missed: My hair is different and my cheeks are pinker.

"You must be the prettiest girl in sixth grade," Dad says, winking. "I bet all the boys will notice."

For some reason, this makes me think of Jeff. I've been so focused on beach umbrellas this week that I've forgotten all about boys.

And I can't decide if I'm still mad at Jeff or not.

After nearly five days of my ducking under stairs, hiding behind lockers, and flat-out walking away, Jeff still has yet to say *anything* to me about what's happened. But when he sees me, when he sees *this*, he'll be the one apologizing.

He'd better.

By the time Friday morning rolls around, I'm still in makeover-mode. Last night, Cristina IM-ed me a list of possible outfits and I picked out the things I liked best: my patchwork jean skirt; a blue, scoop-neck T-shirt with a butterfly design on the front; and a cute, comfy pair of purple sneakers. The new ensemble and the new hair put me in a super mood for the carnival. Mom even offers me a ride this morning. I gladly take her up on it.

Let the games begin.

As soon as Cristina and Leslie see me walk up to the school doors, they let out a little cheer. They're happy to see my hair in the same style from the night before. I've put on a little bit of makeup, too, but not so much. Mom wasn't too happy to see me putting on eye shadow this morning. She's okay with lip gloss, and that's about it.

Some kids in my classes notice my new look, but no one says much. Everyone's way too focused on the carnival.

After morning classes, I follow my nose down to the recreation room. The cotton-candy machine is up and running. That was Mr. Wood's brilliant idea. The school rented food machines to feed the hungry masses: cotton candy, popcorn, and even a hot dog rotisserie. I secretly wonder if Mr. Wood rented them for the crowd or just because he loves to snack.

The carnival is supposed to start at one o'clock, just after lunch. It runs during afternoon class time and after school. Right now, it's noon and almost everyone I know is still in the cafeteria eating lunch, including the eight people on my volunteer list.

I've reminded my team about the time to meet. I even left notes in everyone's lockers. But by 12:40, only two of those people have shown up at their booths.

Where is everyone else?

Five minutes pass and another three kids stroll in. But I still have no one to run the bottle toss and I can feel my neck prickle, like I'm getting nervous hives. What's going on? Plus, I'm missing half of the team that mans the great big Wheel of Fortune, a spin-your-luck game with prizes.

I'm down three whole people?

The carnival doors are about to open wide, and I have to face facts: I'm in big trouble. My stomach clenches right along with both of my fists. How could this have happened? I planned so carefully. Everyone was so excited. I can't believe my team flaked, after all our hard work. I glance around. All of the other team leaders seem to be doing fine. Their games are up and running.

I feel tears well up in my eyes. It figures. The first time I attempt to wear mascara, I get all weepy. Wait. Team leaders can't cry. They need to be strong. I think of Val.

Don't cry. Don't cry.

Then I search the room for a faculty advisor who can help me out. Where is Mr. Wood and his sausage arms? Where are the parent advisors? Where's the janitor? I've got that weird "alone" feeling again, even though there are people everywhere.

The noise around me escalates: clacking shoes on the floor, carnival organ music playing from a boom box, the hum of the cotton-candy maker, the whirr of the Wheel of Fortune, the chatter of teachers and students running back and forth. I see Val across the room, looking cool and collected, of course. She waves and grins confidently, as usual. I'm tempted to run over and scream "HELP!" but I don't. I just grin back. I have to figure this out for myself — fast.

I glance up at a clock on the wall. One o'clock on the dot. The doors to the room are about to fling open and here I am, missing three volunteers, standing like someone just yelled "FREEZE!" in a game of tag. I've gone from excited to panicked in no time. How will I fix this? Think, Taryn, think.

"Surf's up!" a voice bellows.

It's Principal Simms, standing over by the doors. I can't see if he's in swim trunks or not, but he appears to be wearing a blue plastic lei. My eyes scan the crowd of sixth, seventh, and eighth graders as they push into the room. One of the first people I see, heading right for my area of the carnival games, is Emma Wallace.

What else can possibly go wrong?!

I bury my face in my hands and hold my breath, trying to figure out what to do next.

That's when I hear his voice, coming closer.

It's Jeff.

Great, I think to myself. He's here with his crew: Jeff and the rest of the boys have come to the carnival to gloat, I just know it. They've come to see me fall flat on my face. After all, these are the dorks who called me Four Eyes last week.

"Taryn?"

I turn when Jeff calls my name. He's backed up by a cluster of guys from the soccer team. They're all wearing bright red soccer T-shirts.

"Jeff? Wh-wh-what are you doing here?" I stammer. My heart feels like it just stopped. I brace myself for the worst.

And then Jeff does the most incredible thing. He doesn't say anything mean or goofy. He doesn't say anything at all.

He just gives me one of his smiles.

That's when I know everything is going to be just fine.

Chapter 14

••• Jeff •••

No Sweat

When I see Taryn standing in front of that empty booth, I know I have to do something.

Sometimes friendships change, or at least that's what my mom keeps telling me. The other night she reminded me of this kid Chester Leonard who used to live up the block. Chester and I were inseparable for the entire summer after second grade. But then Chester decided to like another kid down the block. So he ditched me. Just like that. Right after he rode my bike over a nail and blew the tire.

That's what it felt like this week with Taryn. All week long, she has avoided me like the plague.

I saw her at lunch a few times. I saw her at her

locker once or twice. She hardly made eye contact. That was weird.

But I'm here now, trying to do something to fix it. I'm huddled outside the recreation room along with everyone else, waiting for the carnival to start. And five guys from soccer came along with me, including Jake.

Some teacher I don't know with a mustache is wearing a clown nose and holding a surfboard. He unlocks the door to the recreation room and welcomes everyone to the carnival. Principal Simms is standing there, too, in bright flowered shorts! Kids press into the room. Some run. Those are the kids looking for the big prizes. The air in here smells sticky sweet and my stomach does a flip-flop. I got super-sick one time at the circus when I ate three blue cotton candies and two snow cones in a row. I've never been the same.

There's beach art up on the wall and everything has some sort of title like SURF SEARCH or BEACH BOTTLE TOSS. It's a little lame, but fun at the same time. Half the teachers are running around in Hawaiian shirts. I can't help smiling.

The moment I enter the room, I spot Taryn standing by this ugly blow-up palm tree. She looks worried. Is she crying? Maybe she's thinking about our fight. Maybe she just misses me. I stride across the room with my new soccer buddies behind me, heading straight for Taryn and the tree.

When she sees me, she does a wild double take. But she doesn't move. It's like she's frozen in place or something.

"Jeff?" she says. "What are you doing here?" She still hasn't moved.

I smile.

"What's the deal? Nice carnival."

We both stand there, just staring, for another moment. All around us, kids rush to different games. The room is really loud with people chatting and music playing. Nearby, there are all these huge soda bottles lined up. Kids stand over them like giants with rings to toss, but there's no one to run the game.

"What's up with that?" I ask Taryn, pointing.

"It's one of the games I'm supposed to help organize," she says, her voice wavering like she's about to cry. "Only . . . no one . . . I don't . . ."

I step a little closer toward her and ask what's really wrong. I can tell when she's about to have one of her meltdowns.

"This is a total disaster," Taryn says, fighting back tears.

"Nah," I say. "It looks great. The room is packed."

"It's a disaster. I'm a disaster."

"What's up with your hair?"

"Hair?" Taryn grabs her head. "Oh. That," she says. "It's a new style."

"Yeah, I noticed." Even though she's about to lose it, Taryn looks good. I tell her, but she doesn't want to talk about it.

A moment later, Principal Simms walks over to us. He tugs on his blue lei and I can read his T-shirt: ALOHA MAN.

I'm tempted to crack up. But Taryn looks like she's about to puke.

"Hello, Miss Taylor," the Principal says in a deep voice.

How does he know her name? That's amazing. Then I realize she's wearing a name tag.

Duh.

"I just want to thank you for your help," the Principal says, shaking Taryn's hand.

She nods politely but I can tell that under the surface, Taryn is majorly unsteady. Her face gets all pink and speckled like it does when she's about to freak out.

As soon as Principal Simms walks away, Taryn sighs and turns to me.

"I'm glad you're here," she confesses.

"I know," I say. "Maybe we could help you out."

"Help? *Me?*"

I nod. "Sure. Who else would I help?"

I'm thrown off balance completely when, all at once, Taryn flings her arms around me and squeezes me like I'm a gigantic lemon. She's never done that before. I quickly look back at the guys. No one's really paying any attention, thankfully.

"Uh . . . Taryn, you can let go now," I plead, pushing her away. Unfortunately, her earring is caught on my shirt. For a split second, we're stuck together.

"Sorry," she says, removing the earring as we pull apart.

"So, do you need any help from us or what?" I ask.

"YES! I do!"

Taryn bursts into giggles. She does that a lot. In between laughs, she shows me and the other soccer guys over to the games and activities that need people to run them. She's all business now, the take-charge Taryn that I've known forever. I grab a trio of large rings and pass them off to the first kid in line.

I can do this. No sweat.

Before I know it, Taryn has put us all to work and things are in full swing. The games are drawing a huge crowd.

But actually, working the carnival is more fun than I expected. I could do it all day. Luckily, after a while the trio of *real* volunteers from Taryn's team shows up to do their jobs, so we stand-ins don't have to run the game for very long. They give Taryn some lame excuse about getting the times mixed up. I expect her to read them the riot act, but instead she thanks them for coming at all. Wow. She really does deal under pressure.

As we're standing there, Mr. Wood comes over and pats Taryn on the back.

"You have to be one of the most organized carnival leaders I've ever had," he says. "You had a team of volunteers — and then you had backup helpers, too. Very fine, very fine. I certainly hope you'll be a carnival leader next year, too."

Part of me wants to laugh out loud and say, "Are you kidding me? You should have seen her about a half hour ago! She was a MESS!"

But of course I say nothing. When it comes to Taryn, I'm learning that sometimes I need to just keep my trap shut.

After being relieved of our ring toss duties, a couple of the soccer guys and I decide to play some games. I win three in a row at the bean-bag toss and snag a princess bear (or at least that's what it looks like, with its cheesy pink plastic crown). Blair will love it. Maybe if she plays with it, she'll leave Toots alone. I can only hope.

At some point, Jake and I hit the jackpot at the Wheel of Fortune, spinning the wheel to reveal a truly grand prize: a supersized Hershey's bar. He's allergic to chocolate, so he gives me the whole thing. I down the bar in only three bites, hardly any chews: a new personal record.

Eventually, Peter and Anthony show up and find me and the rest of the gang, too. Eight of us pose together in a fake beach photo booth where we stand there holding beat-up surfboards and wearing plastic leis. I ham it up, as usual. Some girls standing off to the side make "hoo-hoo" noises. That cracks me up. Then I realize *who* is making all the noise.

It's TLC: Taryn, Leslie, and Cristina.

Humiliation city.

There's one side effect from the whole carnival experience that I didn't even consider. I found five very cool guys on the team to be my friends. We're only a couple of weeks into sixth grade, but I feel like I've been here way longer, and it's all worth it.

It's all good.

Chapter 15

❀ ❀ ❀ TARYN ❀ ❀ ❀

Until the Butterflies Come Back

The air smells like wet leaves because it's raining this morning. I love rainy Saturdays, especially after a long week, and this week was the longest week in the history of weeks. But even though it was tough, I rediscovered all the reasons why Jeff is my best guy friend. He saved me, plain and simple. I guess that means I owe him — big time — and he'll probably collect. But that's okay. The carnival would not have been a success without him.

I stand up from our sofa and stretch. Zsa-Zsa stretches, too. She loves the rain as long as she's inside the house, safe and dry, buried deep into someone's lap or a cushiony chair.

Fall is really here now. I can practically taste it.

Freshly picked apples, pumpkins, and Indian corn are showing up at the supermarket. Tim, Tom, and Todd said something about the four of us hopping in the car this week to go apple-picking up at Brown Farms. We go every year. Last year, we carted home four bushels of apples. Mom made bread, cookies, pies, tarts, and more. In fact, that was when she really got into the whole cooking thing. I blame the apples.

Gazing out of our big bay window, I can see Jeff's porch from our living room. He said he'd come out to see me soon. The moment he appears through his screen door, I hop right out of my seat, grab my slicker, and head outside to join him.

Zsa-Zsa mews loudly as I leave, but she has no intention of following me.

As I step out, I can feel that it's spitting again; not steady rain, but wet nonetheless.

"Hey, T!" Jeff calls out to me.

I race over to his porch, sidestepping puddles on our sidewalk. I can't cut through the bushes today because they're too wet.

"Hey," I gasp, collapsing into one of the wicker rockers. I peel off my jacket. It's too warm to keep it on.

"Can you even see through those things?" Jeff asks, pointing at my glasses.

I take off my glasses to wipe away the raindrops. It's hard getting used to glasses and weather. When it's too hot and I walk into an air-conditioned room, my glasses steam up. When it rains, they get wet, like now.

"You know, they look good," Jeff blurts.

"What?"

"Your glasses. They look good."

"Oh. Thanks," I reply. *Huh*.

"They make you look older," Jeff says.

We sit there, rocking back and forth for a while without saying anything very important. It's been weeks — since just before school started — since we did this together.

I miss Jeff so much, but things feel different now. *Way* different.

"You're wearing your hair down again, huh?" Jeff says.

"Do you like it?" I ask Jeff, tugging at the ends. "It's a little frizzy today with the rain."

Jeff nods. "It's cool. But I like it when you wear a ponytail, too."

When he says that, something inside my belly twists, like butterflies, only I can't quite explain why. Normally, Jeff would make fun of any hairdo long before he'd compliment it. So why is he doing the opposite today?

"Thanks," I say, not knowing how else to respond.

"Yeah, well . . ." Jeff's voice drifts off. He kicks at the bottom of his chair, nearly bonking poor Toots. When the dog lets out a little howl, Jeff reaches down to make sure Toots is okay.

"Hey, did I tell you that I got a new video game?" Jeff asks, completely changing the subject.

"Not Killer Robots!" I squeal. I've been dying to play that game ever since I heard it had come out.

Jeff chuckles. "Yeah, it's Killer Robots. It looks hard, but I haven't really checked out all the levels. You want to play?"

I smile. "Of course I do," I say. I'm wondering if now that I have glasses, maybe I'll be able to beat him at video games. Usually I'm ten thousand points behind.

"I'm warning you," Jeff says, smiling. "I've been practicing a little bit."

I know he's been at it for days. He's always faking me out when it comes to playing games.

"So let's go," he says. "J.D. just hooked up a new TV in the basement."

As we stand up to go inside, I stumble over a loose board on the porch. My sandal flips off and I go falling right into Jeff's arms. This pushes him backward, unsteady. We end up in a big pile right at the edge of his porch steps.

Toots lets out an even louder howl.

"Ouch!" I squeal. But I'm the one squashing him.

"Your superstrength is no match for me, Wonder Woman." Jeff laughs, trying to push me up.

"Watch it, Aquaman!" I laugh back.

We try to stand at the same time, but it's no use. We can't seem to untangle. Rain spills down from the gutters, spraying us like a fountain.

Finally, Jeff gets free, stands up, sticks out his damp hand, and helps me to my feet. It takes me a while to steady myself. For whatever reason, Jeff doesn't let go of my hand right away.

As he's holding my fingers in his, I feel all fluttery again. Thoughts flood into my head. I think of all those things L and C said to me over the summer. I think of how Jeff came to help me at the carnival. I follow him inside, feeling safe — and close.

Wait.

This isn't a crush, I tell myself. Leslie and Cristina don't know what they're talking about. I can't crush on someone I've known since we were in diapers.

No way.

Jeff is my friend. F-R-I-E-N-D. I don't like boys

that way. Besides, all that matters at this exact moment is getting hooked up to Jeff's brand-new video game and destroying every last one of his killer robots.

That's my plan. And I'm sticking to it.

Until, of course, the butterflies come back again.

A **CANDY APPLE** BOOK

CANDY
APPLE

Miss Popularity

Francesco Sedita

SCHOLASTIC

A List of Great People

Here's a list of super-tastic people: my mom and dad; Danielle; Mrs. June Davey, my 7th grade teacher; Ken; Craig, Catherine and Aimee; and Doug.

And, duh, like Sean. Sean.

CHAPTER 1

The Maine Event

Cassie Cyan Knight watched the hideous event unfold:

Erin Donaldson, Cassie's best friend since, well, ever, was in the midst of the most ungraceful spill in the history of Sam Houston Middle School's cafeteria. Her tray of food, including an uncapped Coke Zero, a plate of fried chicken and mac & cheese and an inexplicable quantity of napkins, literally flew in all directions as Erin herself went straight down.

Immediately, Cassie went into crisis mode. She put her tray down on the salad bar counter, took a deep breath, pushed her red tresses behind her ears, and locked her plastic teal bangle high on her arm so it wouldn't bang against her wristbone. Then she marched over to the scene. Kids were gawking and pointing at teary-eyed Erin. Cassie's troupe of girls, Jen, Marci, and Laura, followed in formation, each certain that she was the most important girl on the backup team. Every girl in Sam Houston — in the state of Texas, probably — wanted to be Cassie Knight's best friend.

Cassie waved the gaggle of giggling students off with a breezy, "Oh, come on, like you've never seen someone fall?" And then to a group of awed fifth graders, she added, "Guys, I mean, really? Move it. The show is over." She was firm but sweet. She was a Texan, after all. And Texas girls know how to strike that perfect balance.

Cassie leaned over and offered a trembling Erin her hand. Cassie would get her friend through this. They all would.

In a millisecond the girls — Cassie, Erin, Jen, Marci, and Laura — were in the Ladies Room, de-mac-&-cheesing, reglossing, and de-embarrassing their friend.

"Okay, young lady," Cassie said as she went through Erin's purse, extracting all the needed supplies: lip gloss, shimmery shadow, and, of course, hair spray. "Now it's time to either break down and cry or laugh. Either way, we have some work to do on that gorgeous face, so let me know."

Erin's face was blank. Cassie realized it was time to try a new tactic.

"Okay, so that was quite possibly one of the best falls I've ever seen!" Cassie said, wiping a glob of mac & chese from Erin's shoulder. Sooner or later, Erin was going to laugh. Cassie just wanted to get her there sooner. She made eyes at the other three girls, who were busy hair-spraying themselves in the mirror.

In unison, they said, "Totally!"

Cassie swooped the gloss wand across Erin's lips.

Erin sighed and crossed her arms. "Guys, please, people pointed and stared! Pointed, stared, and LAUGHED!"

Cassie caught her breath fast, hoping to hold back the fit of laughter about to slip out of her. She didn't want to laugh *at* Erin. But it *was* sort of hilarious.

Erin knew her too well. "Cassie Knight, I swear if you start laughing, I am going to add peroxide to your conditioner!"

Cassie put her hand on top of her head, guarding her red curls. "You wouldn't!" And with that, Cassie couldn't control herself and let laughter fly out of her. Through her gasps, she said, "I'm sorry,

Erin, it was so funny!" And then, "I had no idea Coke Zero could explode so much!"

The other girls lost it, too, squealing with laughter.

Erin was quiet for a minute. "Well, I *was* surprised to see mac & cheese could stick to the wall like that." She let out a slight giggle.

And then, the group howled together. Erin did, too, her hand in front of her mouth, her embarrassment slipping away.

"Okay, make me beautiful again," Erin said, pushing back her hair.

"That's our girl!" Cassie beamed, lining up the needed beauty supplies on the counter.

On the way home that afternoon, big Texas sunlight flooded the backseat of Mrs. Donaldson's minivan (the one with the bumper sticker that humiliated Erin: THE ONLY THING BIGGER THAN MY HAIR IS TEXAS). Cassie stretched her fingers apart, admiring the glint and glimmer of her favorite blue crystal ring and loathing the chip in her shimmering, shiny Blue by You nail polish. Blue — and if we're getting specific, teal — was Cassie's signature color. Oh, it was just so yummy! And it was the basis of Cassie's #1 Design Rule. *Teal: good. Teal and tons and tons of warm sunlight: um, delicious.*

"So, what are we doing this weekend?" Laura asked from the backseat.

Cassie turned around. "I heard that everyone's going roller skating on Saturday for Donny McMahill's birthday."

"Really?" Erin asked, dreamily. She'd had a total crush on Donny since second grade.

"We should go. And maybe hit the mall first?" Cassie asked.

All the girls nodded.

"Erin, what are you going to wear?" Cassie asked.

Erin went white. "I have NO idea!"

"We'll figure it out. We have plenty of time," Cassie said, confident. "You can borrow my new flouncy denim skirt if you want. It would look SO cute on you!"

"Really? Thanks!" Erin said. "Because, really, Coke Zero is *not* my color."

The girls started to laugh again. Cassie was relieved Erin could joke about her spill.

"What's going on back there?" Mrs. Donaldson asked, her eyes in the rearview mirror.

Cassie leaned forward and said, "It's nothing, Mrs. D. Your beautiful daughter had a relatively un-beautiful moment today. But we handled it. She's still as beautiful as ever, right?"

Mrs. Donaldson smiled. "Of course!" She lightly bounced her hand against her hair-sprayed head.

They turned past Palace Boot Shop, where Cassie got a new pair of cowboy boots each year for her birthday, and entered Houston Heights, Cassie's neighborhood.

Before she stepped out of the car, Cassie turned to the girls. "Okay, wrap-up calls in half an hour? Because we have some major homework to do. I can't believe it! It's like, welcome back from winter break, here's enough work to make you forget you had a vacation."

"Oh, please, Cass," Jen said, her copper-shadowed eyes twinkling in the sunlight, "you probably already did it all during free period."

Cassie grabbed her bag. "Thanks for the ride, Mrs. D!"

"Of course, sweetie. Tell your mom I'll call her later tonight."

"Will do!" Cassie looked at Erin, wanting to make sure her best friend was still okay after the unfortunate fall earlier. "How are we? Tell me before I go, so I don't have to start up CheerErinUp-dot-com when I get upstairs."

Erin laughed. "We are fine. Really. Thanks, Cass."

"It was funny. But so what? Funny is the best."

Erin smiled. Cassie reached over and gave her a hug.

Cassie blew kisses to the rest of the girls and slid out of the car, her teal blue Candies clicking on the cement. Feeling the slight chill of January in the Houston air, she walked through the yard toward her house, a reddish-brown brick beauty. Before Cassie crossed the lawn, she stopped to look at the big stone archway over the door. When she was a little girl, she used to imagine it was the entrance to her princess castle. Truthfully, she still did. She just wouldn't admit it to anyone!

"I'm home!" Cassie called, the heavy door sighing open. She dropped her backpack and ran upstairs to her room.

She put her purse down on her desk, next to her blue rhinestone laptop. Design Rule #11 was obvious — basic, really. *Glitter, sparkles, and marabou make a perfect accent to anything.*

Cassie sat carefully on her bed, making sure she didn't upset her perfectly arranged pillow pile. She reached for her cordless phone to call a few of her other girls, to report on a *fab* pair of wedge heels she'd seen at the mall. This was Design Rule #8: *The cordless (teal, of course, and not so easy to find!) must get killer reception, anywhere in the house.*

Cassie knew that might not technically be a Design Rule. But it was a rule. And it was important.

Just then, her mother called from downstairs. "Cassie, can you come to the kitchen, please?"

Cassie swung her feet onto the floor, slid on her marabou slippers, and walked to the mirror. She frowned at her frizzy mane, then sprayed hair spray with a flourish. Humidity in January was a real downer.

She clicked her fingernails against the banister as she walked down the stairs. She had to fix that chip. It was driving her crazy.

Her parents were at the kitchen table, papers spread in front of them. *Paul is home from work already?* she thought. This wasn't a good sign. Cassie's parents only asked to speak with her like this when something was really up. Like when she was little little and her hamster, Peteykins, had gotten really sick.

Uh-oh.

"Hey, Cass, how's it going?" Her dad stood up and gave her a kiss on the head.

"Great." Cassie bit her lip. "Um, guys, what's going on?"

"We wanted to talk to you about my job," her dad said.

Oh no! Paul must've lost his job. (Cassie called her parents by their first names, Sheila and Paul. She had total respect for them — they ruled! — but "Mommy" and "Daddy" was just so, well, *7th Heaven.*) Cassie was ready to tell him that everything would be okay, that she would limit her clothes buying, and that she would do everything she could possibly do to help, even if that meant not getting manicures and pedicures every other week.

"Your father got a promotion, Cassie."

"That is so amazing!" Relieved, Cassie sprang out of her chair and hugged her dad.

"But it means that he has to move — we all have to move," her mom added.

Cassie plunked into her chair, her stomach sinking. *Move? To a new neighborhood?* "Where?" she asked.

"To Maine, honey," her mother said gently. "All the way up north."

Cassie looked from one parent to the other in shock. How could this be happening? Just a few minutes ago, her biggest issue had been frizzy hair, and whether or not to run for class president. And now — *now* — Cassie couldn't even process it. Her stomach turned and her heart began to pound. Leave Houston and all her friends? She was about to cry, she could feel it.

"I know this must be really scary and disappointing, Cass," her father said. "But it's going to be okay, you know?"

"I know," Cassie said, her voice trembling, a big wave of tears working its way through her. "But Maine? Really?"

Her dad laughed. "I know. It's far. And cold. But Maine is beautiful. And there's a great school that wants you to start as soon as you can."

A new school? Cassie hadn't even thought of *that* yet.

Maybe it wouldn't be for a while. Maybe they were telling her now so she could really get ready over the next few months. "When?" she asked, her voice trembling.

"In two weeks. We wanted to wait until after the holidays to tell you."

Cassie couldn't help it anymore. Her big eyes filled with bigger tears. "Okay," she managed to say.

"Cass, we'll all be together. And you'll make friends there, too. You'll see." Paul smiled and walked to her.

"Your father's right, honey," Sheila said. "I promise."

Her parents both hugged her, but their reassuring words weren't helping Cassie feel any better.

"I'm going to go up to my room for a little while. Is that okay?" she asked, pulling away.

"Of course," Sheila said, petting Cassie's hair.

Before Cassie left the kitchen, she turned around. "I'm really proud of you, Dad." She hadn't called him that in forever, but she knew this was the right time.

Cassie closed her bedroom door and walked directly to her closet. She reached toward the back, behind all her shoes, and found him: Bobby the Teddy Bear. He'd been Cassie's teddy since she was two, and since Cassie was an only child, she secretly felt she could confide in Bobby as she would a sibling. Of course, *no one* knew that Bobby was still around.

Except for Erin.

Cassie slid off her marabous and sank onto her bed, holding Bobby tight. The tears came down and down and down. Moving to Maine! This was not supposed to happen. It just wasn't. Everything had been feeling so good. She was going to run for class president. She and her friends were going to *rock* the sixth grade. There was Donny McMahill's birthday party. Her mind raced. Maybe she could stay in Houston and live with Erin's family. That would be okay with the Donaldsons, she was sure of it. Maybe that would be the way to make this better. Cassie sat up, feeling a huge wave of relief.

But just as soon as she felt the relief, it went away. She couldn't be without her parents. She would miss them more than anything. Cassie plunked her head down on the bed, all cried out.

Her galloping thoughts were interrupted by the *ding* of her IM. Cassie gave Bobby one last hug and then sat down at her desk.

4EVERERIN: Okay, I'm over it. I swear.

Cassie smiled. What was she going to do without Erin?

MISSCASS: I'm so glad.

Cassie twirled her hair between her fingers. How was she going to tell Erin her awful news?

MISSCASS: I have something to tell you.

4EVERERIN: Celeb gossip???!

MISSCASS: No.

4EVERERIN: Newest gloss color?

MISSCASS: Uh-uh.

4EVERERIN: Okay. Last guess. New shoes?

MISSCASS: LOL! I wish!!!! Okay, are you ready?

4EVERERIN: You're scaring me. Is Bobby out?

MISSCASS: Yes.

4EVERERIN: Uh-oh. Okay. I'm ready.

MISSCASS: We're moving. Because of my dad's job.

Even writing it was hard. The tears filled Cassie's eyes again as she stared at the blank screen, waiting for Erin's response.

The phone rang.

Before Cassie could even say hello, Erin said, "Where?"

Cassie took a deep breath. "Maine."

Silence.

"Are you there?"

"I'm here," Erin said. "I can't believe it." Cassie could hear the tears in Erin's voice.

"Neither can I!" Cassie said, flopping back down on her bed.

Erin groaned on her side of the phone. "This *sucks*!" she said. "Isn't there a way you could get out of this? Oh, I know — you can move in with me and —"

"I can't do that, Erin. I thought about it, but . . ." Cassie sighed. "I mean, I know it's good for Paul and everything, but hello, did they even think of me at all?" Cassie knew the answer to that question. Of course her parents thought of her. But for the moment she just wanted to be whiny and complainy. "What am I even going to *do* in Maine?"

There was silence on the other end.

"Are you there?" Cassie asked.

"I'm here," Erin said, sounding determined. "I'm just Googling it. Let's see what I want to do when I come visit you."

A flicker of happiness went through Cassie. Leave it to Erin to look on the bright side of things.

"Ooh, we could rock climb!" Erin was trying hard.

"Can you rock climb in sparkly flats?"

"Hmm, good point. Hold on. I'm clicking on PERFORMING ARTS. . . . There's ballet! And theatre! Oh my God, they're doing a production of *Annie* right now! Cass! This is a good sign!"

They both laughed. Cassie and Erin could perform "It's the Hard-Knock Life" like no one else.

"Wow. People are going to *freak* when they find out," Erin said.

"I mean, some, I guess. Yeah."

"Don't even, Cass. You've been the most popular girl since the first grade."

Cassie blushed. "No, that's not true," she protested, even though, well, it was true.

"Cassie! Everyone adores you!"

Smiling, the tears welling up, Cassie just said, "Thanks." She thought for a moment. "Wait, *how* am I going to tell everyone? I *so* don't want to have to say it, like, a thousand times. There's not enough waterproof mascara in the world for that."

Both girls were quiet, thinking.

And then, Erin, brilliant genius that she was, said, "I know: Call Jen. Tell her. And tell her not to tell anyone. She has the biggest mouth in all of Texas!"

Cassie laughed. Jen really didn't know how to keep a secret. "Ooh, that's a good plan."

"You're going to be okay. And we're going to get you through this. I promise."

Cassie felt better. It wasn't going to be easy, but with friends like Erin, she knew she would survive. "I'm going to call Jen right now."

"I'll check in on you later," Erin said. Cassie was sure she was still looking for things for them to do in Maine when she came to visit.

"Thanks, you," Cassie said, the tears coming back.

"Please, thank YOU. Now no one will remember my little incident in the caf today!" Erin laughed. "Love you."

"Love you, too."

Cassie clicked the phone and dialed Jen's number. And within a few hours, everyone knew. Cassie did her best to sound excited when her upset friends called her. But she was scared. Maine seemed so far away.

CHAPTER 2

Can You Wear Cute Shoes in a Snowstorm?

As Sheila drove up the long driveway to The Oak Grove School, Cassie's stomach flipped over. It was her first day at a new school in a new state, complete with a new weather pattern. The Knight family had moved just three days ago and *whoomp!* an enormous, welcome-to-Maine snowstorm had walloped them. Twenty-five inches of snow. Cassie didn't even know that was possible. Except for maybe in Antarctica or somewhere like that.

Sheila pulled up to the big, dark, castle-like building. Cassie had visited it over the weekend to pick up her class schedule and meet Principal Veronica, the way uptight leader of the school.

"Okay Cass, good luck, honey. I know this is going to be great. I do. Just give it some time."

Cassie had to admit that, despite being nervous, she was a little excited. She was going to meet so many new people. She looked out the window at the snow-covered lawn in front of her. There were kids everywhere, bundled up in puffy jackets, laughing and throwing snowballs at one another. *Snowball fights! Cool!*

"Thanks, Mom. It's going to be great!" Cassie smiled at her mother. This was hard for Sheila, too, she knew that. She gave her a big kiss and a hug. And with that, she opened the door and stuck one glamorous beaded flat out onto the ground.

Watch out, Oak Grove Middle School. Here comes Cassie Cyan Knight.

As she stepped out of the car, her foot slid out from underneath her and with a completely ungraceful *whoosh*, she landed — on her behind — in a snowbank.

Fabulous.

Sheila ran around the car to help her up. But Cassie was on her feet before her mother got there. "I'm fine. I'm fine." They looked at each other and laughed.

"Oh, Cass. Are you okay?" Sheila brushed snow from Cassie's new ugly down parka, which would have been embarrassing even without the big fall. "Honey, you have to let me buy you some good boots. You're going to break your neck. After school today, we're going straight to the mall."

The very thought of big clunky snow boots sent down Cassie's spine a chill colder than the sub-zero temperatures. But Sheila was right. She knew it.

"Okay," she said, distracted by the thought of what her hair looked like post–snow attack.

She hugged Sheila good-bye and walked into the school, careful not to have an additional spill. The hallway was so quiet, Cassie felt like she was in a cornfield in the middle of nowhere. No, wait: in a *library* in a cornfield in the middle of nowhere. It was all dark and musty and dusty. Oak Grove used to be a mansion that some family lived in.

Like, a haunted *mansion, maybe.*

When Cassie got to the principal's office, she smiled politely at the secretary behind the front desk. The whole place was all dark wood and dim light. There wasn't *one* splash of color or sparkle. As Cassie removed her parka, she felt like she practically glowed in the dark in her teal Chick by Nicky Hilton dress and flats.

The secretary was talking on the phone, obviously to a disgruntled parent. She didn't even look up at Cassie, just kept shaking her head and saying "mm-hmmm." Cassie gently cleared her throat. The woman looked up with a hideous, frightening glare and stuck her completely unmanicured pointer finger up in the universal "Just wait a minute, sister" sign. Cassie smiled as politely as possible.

Suddenly, Principal Veronica opened the heavy wood door. She wore a dark gray suit that she must have bought before Cassie was born. And worse, she had on unshined black shoes and her gray hair was in a messy bun. Another chill ran through Cassie.

"Hello, Principal Veronica!"

The principal looked Cassie up and down, seemingly stunned to see her.

"I'm Cassie Knight. Remember me?"

"How could I forget," she said, the corner of her mouth curling into a smile. She checked her watch. "You're late," she added sternly.

Cassie looked at the clock on the wall. She *so* wasn't late. But she wanted to make a good impression. And, besides, she didn't have the will to argue when all of her energy was being sapped trying to warm her feet up. "Sorry," she said, picking up her purse and following the principal out of the office.

Cassie walked alongside PV. That's what Cassie would call Principal Veronica from now on, at least in her mind. It just took the edge off her big, scary presence. And initials were *so* right now. She followed her through the narrow hallways. There was dark wood everywhere. The thin tan carpeting seemed to drink up sounds in the creepiest of ways. Unflattering yellow lights glowed from above, and Cassie was certain the glare turned her auburn locks carrot.

"At Oak Grove Middle School, we believe in educating the complete student, Ms. Knight. It is vital that education come not only from books and literature but also from the quest for self-knowledge."

Cassie did her best to stay focused. *Education was important. Yes, of course. Quest for self-knowledge? Wow, sure. But you know what else is important? A deep power-pack hair conditioner.* Cassie studied PV's unfortunate bun and rolled her eyes.

"Your homeroom is just up on the left," PV said.

I need to check my lip gloss and spray my hair before I meet people, Cassie thought. Before the move from Texas, she'd had one last cut and blowout from Fabrizio, her über-cool, über-rocking hairstylist. There were a lot of things Cassie was going to miss about Texas. But leaving Fabrizio had broken her heart.

"Is there a bathroom I can use before I go in?"

Principal Veronica looked at her watch for the third time since they'd been together. "Yes. Just to your left." She stopped walking, pointed to a varnished wooden door, and checked her watch. Again.

"Thank you so much. I'll just be a sec!" Cassie pushed through the door. The bathroom fixtures were old and cracked. Her shoes echoed loudly as she walked to the mirrors. The windows were open slightly, and outside, snowy hills rolled out far, far, far away. Cassie was so not in Houston anymore.

She reached into her purse for her cell, desperate to talk to one of her girls. But she stopped herself: new leaf, new life, *just relax*. Instead, she grabbed her most valuable tool from her purse: Cargo lip gloss. *LuLu Island, thank you very much.* She slid her finger over the dark side of the gloss, painted it onto her lips in two evenly pressured swipes, and then dipped into the light side. She smacked her lips together twice, a *thwack* echoing from the pale green tiles. She swiped her lashes with her Benefit BADgal Lash Mascara. *Roar!* Her lashes were fierce. Finally, she pulled out her hair spray and covered her red curls, scrunching them to new heights in a haze of super-holding goodness.

She smiled at the mirror, feeling much more like her old self. *It's time for a new adventure, Cassie.*

Refreshed, she did an about-face and marched

out of the bathroom. PV was waiting for her, tapping her poorly shod foot.

"Sorry about that!" Cassie smiled.

Taking a deep breath, she followed the principal into her new homeroom. It was much smaller than her classrooms in Houston. And there were no bright paintings on the plain white walls. It seemed so bare and dull.

Principal Veronica was talking to the teacher, who was in khakis and a white button-down shirt, buttoned too far up. Thick black curls framed his face and he had a big, toothy grin. He seemed young for a teacher, but nice. "Ms. Knight, this is Mr. Blackwell, your homeroom and English teacher," PV said crisply.

Cassie extended her hand. This was a major Life Rule for Cassie.

Life Rule #31: Shaking hands is a really mature, I'm-gonna-be-a-woman-who-runs-a-BIG-pretty-company thing to do!

He met her hand and shook it firmly.

"It's Robert. Robert Blackwell."

Cassie flushed with embarrassment. Oh no! All of this was so different and so new — a teacher offering his first name? It was one thing to call her parents by theirs. But a *teacher*? That was just crazy.

"You can call me Mr. B," Mr. Blackwell added.

"Hi, nice to meet you. You can call me Cassie."
Duh!

Embarrassed, Cassie ducked her head. She didn't know what to do with herself, her arms, her anything! She decided to rest her hand on her hip.

"I'll leave you here, Ms. Knight. I wish you luck in your academic pursuits." PV nodded briskly, then strode out.

Mr. Blackwell leaned against his desk and crossed his arms. He slid his smarty-pants oval glasses onto his head. "So, Cassie, welcome to Oak Grove. Tell us a little bit about yourself."

For the first time, Cassie turned her head and looked at her new classmates. She was frozen. Totally and utterly frozen. Thirty eyes were blinking at her through the pea-soup heat seeping from the radiators. She could feel her stomach doing cartwheels. She had to pull it together. Her eyes ran the length of the mahogany bookcase.

"Wow. You guys have a lot of books here!"

Jaws dropped.

"No! That's a good thing! Like, I mean, we had books, too, at my old school."

Uh-oh. This was not so perfect. Cassie had to find her way through this. She cleared her throat. "What I meant is that, in Houston, we had a lot of books and smart stuff, too."

Nothing. Not even eye contact from most people.

"I guess we just had more, like, sports trophies and things."

More jaws dropped. Cassie was sure her new classmates could see her heart beating through her satin dress. She took the moment of stifling silence to check out what the other students were wearing: gray. Gray, gray, and a little navy-blue. Sometimes, there was a "daring" splash of white or black. But the standard look for girls was: white turtleneck or button-down, navy blazer, gray skirt. And for boys, gray pants, navy sweaters.

Cassie felt a huge wave of homesickness.

Mr. Blackwell stepped in to save the day and became Cassie's favorite person in the universe when he said, "Cassie, why don't you have a seat at that desk over there?" He pointed to an empty desk near the back of the room.

Cassie began her walk, smiling as she did. All eyes were glued to her. She did her best to make eye contact and whisper hellos, but still only stony silence greeted her.

Finally in her seat, she dropped her bag on the floor and exhaled. She was exhausted, and the morning had just begun.

"All right, guys," Mr. Blackwell said, still leaning on his desk. "I want to make sure you all take care of Cassie. It's no fun being the new kid." He smiled out at the class. Cassie felt a prickle of relief. There *were* nice people in Maine.

Cassie fumbled through her bag to pull out a pen. She grabbed her favorite — teal, complete with silver glitter and a maribou tip. She smiled when she saw it, but then realized that no one at Oak Grove would appreciate it. She stuffed it back into her purse.

"Does anyone have any questions before we start our day?" Mr. Blackwell asked.

A girl raised her hand. She had pale skin, was wearing a gray fuzzy sweatshirt thing, and her brown hair was pulled tight into a ponytail. "I have a question," she said.

"Go ahead, Mary Ellen," Mr. Blackwell said.

"It's actually for Cassie. . . ." The girl turned in her seat to look at Cassie. "I'm Mary Ellen McGinty," she said sharply. Soon to be known as, Cassie would learn, *Mean, Mean Mary Ellen McGinty*.

"Hi," Cassie said, slightly relieved that someone was introducing herself.

"I know you're new here," Mary Ellen said, her lips forming a perfect heart. But when she next spoke, the heart broke. Into ten million pieces. "I'm just wondering why you aren't following dress code. It's an Oak Grove rule. We're not here for a fashion show, you know."

Now, THAT was apparent. And a real problem. Muddy snow boots were SO not on the runways this season, as far as Cassie could recall.

"I am in code!" Cassie gasped. "I'm wearing a dress that is at fingertip length," she said, jumping up and turning to the side, stretching her arm down so she could show that her hem was longer than her fingers. "I am not wearing any 'overly colorful' makeup." She put her hand to her cheeks to draw attention to her flawless application. "And I am wearing flats, which is far less than the two-inch maximum on heels."

"But we don't wear dresses. We just *don't*," Mary Ellen said, her words sharp.

Cassie gulped. They could take the sun away from her. Her friends. Her princess house. But her clothes? Never.

Oh no. Things were not going as well as she had hoped. Not at all.

351

CHAPTER 3

Hello, No Frozen Yogurt? Really?

Cassie was starving. She made her way into the cafeteria, surrounded by a sea of people she didn't know. And she was quickly learning that most of them didn't want to know her.

Her eyes quickly surveyed the caf. Long, wooden tables with worn-in plastic chairs, a gray marble floor, and brown trays. Like everything else about Oak Grove, it was colorless and blah. *I miss my Houston*, Cassie thought. She just wished she could sit with Erin and all the girls at their fave table, eating frozen yogurt and giggling.

Frozen yogurt! Cassie was newly inspired. That would bring her spirits up. She hoped they had the classic chocolate/vanilla swirl.

As she neared the counter, her eyes scanned for the frozen-yogurt machine. Soda machine: check.

Fridge filled with Snapple and Vitamin Water and water water: check. Little, cute, tiny fridge filled with little, cute, tiny ice creams: check. But Cassie was getting nervous. Where was the yogurt? Her eyes shot back and forth. Nothing! No FroYo! No oodles of sprinkles and crushed, delicious candy bars and cherries and other forms of deliciousness to top it all off!

It was official: This *was* a bad day.

Always a trooper, Cassie tucked her red tresses behind her ears, squared her shoulders, and took a deep breath; she'd been through tougher things than no frozen yogurt in her life. She headed to the sandwiches and picked up a turkey and cheese. It looked surprisingly edible. She made a mental check in her brain in the *Pros* column.

She grabbed a Coke Zero, smiled again at the thought of Erin and the girls back in Houston, and walked to the register to pay. She put her tray down on the ledge, balancing it with her hip. Just as she was opening her purse, the tray wobbled. Cassie panicked: Save the food or save the purse? Against her better fashion judgment, she opted for the food and both hands flew to the tray. And of course, her purse — and all of its contents, including lots of change — slipped out of her hands.

It all seemed to happen in slow motion. The purse flipped in the air, and her products, her mirror, her Arctic Chill gum, and her sunglasses flew everywhere. Cassie looked to the left and then to the right, and saw everyone in the cafeteria stop and stare. No. Not this. Not today! Cassie felt her face heat up, redder than her hair.

I've become Erin!

Maybe this was a mistake. Maybe she should have asked to be homeschooled. That would have been so much easier.

The woman behind the register, a kind, grandma type with curly silver hair, scurried around the counter to help Cassie collect her things. As she deposited a fistful of mascara, lip gloss, and cell phone into Cassie's purse, she looked at Cassie with big green eyes.

"First day?"

Cassie scrambled to pick up the glimmering change, some of which was still rolling away in various directions. She stood up, inexplicably out of breath.

"How'd you guess?"

The woman smiled. "Oh, I don't know."

"My unbelievable grace?" Cassie laughed at herself.

"Maybe that. Maybe the fact that no one here wears such beautiful colors as you do. I love your dress!"

"You do?" Cassie felt happiness wriggle through her. The lunchroom lady and Mr. Blackwell. That made two nice people in Maine. "Thanks so much! It's a Nicky Hilton!" A line was forming behind her. "Sorry, I should get out of your way," Cassie said, her eyes scanning the ground for any last evidence of her mishap. "How much is it?"

"It's on me," the woman said with a wink.

"Are you sure? Thank you so much!" Cassie grinned. "My name is Cassie Knight." She extended her hand.

"So nice to meet you. I'm Rose Miller."

"Oh! What kind of moisturizer do you use? Your hands are so soft!"

"Whatever's on sale at the grocery store," Rose said, smiling.

Cassie dug through her purse quickly, knowing she was making the line of people wait even longer for her. Finally, she found the small tube of L'Occitane Shea Butter Hand Cream, a product she thanked the goddess for each and every day, and gave it to Rose.

"You must try this. It will change your life!"

Rose took the tube and smiled. "You don't have to do that."

"Oh yes, I must! The fate of beautiful skin like yours can't be left up to supermarket sales! We must work to maintain it!" Cassie smiled again, picked up her tray, and walked out to the seating area, feeling ten times better.

But now, another problem: Where was she going to sit? This had *never* been an issue for Cassie, and it felt so weird to be in this new, awkward position. She looked out into a Milky Way of unfamiliar faces and bit her lip, her heart pounding.

She was certain no one was going to ask her to sit with them, so she would just approach a table.

Life Rule #37: When in doubt, be bold.

She surveyed her prospects, stopping for a moment at the napkin stand, praying to look less conspicuous. As she slowly pulled a napkin from the dispenser, she found her table of choice. Located at three o'clock sharp. Two girls were laughing together and seemed friendly. Like everyone else at Oak Grove, they wore navy blue sweaters over plaid and gray skirts. Who were they? Would they be her new Maine friends? She hoped so!

With new confidence, Cassie walked the length of the cafeteria, her target in focus at all times. When she neared the table, she widened her smile.

"Hi! I'm Cassie. Do you mind if I sit here?"

The laughter immediately stopped and the girls looked up in disgust.

"Yes."

This was a joke, right? It had to be. Cassie stepped closer to the table and put her tray down.

"So, what are your names?" she asked, her right fist scrunching up some curls.

"Our names are 'Go' and 'Away,'" one of them said.

"Tex-*as* girl," the other added with a twang.

Both girls laughed, their faces twisting into a very special form of hideousness.

Really? People actually acted like this in real life?

Cassie took a deep breath, the pressure of tears filling her eyes. *Do not let them see you cry.* She turned abruptly and began walking over to the first table she saw. She recognized some people from her homeroom, but she sat at the very end.

Cassie unwrapped her sandwich, taking far longer than she needed to get the plastic off. She didn't know what else to do. No one was really talking at the table and she wasn't sure why.

"So, do any of you guys have Mr. Blackwell for English?" she finally asked, careful of her accent. She hoped she didn't sound as twangy as that girl who'd made fun of her.

Of the six people at the table, only one looked up to acknowledge Cassie — a dirty-blonde with a tartan headband. "Everyone in sixth grade has him for English." She scowled at Cassie.

Is this for real? Or am I on one of those reality shows about mean kids? Cassie wondered.

"Well, I've only been at this school for, um, like, three hours," Cassie replied, hoping for some laughter.

But nothing. No one made a sound. They just ignored her.

Then, a prepped-out boy in an unseasonable pink polo turned to her and said, "You're from *Houston*?"

"Yes," Cassie responded cautiously.

"I've never met anyone from Texas," the boy replied.

"Looks like your luck has run out," another girl at the table muttered.

Cassie took a breath. "It's a nice state. The people are actually *friendly*." Cassie grabbed her purse, scooped up her tray, and said, "Thanks for letting me sit with you." As she turned to walk away, she felt the tears starting. There was no holding them back now. She caught her breath, placed her tray on the counter, and hurried to the *toilettes* again. (Cassie preferred the French word for *bathroom*.)

After carefully navigating the dark and long hallways, she ran into the Ladies and shut herself in a stall.

And burst into tears.

Her cell phone buzzed. She dug through her purse. It was a text from Erin.

Hope UR smiling!

Just the opposite, Cassie thought. Her heart melted as she realized what a good friend Erin was. Who needed new Maine friends?

Am now.

Cassie grabbed a tissue from her purse and carefully blotted her cheeks.

TNN. TNN. Tears Not Necessary.

After a makeup redux, Cassie headed to her locker. The lockers weren't even metal — they were that same old dark wood that was everywhere. (But they did allow more room for shoes. You never know when you might need a heel change in the middle of the day.) Cassie walked the quiet hallway, hoping she remembered her combination. As she ran the numbers through her head, she spotted a girl at a locker near hers. Cassie couldn't decide if she should say hello. Maybe she should just keep going.

But no, a Texas girl would never do that!

"Hi," Cassie said, trying to control her accent, so she didn't say *haaah*.

The girl — a super-pretty brunette in a surprisingly cool outfit — white blazer, cute gray skirt, and tortoise-shell glasses — jumped a little and clumsily slammed her locker shut. And just as she did, Cassie caught the glimmer of something sparkly in her locker.

Before she could say another word, the girl scurried away down the hall. Cassie sighed, her eyes on the locker. There was something good in there, and Cassie was going to find out what it was!

CHAPTER 4

Not Even the Mall Is Safe!

By the end of the day, Cassie was a fading flower. No one had spoken a word to her, except to comment on her Texas twang, which she didn't even know she had. The homework didn't seem like it was going to be more or harder than it was in Texas, just different. There *was* one thing Cassie decided she could manage in Maine: the schoolwork. Cassie had been an A student in Houston, and that was not going to change in Maine — regardless of how socially B-list she felt.

Cassie sighed as the bus carried her home through the snowy streets. She was so relieved to have the day behind her.

The bus let her off just in front of her house. She smiled at everyone as she walked past them and even said "Bye" to a boy and a girl she recognized from math class. They sort of smiled back, but didn't say anything.

What did I expect?

Before she hopped down the steps, Cassie turned her head and looked out at everyone, the dark green leather seats framing their heads. Then she glanced at the bus driver.

"Thanks so much." she said to him.

This was a major Life Rule.

Life Rule #46: You thank people for the work they do. Always.

"See you in the A.M.!" she added.

Even though Sheila had offered to drive Cassie to and from school, Cassie knew she had to take the bus no matter how nervous it made her.

Surprised, the driver smiled. "You, too!" he said.

Cassie walked down the steps, careful not to slip on the ice. She stopped for a moment to take in her new house. It was nothing like the old one. This house was an old farmhouse, built, in like, 1800 or something, drafty and old, stained gray with black shutters. There were blueberry bushes in the front yard, now covered with snow, but Paul said they would be really pretty in the summer. He said they could even eat the berries right from the bush. Cassie wasn't sure how she felt about that. What if there were bugs on them? *Gross.*

On the way up the front stairs, Cassie fumbled with her keys in her purse. *It's hard to use your hands when they're wrapped up in gloves.* Cassie hardly ever had to wear gloves in Texas.

Inside, the heat immediately soothing her, she put her bags down, took off her hideous parka, scrunched at her hair in the mirror, and ran up to her room. Well, it wasn't totally her room yet. All her stuff was there, but she hadn't Cassie-fied it yet. *Design Rule #51: A room must reflect its owner's sparkle.*

Before Cassie could settle in, her mom stuck her head into the room to see how the first day went and to announce that it was time to hit the mall.

"I have a vision for boots," Cassie said to Sheila as they walked through the mall, a place she finally felt at home. Cassie wanted something suede-y, nice and cozy on the inside, but nothing too Ugg-ish. Ugh to Uggs! Even girls in Texas wore them! Now, *that* was crazy.

Upon entering the shoe department, Cassie's eyes widened. Oh, *shoes.* They always had a dangerous effect on her! Her eyes flitted back and forth across all the styles and colors. So much to look at and choose from!

But Sheila was on to Cassie fast. "Earth to Cassie. We are here for *boots*. One pair of boots. And a pair of boots that you can actually wear in this ridiculous cold!"

Cassie looked up at her mom. She knew this was a hard move for Sheila, too.

"It is *so* cold! I had icicles on my face before when I was waiting for the bus!"

Sheila smiled. "Icicles, huh?"

"Totally!"

"C'mon, you." Sheila grabbed Cassie's hand and led her to the boots.

Even though Cassie and her mom had very different styles, they understood — and respected — those styles completely. Sheila was all *matchy-matchy* with sweater sets and pearls and stuff. Cassie was more *pizazz-y*.

Life Rule #2: You don't have to agree. But you do have to respect.

As she followed her mother, she caught sight of one of the most beautiful pair of boots that was ever created. Ever. Leather, with a lace-up back and gorgeously embroidered flowers up the side.

They were divine. Fast and furious, Cassie headed toward them, her hand outstretched, in serious need of a *TE* (textural experience). Just as she made contact and shivered in delight, something else caught Cassie's eye: Mary Ellen McGinty.

What was she supposed to do now? Cassie hated having weirdness with anyone, and this was going to be weird. She just knew it.

But she squared her shoulders, picked up the boot, and walked over to Mary Ellen, who was looking at the frumpiest pair of Keds Cassie had ever had the misfortune of encountering.

"Hi!" Cassie said.

Mary Ellen looked up with a grimace. "Oh, hi."

Cassie stuck the boot in between them, trying to make friendly conversation. "Have you seen these boots? Aren't they to die for?"

"Maybe if you're from Texas," Mary Ellen said coolly. "You're Cindy, right?" she snarled.

"No, I'm Cassie." *I mean, really?* Cassie knew Mary Ellen had said the wrong name on purpose. They had met just hours ago! "These boots are fabulous, no matter where you're from."

Mary Ellen rolled her eyes. "Cindy, you don't get it, do you? You're not the princess of Texas anymore. If you hadn't noticed, there are no runways around here. There's snow and ice — and pavement. So do yourself a favor and get a fleece and some real boots."

Cassie jerked back, worried that her hair might ignite from Mary Ellen's fiery words. No one had ever treated her this way. She wanted to ask Mary Ellen what a fleece was, but she was too startled to speak.

Finally, Cassie managed an icy "Have a good night." And with that, she flipped her hair dramatically and walked off to find a salesperson. She would try on the boots, no matter what Mean Mary Ellen McGinty had to say.

CHAPTER 5

So, Fine, This Isn't Going to Be a Fairy Tale

On Cassie's fourth day at Oak Grove, she gave in and decided to wear jeans. It was just too cold in Maine, and she needed to be smarter about her fabric choices. She chose a beautiful green peasant blouse with three teal flowers on the bodice and a pair of Sevens. Sevens, Cassie knew, are perfect when a girl needs some cheering up. Cassie wasn't *completely* depressed, but she needed some help. And her Sevens were always there for her. Not to mention the peasant shirt, which Erin had given Cassie last year for her birthday.

As Cassie entered Oak Grove, shivering and stomping snow off her lovely new boots, she wondered what Erin was doing right now, back in sweet ol' Texas.

There were exactly seven minutes to the first

367

bell and only one way to find out. Cassie ducked into the girls' room and shut herself in a stall. She pulled her cell phone out of her purse and smiled at the picture of herself with Erin on the main screen. Then she hit #1. Of course, Erin was the first person on her speed dial.

The phone rang almost one full time before Erin picked up. She must've been doing her hair or something.

"CCK? What's up?"

Cassie suddenly didn't know why she was locked in the stall again. It was so *dramatique*! She decided to go with it.

"I'm in a stall in the bathroom," she whispered, trying not to laugh at herself.

"Are you doing the drama thing right now?" Erin asked.

Cassie laughed. "Yeah, totally."

"Is everyone still being ridiculous and not noticing how utterly cool you are?"

"Kind of." Cassie sighed. It had been a lonely four days. "I just don't blend in." Cassie looked down at her vibrant shirt, suddenly convinced that it was fluorescent.

"So what?" Erin asked. "You are *not* a blender. You're Cassie. You ruled the school here in Houston. Remember?"

"I know. But *everything* is different here in Maine."

"But, Cass," Erin argued. "Don't change yourself to try and fit in, okay? I promise you everyone will see the light that is Cassie one day soon."

"All right," Cassie said, not quite convinced.

"Now, I have to go. I have rollers in my hair still and the bus is, like, going to be here in, oh no, ten minutes!"

"Rollers?!" Cassie squealed.

"I'm trying something new, okay? The girl with the prettiest curls is gone; it's free rein now."

"Oooh, really? Send me a pic later! You're going to look so good!"

"I will. Thanks!"

"Okay. Miss you!" Cassie said, loud enough that her voice echoed.

"Bye!"

Cassie stepped out of the stall, relieved that no one had come in during her pep talk with Erin. She stood in front of the mirror and applied just a little more Forest Green Lorac Eye Candy to her lids and a swoop of Pout Lip Polish on her lips. She pulled out her hair spray and covered herself in a fog of holding fumes. Just then a few older girls walked in, and as they passed Cassie, they waved their hands in front of their faces, batting the spray out of the way. Cassie rolled her eyes, made an about-face, and left. It was clear they had no idea what the purpose of hair spray was.

That afternoon, walking to the cafeteria for lunch, Cassie slowed down when she saw the Girl With the Sparkly Thing in Her Locker. Cassie had seen her a few times since that first day, but hadn't spoken to her.

Today, she decided to change that. There was something different about this girl. She didn't look or dress very differently from the others. But somehow she had . . . style.

When she got close, she said, "Hi. I'm Cassie." She extended her hand.

Looking surprised, the girl glanced up, her chestnut hair falling in a perfectly conditioned sheet across her face. *Finally*, Cassie thought. *Someone who conditions!* She had glasses on — sort of vintagey, sort of nerdy, somehow chic. "Hello. My name is Etoile."

Wow! Cassie had never heard a name like that.

"Can I ask you a question?" Cassie said hesitantly.

"Um, sure," Etoile said, smiling shyly.

"Well, the other day you had a tweed blazer-ey

thing on," Cassie began carefully. "It had really pointy lapels."

Etoile's face drained of all color. "What about it?" she whispered. She looked past Cassie, down the empty hallway.

"I was just wondering where you got it," Cassie said, certain she was on to something.

"Why?" Etoile crossed her arms over her chest, clearly suspicious.

"Because I loved it. It was so adorable."

"Really?" Etoile's face flushed. "Do you mean it?"

"Yes! Of course!"

"Well . . . I made it!" Etoile said, beaming.

"NO!" Cassie was awestruck.

Etoile nodded proudly. "I bought it in a vintage store and I totally redesigned it."

"That is so cool, Etoile." Cassie grinned, careful to say her name the right way.

"Do you think so? I was worried it might be too . . . *flashy* for Oak Grove."

"I bet," Cassie moaned. "There's no *color* at this school."

"Well, there wasn't — until you got here."

Cassie blushed. "But people look at me like I'm crazy."

"I know. But — oh, wait!" Etoile exclaimed. "Can I get your opinion on something?"

"Of course," Cassie said.

Etoile turned and fiddled with her locker. At first glance the inside was normal and blah, but then Cassie saw some of that mysterious sparkle. Etoile reached for it and held it out in front of her. It was a big swath of fabric — pink with white and blue crystals. It was totally amazing!

"Wow!" Cassie said.

"It's nice, right?"

"More than nice. Gorgeous. What's it for?"

"I was thinking about making a jacket out of it for spring. But I don't know."

"You have to — it will be incredible!"

"I just don't know if I can do it. I never really make my own stuff from scratch. I just fix things that I buy."

"I'll even help you if you need me to."

Etoile examined the fabric for a moment. "Really? Okay. I'm going to do it," Etoile said, carefully folding the fabric up into a square and putting it back in her locker. "Were you on your way to the cafeteria?"

"I was."

"Want to sit with me?" Etoile asked, pulling her backpack on.

"I'd love to." Suddenly, Cassie felt happier than she had since setting foot in Maine.

* * *

Cassie was so relieved to have purpose in the caf. After that first day, she'd been eating quickly by herself, pretending to catch up on homework. Today, Etoile chose a table by the window, which made Cassie happy. There was a little sun out and she was so glad to be able to enjoy it.

"Your name is really Etoile?" Cassie asked.

"Yeah. It means 'star' in French."

Cool, Cassie thought, unwrapping her sandwich. She was obsessed with France — she couldn't wait to be able to go someday.

"And I'm not telling you that because I want you to think I'm a star — or that my parents think of me that way or anything. Like, could they be more annoying than to name me that?" Etoile laughed at herself and covered her mouth. "And besides, when my parents see the grade on my latest math quiz, they *really* won't think I'm a star!" She laughed again.

"Are your parents French?" Cassie asked eagerly.

"No. Just slightly pretentious! We're from Maine."

"Well, it's still an awesome name."

"Thanks. But people always say 'E-toy-el' when they see it written out instead of 'Ay-twal.' It drives me crazy!"

373

"Well, I don't think I would ever be able to spell it, so at least I know how to say it!" Cassie smiled. "Really, it's amazing."

"You know what's *really* amazing?" Etoile asked.

"No — do tell!" Cassie sat up straighter in her chair.

Etoile dug through her backpack and pulled out a glossy magazine. She flipped through several pages and pointed to a pair of rose-colored, flowery flats. *Oh, divinity!* Cassie thought. Shoes like that would make any girl feel like Cinderella at the ball. "Are these killer, or what?" Etoile asked.

"I need those in my life," Cassie said, mesmerized.

Etoile put the magazine between them and moved her chair closer to Cassie's. She flipped another page and pointed to a celebrity dog dressed up for an event. "So cute! Look at that little tuxedo!"

Cassie giggled at the silly dog. It felt good to laugh in school again.

As if reading her mind, Etoile looked up at her. "How have your first few days at Oak Grove been?"

Cassie sighed. "It's so different than what I'm used to."

Etoile looked at her in complete understanding. "You'll get the hang of it. It must be really different from Texas."

"It *really* is!" Cassie took a bite of her sandwich, and Etoile flipped the page again. "So, can I ask you a question?"

"Okay."

"Well, I can't point right now, but can you tell me who two people are?"

"Sure."

Cassie looked back over her shoulder at the two girls who wouldn't let her sit with them on her first day. Mary Ellen was sitting at their table today. Cassie had done her very best to avoid any contact with Mary Ellen since the mall incident. She slowly turned back to Etoile, hoping she was being nonchalant.

"Those girls sitting with Mary Ellen," Cassie whispered. She took another bite of her sandwich.

"You mean the Nightmare Sisters? Lynn Bauman and Deirdre Donahue. Don't think twice about them. They are totally the founders of the Mary Ellen Fan Club. They are so obnoxious!"

Cassie laughed. "The Nightmare Sisters? That's genius!"

And as she and Etoile laughed together, Cassie knew that she had found her first friend at Oak Grove.

CHAPTER 6

Can You Say "Friday?"

That Friday, Cassie was completely relieved. At last, this first, unbearable week would be behind her. It *had* to get easier after this.

She hurried to the gym for a special assembly and stopped short when she walked in. The gym was filling up. There were kids everywhere, clamoring for spaces in the bleachers, and Cassie felt beyond intimidated. Her phone buzzed in her purse — a LeSportsac, designed by this rad graphic artist, with all of these sweet blue birds all over it.

Cassie discreetly pulled out her phone and looked at the screen. It was a text from Etoile!

Sit with me! ★

Signed with a star! It was so adorable.

Cassie looked up at the bleachers and finally, like a lighthouse on the edge of the stormiest of beaches, she saw Etoile.

Maybe her week hadn't been *so* unbearable.

Cassie wove her way up the bleachers, stepping around people and over backpacks, her boots thumping against the wooden planks.

"What's up?" Cassie said when she reached Etoile.

"Hey!" Etoile said, smiling and patting the space next to her.

"So, what's this assembly about?" Cassie asked, arranging herself and her stuff on the seat.

Etoile rolled her brown eyes. "They do this all the time. You never know what it's about." She pulled out a bag of dried fruit. "Here," she said, pushing the bag toward Cassie.

"Thanks." Cassie put her hand in and extracted a banana chip and a piece of mango. No one at school in Houston ever had dried fruit in their bag. Cassie took a bite. *Delicious!*

Life Rule #98: Always try new things—you never know, you might like them!

Just then, the microphone squealed, setting Cassie's hair on end. Principal Veronica stood under the basketball net, the amp in front of her. She was dressed in a blue grandma suit and black flats, with an unmatching blue band in her hair. *Oh, poor thing!* thought Cassie.

"Good morning, Oak Grove ladies and gentlemen. It's a brand-new semester, and I hope you all are settling into your new routines beautifully. I just wanted to take a moment to say hello to all of you and wish you very well. It's been a wonderful school year thus far and I hope it only gets better and better. . . ."

Cassie was zoning out when she felt a tap on her leg. When she looked down, she saw a notepad on the bench between Etoile and her. There were two words written on it:

HELP US

Cassie caught a laugh before it escaped. She picked up the pen and slowly wrote:

I WISH I KNEW HOW

She looked up. PV was going on. ". . . because there is nothing like the joy of academics. You are only starting on your academic journey. And for some of you, your lives will be filled with school-ing. Fine schooling. You know who you are. . . ."

Cassie looked down at the notebook. Etoile's next entry was simply:

☹

PV droned: "Harvard, Yale, Princeton! I am so excited for your futures, Grovians!"

Cassie picked up the pen:

Did she just say "Grovians"?

"Now," PV said, the mic echoing, "I would like to introduce Mr. Robert Blackwell, who has some wonderful things to share with you."

From the crowd, some of the boys shouted, "Mr. B!"

Mr. Blackwell walked to the mic, and Cassie smiled to see her energetic teacher. "Hey, guys. How's your Friday?"

A bunch of "whoops" and "good"s came from the bleachers.

"Good. Really good. You all sound really excited to be here."

Everyone laughed.

"So, I want to talk to you about this year's annual fundraiser. Now that Rebecca McGinty has graduated, we have a lot of work to do. I need you all to stay focused on it, okay?"

The room was silent.

"Guys? Hello? Do you hear me? Okay?"

Finally, the room responded with murmurs and nods.

Cassie looked at Etoile. "What is *it*?" she whispered.

Mr. Blackwell continued, "So, if you want to be on the committee, you should speak to Mary Ellen McGinty, our student rep, or me about it. Mary Ellen, do you want to come up and say a few words?"

Etoile rolled her eyes. "A Mary Ellen project," she whispered back.

Mary Ellen stood up from the front row and walked to the mic. She took a moment before she started to speak and cleared her throat. Then, in the cheeriest voice Cassie ever had the displeasure of hearing, she said, "Hi, I'm Mary Ellen McGinty. And I want to make sure you all take part in the charity fundraiser this year!"

Cassie was shocked. Stunned! Was this the Mary Ellen McGinty that she saw at the mall who couldn't even lower herself to share the beauty of a boot?

Cassie stared at Mary Ellen standing at the mic, her shoes brown and drab, her complexion tight from an overly astringent cleanser. Really, too bad. Because her skin was . . . No! No! Cassie would not feel bad for this girl. No! Stop!

"I will be arranging a meeting next week to get everything started. And please don't come to the meeting unless you really are committed to working hard. The charity fundraiser was my sister Rebecca's idea. And now that she's graduated, I need real team players who can help me realize it for the third year." Mary Ellen took a stupidly dramatic breath. And then, "In a row."

With that, she smiled out at the crowd and the Nightmare Sisters began to clap. The rest of the room quickly followed.

Mr. Blackwell stepped forward. "Before we end, I just want to make sure no one has any questions."

Cassie wanted to ask for more details. And she wouldn't have thought twice about it if Mary Ellen weren't up there, waiting to pop out her unmanicured claws. The Cassie of just a month ago wouldn't let that stop her, though. She rubbed her hands together quickly to warm them up, and scrunched her curls. She stood up. Etoile was staring at her in disbelief.

"What's up back there, Cassie?" Mr. Blackwell asked.

"Mr. B, I'm sorry, but I don't know what the fundraiser is," Cassie said.

"Oh, of course!" Mr. Blackwell said. "Mary Ellen? Would you please tell Cassie about it?"

Mary Ellen turned to face the crowd, her eyes dark now — stormy — as they surfed the bleachers for Cassie. "My sister started it three years ago because we wanted to do something to help the environment," Mary Ellen said crisply. "And so, each year, we plant fifty trees on campus and raise money for the National Arbor Day Foundation with a bake sale. It's always been *very* successful."

Cassie smiled and nodded. A bake sale? That all sounded so boring. Totally good and the right thing to do but *boring*.

"Does that help, Cassie?" Mr. Blackwell asked.

Cassie smoothed her shirt and said, "Actually, I have a question." She bit her lip, knowing she was about to anger Mary Ellen further. "I know I don't know much about Oak Grove but . . . why are we planting *trees* for charity?"

Mary Ellen shot a glare at Cassie, scowled, and stepped closer to the mic. "Maybe you don't know about the environment back in Texas, but our planet is in serious danger of succumbing to something

382

called the greenhouse effect." Mary Ellen spoke deliberately slowly, like she was addressing a five-year-old.

Cassie gritted her teeth. She had not been the secretary of the Environmental Club in Houston by accident. "It's Mary Ellen, right?"

Mary Ellen was thrown off by the question.

Cassie repeated herself and said again, slowly, like they do on soap operas, "Your name is Mary Ellen, right?"

"Yes," Mary Ellen said, confused.

"Hi, I'm Cassie."

Confused no more and back to her nasty self, Mary Ellen said, "I know. We've already *met*."

"I know we did," Cassie replied. She caught her breath and made sure she was staying calm and considerate — but to the point. "I just wanted to be polite and reintroduce myself before we had what might be our first public disagreement." Cassie swallowed hard, staying as calm as she could, holding her hair for a moment in a twist and then letting the red curls fall gracefully down her back.

Etoile fidgeted in her seat, and so did everyone else. Hello, drama!

Before she began, Cassie pushed her turquoise bangle to the top of her arm, so it wouldn't jangle around. "I am well aware of the greenhouse effect,

Mary Ellen. Thanks for reminding me — for reminding all of us — because, well, you can never be reminded enough of such environmental travesties. I'm just wondering why we're planting trees in *Maine*." She paused and looked around at her new classmates. "While I think there are a lot of things missing here, there's one element that I am certain is plentiful: trees." Cassie looked around the gym — the cavernous, oh-no-what-am-I-doing-the-whole-school-is-looking-at-me gym.

There were whispers. Cassie felt slightly nauseated. At least her green face matched her turquoise flowered tunic. Sometimes her mouth got the better of her.

"Wow, that's a good point, Cassie. Do you have another idea?" Mr. Blackwell asked, stepping slightly in front of Mary Ellen.

Cassie twisted her hands together. "Um —"

Just then, Mary Ellen, hands in tight fists at her sides, snapped like cheap spaghetti. "Well, until you have a better idea, maybe you should keep your mouth shut." She stamped her foot, her blue eyes blazing.

Cassie didn't want this to be a fight. She didn't want to come across as a troublemaker. She just wanted to help make something better. She put her

384

head down, thinking, her colors loud against all the muted tartans and beiges around her.

And then, just then, she had an idea. The best idea ever.

She lifted her head.

"What if we raised money to buy saplings for communities throughout the country — the world — that needed them more than we do?"

"What?" Mary Ellen hissed.

Cassie could feel the vibe in the gym change — she was suddenly surrounded by softly growling, drooly, Mary Ellen watchdogs. Badly accessorized watchdogs, baring their teeth at Cassie.

"Mary Ellen, please don't think I'm trying to change anything," she stammered. "I'm not. But sometimes, a new eye on something really changes how you think about it."

"Tell us more, Cassie," Mr. Blackwell said. "What does your new eye see?"

It all came to Cassie in a wave, like most of her good ideas — including the one that had led Sheila to get caramel highlights.

"What if we did a charity fashion show?" she burst out, her cheeks flushing. Her heart started to beat faster, not because she was nervous, but because this *was* a good idea. "We could ask people to buy tickets to see the show. We could even invite newspapers and stuff to come to our big event!"

The entire gym fell silent. Cassie looked down at Etoile. She was pale but smiling enormously. Too bad no one else was.

Before Cassie could slump back down in defeat, Mr. Blackwell stepped closer to the mic. "Cassie, that's a terrific idea. I'll talk it over with the faculty and we'll see if it's something we'd like to consider."

"Okay, thank you." Cassie nodded, sitting back down.

"That was genius," Etoile whispered to her, but Cassie could only sigh. Based on the cold looks her other classmates were giving her, she was sure no one else felt that way. Not even Mr. Blackwell. He was probably just being nice.

CHAPTER 7

Sh-8-kn in My Pumps

By Monday, Cassie assumed that everyone would have forgotten all about the assembly. But Mr. Blackwell asked her to stay behind after homeroom.

"How has everything been going?" he asked.

"It's good!" Cassie said, not really wanting to have another *How are you, New Kid?* conversation.

"Glad to hear it. I wanted to let you know that we discussed your fashion show idea in our faculty meeting on Friday."

The butterflies started waking up in Cassie's stomach. "Oh, really?" she said, trying to keep calm.

"And we all loved it. We think it's fresh and exciting and will really be a great event for Oak Grove. And we'd like to do it this year. Can you meet with us today after school to tell us more?"

387

Cassie was speechless. They'd *liked* her idea?

"But . . ." she began, her pulse racing. "What about . . . Mary Ellen? Does *she* like the idea?"

"I wouldn't worry too much about Mary Ellen. We never said we were definitely doing things the same way this year. We'll talk to her after everything is finalized and she'll come around. She has to — she's been on the committee forever."

"Okay," was all Cassie could say.

"Really, it's going to be fine. There are far more important things for you to think about. You're psyched, right?" Mr. B asked enthusiastically.

Cassie had to admit that she was. "I am really excited!"

"Great. So are we. So, do some thinking today before the meeting, if you can. Sound good?"

"Sounds great!" Cassie walked away from Mr. B, a huge smile on her face. This was going to be amazing!

But as the day went on, Cassie found herself tippie-toeing through the halls. Even when she was telling Etoile the news during lunch, she whispered, afraid that someone would overhear. And she made Etoile promise to keep it quiet!

After lunch, Cassie decided she needed some

major reinforcement. She pulled out her cell and texted Erin:

Sh-8-kn in my pumps

It didn't matter that Erin didn't know the latest development. She would still send Cassie nice, big, twenty-gallon Texas vibes. And Cassie needed as many as she could get! She felt like a total school-wrecker.

Cassie was so relieved she'd worn an especially perfect outfit, consisting of one of the most confidence-inducing items in her collection: a super-fab frock she scored from a vintage shop in Houston. And this dress was a beauty: coffee and cream paisley swishes, set against an inky purple. *Design Rule #17: Personal style should always be of the moment, with a wink at the future and a grateful nod to the past.*

Cassie knew her confidence would falter the moment she entered English class. Mary Ellen was going to be there and it was going to be awkward. What if Mr. B said something to her in front of everyone?

She ducked into the *toilettes* and gave a good spray of the hair just before class, then took a deep,

deep cleansing breath as she walked into the room.

Everything seemed normal. Mr. Blackwell was at his desk; the windows were open to let some cool air in over the steamy haze of the radiators; kids dressed in gray and beige sat at their desks.

Mary Ellen was talking with the Nightmare Sisters. As Cassie settled into her seat and got herself ready for class, she avoided eye contact with Mary Ellen at all costs.

"Good afternoon, guys," Mr. Blackwell said. "I thought we could start class with a quick and easy writing exercise. You can write about anything you want. Anything at all." He paused for a moment and smiled. "But there's just one catch. You only have five minutes." He looked down at his watch. "Okay, go."

Just as Cassie's pen hit her notebook, she heard someone speak. Well, not just someone. Mary Ellen.

"Excuse me, Mr. Blackwell?" she said.

Cassie popped her head up, along with every other person in the classroom, like gophers from their holes.

"Yes?"

"Before we begin writing, I just wanted to ask a business question."

Mr. Blackwell crossed his arms. "Shoot."

"I was wondering if you could tell the class what you and I discussed earlier today?"

Mr. Blackwell didn't miss a beat. "I don't think this is an appropriate time, Mary Ellen."

Cassie hoped this wasn't what she thought it was.

Mary Ellen looked hesitant, but then she plowed ahead. "But, Mr. Blackwell, I am the student rep and I want to know what the students think about the new idea for the annual fundraiser." Mary Ellen turned and glared at Cassie.

"Well," Mr. Blackwell started, seemingly unpetrified by Mary Ellen's wrath. "Like I told you, we are having a *faculty* discussion today." He looked out at the class. "As you all know, a new idea has been thrown into the ring for this year's fundraiser. And we would like to take the time to review that."

"The *fashion show* idea?" one of the Nightmare Sisters asked.

"Yes. Cassie's plan for a charity fashion show." Mr. Blackwell pulled his glasses up on his head.

Cassie didn't know what to do. All eyes in the

classroom were split between looking at her and looking at Mary Ellen.

"To be honest," Mary Ellen said, "I don't think most people would want to do a fashion show." Mary Ellen craned her neck around to see Cassie. "Right, guys?" Mary Ellen asked the room. "Don't you all agree?"

The room was silent. The radiator hissed. A tiny breeze blew in through the windows. In unison, the Nightmare Sisters said, "I agree."

And then, suddenly, the class was filled with robotic murmurs of agreement. Mary Ellen triumphantly nodded her head.

"People have different interests, you know," Mr. Blackwell said. "It's what makes the world go 'round."

"Really? I thought being smart and successful and giving back to the community was what made the world go 'round. Not hair spray and tacky dresses."

The Nightmare Sisters snickered.

Cassie wrapped her arms around herself, protecting her dress from such rude words.

"Mary Ellen, let's watch our mouths, okay?" Mr. Blackwell said.

"Do *you* like fashion, Mr. Blackwell? Do you care

about a fashion show? Would any *boy* in this room care?" she snapped back.

Silence crawled through the room like an icky snake.

C'mon! Cassie wanted to cry. *She's playing the boy card! Boys are way too shy to admit that they like to get dressed up and stuff.* But Cassie decided to keep her mouth shut. A new Life Rule was forming. It was something like, *Sometimes it's better to not say anything at all.*

Just then, her phone buzzed in her Jordache bag. She reached for it, against all better judgment.

Life Rule #21: No techno-thingies in class. Just rude. And pointless. You're in school to, well, learn.

But this was an emergency. She slid the phone out. It was a text from Erin:

Ms. Cassie Cyan Knight never sh-8-ks!

Everything changed at that moment for Cassie. There was no point in being scared of Mary Ellen. Or of anyone. Fine, she had only been at Oak Grove for a week, but that didn't mean her idea wasn't a good one. She stood, her knees pushing her up just a second or two before her mind was ready.

Darn! That always happens!

"Excuse me," Cassie said, her voice more powerful than she expected it to be.

All heads turned.

"Since the faculty is going to decide today, I think we should just let them worry about all of this," she said. "And, just so you know, Mary Ellen, I have been asked to go to the faculty meeting to talk about my idea."

Mary Ellen's fists clenched. One of the Nightmare Sisters gasped. Cassie wasn't yet sure which was Lynn and which was Deirdre.

"And if you'd like to join us for the discussion, then I'd love to see you there."

More gasps in the room.

And with that, Cassie scrunched some curls, sat down, picked up her Deery Lou pen and began to write.

But she *was* worried. What if the faculty thought the fashion show was a terrible idea? What would she do then? No one at Oak Grove would ever take her seriously if that happened.

Cassie swallowed hard and did her best to concentrate on her work, but her worries continued to plague her.

CHAPTER 8

With So Much to Say, Why Is There No One to Talk to?

Cassie paced outside the school, waiting for Sheila to pick her up. She'd missed the bus so she could attend the faculty meeting, and now, she was bursting to talk to someone! Erin was in ballet class back in Houston and all the other girls were probably still at their extracurriculars. And Etoile wasn't picking up her phone! How could there be no one to talk to? *This is the twenty-first century, people!* she thought.

She looked up at the big Maine sky, the cold wind against her face, her feet freezing in her boots.

When she glanced back down, she saw her mom's car turn onto the long driveway. She watched the blue car get bigger and bigger as it came closer. She could see Sheila behind the wheel with her sunglasses on.

Cassie popped into the car. Before she could even slam the door, Sheila slid her sunglasses onto her head and asked, "So?"

Cassie wanted to play it coy. Even for a minute. "Yes?" she said.

"Are we throwing a fashion show?" her mother said, clapping her leather-gloved hands together in excitement.

"Can we go to the mall?" Cassie asked. "I really want to get more scarves and stuff. This cold weather is crazy!"

"Cassie Cyan Knight, you stop toying with my emotions."

Cassie squealed. "Yes!" she said. "Yes! We are throwing a fashion show!"

Sheila threw her arms around Cassie. "Oh, honey! This is wonderful. I am so proud of you!"

Cassie hugged her mother back hard. Nothing was better than a good hug. "I can't believe it!" she said, her mouth shmushed into her mother's hair.

"Tell me everything!" Sheila said as she put the car in drive.

"Well, I went into the meeting right at three, and all these teachers were sitting there. The room was chocolatey wood with leather chairs and stuff — it was so official. And Mr. Blackwell sat next to me. And he introduced me and I talked about my idea and everything. And then PV was like, 'I think it is a marvelous idea!' *Marvelous!* I didn't even know people really, like, said that word. And so they want to do it!"

"Oh, honey, that's wonderful. It's . . ." Sheila looked at Cassie and together they both cried, "MARVELOUS!"

By the time they got to the mall, Cassie had told Sheila all the details of the meeting. And she never once mentioned Mary Ellen (who had been a total no-show). She didn't want to ruin her excitement by worrying about Miss Meanie.

They walked to the food court to get bottles of water before they started. They knew all too well that they had to stay hydrated while shopping! As they waited in line to pay, Cassie saw Etoile sitting at a table with her mother. It must have been her mother — she had that same chestnut-y hair.

Cassie handed her water to Sheila. "That's Etoile! I'll be right back!" She ran straight to them, her boots clunking against the marble floor.

"Etoile!" she shouted as she ran.

Etoile looked in Cassie's direction. When she saw her, she stood up, her face filled with anticipation.

"Cass! What happened?"

"I tried calling you but couldn't get through!" When she got to Etoile they hugged.

"What did they say?" Etoile's eyes were big and bright.

"Well . . ." Cassie said teasingly.

"C'mon! I'm dying to know!"

Cassie smiled big. "They said yes! They said they thought it was the best idea they'd heard in a long time!"

"I knew it!" Etoile said. "You're the best!"

Cassie's eyes filled with the happiest tears and she hugged Etoile again. Arms tight around each other, the two girls bounced up and down, squealing.

Sheila walked over then. "Let me guess, you're Etoile's mom?"

The woman laughed. "I am. And you're Cassie's?"

"I am!"

The two girls unlocked from each another.

"Mom!" Etoile said. "This is Cassie and her mom!"

Cassie shook Etoile's mother's hand. "Mom!" Cassie said to Sheila. "This is Etoile's mom and Etoile, my executive vice president of the entire show!"

"What? Really?"

"Of course!" The girls shrieked again and hugged.

"I have an idea. Why don't you two go shopping and meet up back here in an hour?" Etoile's mother asked.

"Perfect." Etoile said. "I can teach Cassie what a fleece pullover is."

Cassie scrunched her nose. It just sounded so terrible.

"Cassie, you better come back with something warm and Maine-ready," Sheila said, handing her some money.

"And some nail polish?"

"ONE bottle only," Sheila laughed, and the two girls ran off together.

As they shopped, Cassie and Etoile worked out a plan for the show. Cassie was afraid she was going to have to convince Etoile to be on the committee, but she said yes right away. They decided they would have sign-ups at lunchtime tomorrow, and then have their first meeting. First they would assign each person to a committee like accessories, skirts, and set design. Then they would ask stores at the mall to donate clothes to the show. Etoile even offered to ask her friend Jonah, who was the best artist in the school, to do the set building.

To celebrate their brilliant ideas, the two girls decided to get serious about some shopping. Soon Cassie was surrounded by a pile of clothes in a dressing room, directly across from Etoile's. As she navigated the pile of picks, Cassie had another idea, maybe the best one of the night. She just needed Etoile to agree to it.

"I have one more thing I'd love for you to do for the fashion show," Cassie called out to Etoile through the dressing room door. She was trying on a darling Guess? top.

"Okay, what is it?" Etoile asked, pulling on a pair of corduroys.

"I want you," Cassie said, poking her head through the top of the shirt, "to design that fantastic jacket for the show and premiere your talent to the world."

Etoile was silent. Then Cassie heard her friend say, "Are you crazy?"

Cassie fluffed her hair and opened the door, just as Etoile opened hers.

Even though she was flustered, Etoile couldn't help herself. "Caah-ute! You have to get that!"

Cassie did a little spin. "Are we sure?"

"Totally sure. What about these?" Etoile asked, going up on her toes.

"Like, perfection. Really. Get them!"

Etoile stepped back to the mirror and checked herself out. "Okay."

"And, you *are* going to make that jacket for the show. You don't have a choice."

Etoile crossed her arms over her chest. "Cassie, I just can't. Thank you so much for thinking of me that way. But it's too much pressure." Her eyes were big and pleading.

Cassie shut the door to change. "Okay, how about this?" she said through the door. "You make the jacket and we decide then if it's going in the show? Okay?"

Etoile was silent.

"I'm going to count to three. And if you stay quiet, I will just have to assume that it's a yes." Cassie stood, not moving, hoping she wouldn't get a response. "One . . . two . . . three."

She fluffed her hair and opened the door. Etoile stood there, her arms full of clothes, grinning.

"Yay," Cassie said, her heart bursting. She leaped forward and gave Etoile a giant hug.

"Yay," Etoile said and hugged Cassie back.

CHAPTER 9

Rope Climbing Is So
Not a Fashion Statement

The next day, Cassie was planning on being all business. She had to be. There was a lot of work to be done and not much time to do it! Whatever Mary Ellen had to say, Cassie knew she had a job to do. And that job was to create the most successful fundraiser ever! To mentally prepare, Cassie wore one her favorite outfits: a black and white checked Betsey Johnson dress with a black bolero and a pair of red pumps that were just heavenly.

Her mind was reeling as she sat in homeroom. So much was happening so quickly. She pulled her marabou pen out of her purse and began a to-do list while she waited for Mr. B.

Just as the glitter ink rolled onto the paper, Mr. B walked into the class with Mary Ellen. She looked really upset.

Oh no. She must have gotten the news about the show.

Cassie didn't want her to be mad about it, but there was nothing she could do. After a good shop last night, Cassie, Etoile, and their moms had a solid powwow over some FroYo (finally!) and all of them agreed: Let Mary Ellen be upset and give her some space.

"Good morning, everyone," Mr. B said as he unpacked his worn leather briefcase. "I want to let everyone know some news about the fundraiser. This year, we have decided to take the project in a new direction and hold a charity fashion show. And, as you can probably guess, Cassie Knight back there is going to head up the student committee." He gestured to Cassie. "So if you want to sign up, you should speak with her." He stopped and smiled at Cassie. "Is there anything you want to say, Cassie?"

Cassie sat up straight and folded her hands on her desk. She didn't know she was going to be asked to say something so soon, but that was okay, she was ready.

"I just want you all to know that I am so excited to do this. And if anyone wants to be a part of it, just let me know. There's room for everyone!" she said. She turned toward Mary Ellen, hoping she was smiling, ready to be a part of it all, and volunteer a design idea.

But of course not. The room was silent. Mary Ellen didn't even acknowledge her. Cassie continued on. "So, if you want to sign up, just stop by my table at lunch and we can take it from there. Our first meeting will be tomorrow after school."

"Principal Veronica will be making an all-school announcement today, so be on the lookout for that," Mr. B said. "And don't be thrown off by the fashion part; we need all hands on deck for this. This is a fundraiser. It's not only about the clothes."

"Well, it sort of *is* about the clothes," Cassie said truthfully. "But the other stuff is super-important, too," she added with a grin.

No one laughed.

Would she *ever* get through to her classmates? Ever?

Third period was gym class. Dreaded, hated, hideous, and horrible gym class. It's not that Cassie had any problem with sweating and running and being healthy and stuff. Of course not. *Duh, being healthy, like, makes you live longer.* (This was not yet a Life Rule, but she realized she needed to make it one soon. She just needed to work out the exact language.) And she loved her gym outfits. Today's featured two wristbands, left arm white, right arm blue, her Grid Propel Plus Sauconys with delicious blue laces, and her pearl Danskin unitard with her midnight Cobweb Crop Tie-Front Sweater and matching skirt. And matching leg warmers, of course.

But here were the bad things, and there were a lot:

1. Getting all sweaty.
2. Getting all sweaty with other people. Especially boys. They _really_ get all sweaty.
3. The things you have to do! Like swinging a bat, or running in circles, or the worst: throwing a ball.
4. I mean, hair!!! What's a girl supposed to do with her hair when she has, like, ten minutes to de-sweat, re-glamor, and bejewel?
5. Feeling kind of clammy and sticky for the rest of the day. So not cute.

Cassie walked into the locker room and put her backpack in a locker. She pulled out her gym fashions and changed. There were girls around her,

405

laughing and talking, but she couldn't think of a word to say. They were talking about such boring things, like debate club and what they thought was going to be on such-and-such quiz.

She sat on the bench to put on her leg warmers and slouch them just so. While she did, someone walked toward her and stopped. Cassie looked up and saw a pair of pasty white legs.

Oh, this was going to be Mary Ellen. It had to be.

And it was not going to be good.

Cassie sat back and looked up. The flourescent light glowed above Mary Ellen. The Nightmare Sisters stood behind her, looking more green in the bad lighting and gym gear.

A Texas girl always starts out polite. "Hi there!" Cassie put her hands on the bench and crossed her legs. She worked hard not to wrinkle her nose when she saw what Mary Ellen was wearing. A pair of hideous boys' soccer shorts and a big, dingy white T-shirt. *Aaaaaagh!* This fashion situation was worse than Cassie thought.

"Hi there," Mary Ellen said back, mockingly. Some girls stopped talking.

"What's going on?" Cassie asked, her heart picking up speed.

"I know fashion's your thing and all," Mary Ellen began.

Cassie stood, her sweater and skirt overly adorable. The other girls were blatantly staring now. "It's one of my things, yes," she said, putting her hand on her hip.

Mary Ellen went on. "You know, we really try to take gym seriously here. I thought you would have at least figured *that* out by now." She gave Cassie the old up-and-down eyes.

Cassie knew she was SO NOT the one who should be looked up and down in this situation!

"I try hard to excel in all areas, so I'm ready!" Cassie said. "What are we playing today?" Cassie was trying to sound tough, but she didn't want a gym showdown. She knew herself. Gym wasn't her strongest suit.

"We're climbing ropes today."

Climbing ropes? What's the point? Where are we going? To the ceiling?

The bell rang and the other girls ran into the gym. Mary Ellen gave Cassie one final look and walked away.

All of Cassie's hopes and dreams of a successful fashion show seemed to slip out of her hands. What had she been thinking? She would never get people on her side.

When she entered the gym, she saw four ropes hanging from the ceiling. Kids were lining up at each one, ready to take turns climbing up and down. Cassie had never seen such a thing before. They did square dancing and aerobics and fun stuff in her Houston gym class. Nothing that involved ropes!

When it was her turn, all eyes were on her. She knew Mary Ellen's were, for sure. For super sure.

Maybe she would perform better under pressure.

Or maybe not.

By the time she got halfway up the rope, which was surprisingly easier than she thought it would be, she became nervous. The more she tried to think about not falling, the more she was certain she would. So, she stayed mid-rope for a minute, looking down and then trying not to look down but not not looking down because how could you not look down?!!

"Everything all right up there, Cassie?" Mrs. Simmons called.

Why was she being spoken to? She was dangling from a rope, people! No one should be shouting at her. Of course, she looked down again — because it's rude not to at least try to make eye contact — and all she saw was Mary Ellen. She just stood there, staring up at Cassie, a mean grin on her face, her unmanicured hands on her hips.

What was Cassie supposed to respond, anyway? "No, it's really not okay up here at a trillion feet above sea level!" *The fact that I might fall and maim myself is not an issue at all.*

She settled on "Yes, just super!"

She took a deep, cleansing breath, flipped her red curls back, and started to pull herself up. She counted in French in her mind. This was the best and only thing she could do to stop herself from thinking about plummeting to an ungraceful crash on the plastic, sweaty, yellow vinyl gym mats beneath her.

She was feeling a little more confident by the time she pulled her way to the top. Her hands burned from the rope, her upper lip was dewy, but her hair, of course, was perfectly in place (at least she hoped it was!). When she got to the top, she slowly looked down. And what Cassie saw from the top of the gym ceiling surprised her. Everyone down there looked kind of normal. Cassie was sure that they were all feeling a little stupid having to climb ropes. And, most of them were just hanging out and talking. Some girls were even cheering their struggling ropemates on.

Suddenly, Cassie wished Etoile was in her gym class so she had someone to cheer *her* on. But even without her, from up there, nothing looked so bad. Even Mary Ellen had stopped her staring and was helping one of the Nightmare Sisters up onto the rope. Boys were goofing around and about to get into trouble. It was all sort of like her old school. Well, without all the girls that she loved. And with, like, zero hair spray. Or gloss. Or color. Oh, no, stop!

Before she let herself down, Cassie gave herself one second for a victory smile. She realized that she would NEVER be up there again, so she savored this life millisecond. Then she took a deep breath and happily let herself glide down the rope, her cobweb sweater perfectly fluttering in the breeze.

CHAPTER 10

I'm Sitting Right Here, Just Come and Sign Up, Already!

At lunch, Cassie and Etoile hung a sign advertising FASHION SHOW TEAM on the cafeteria table and held a clipboard with a sign-up sheet. Cassie kept her eyes on the crowd.

"Cass, you have to chill out!" Etoile said, taking a bite of a Rice Krispie treat. "People will sign up. I'm sure of it."

"It doesn't feel that way at all. I mean, we've already eaten our lunches. And unless we nibble at that Rice Krispie treat krispie by krispie, I just don't think we have that much time left." Cassie was tapping her nails on the table. She was trying her best to keep her spirits up, but this wasn't feeling so good. There were only eleven minutes left before the bell and *no one* had signed up yet. Even though it was mortifying, Cassie was relieved that PV helped to get the word out when she made her morning announcements after homeroom, telling everyone about the show. But she practically fainted when PV started going on about "the importance of new ideas" and once referred to Cassie as "our new Texan friend." It was twenty seconds of total eyes-to-the-ground embarrassment.

New Texan friend? People would actually have to be my friend to say that.

But Cassie had Etoile. And she knew she was lucky for that — to have someone sit next to her at the unpopular sign-up table. But the girls sat there in total silence, the seconds ticking by as they stared out into the crowd.

And then —

"There's Jonah!" Etoile said, jumping up. A boy was approaching their table. Cassie had seen him in the hallways but didn't know he and Etoile were friends. He was all freckles, with a big smile and a mess of sandy waves on his head.

"Jonah Thomas, this is Cassie Knight," Etoile said.

Cassie extended her hand toward Jonah. He met her hand with a good shake.

"Jonah, Cassie has just moved here from Texas

and she is in charge of the fashion show. And we need you to get your friends involved."

Jonah shrugged his shoulders. "What for?"

"Because we need your support. And because I said so," Etoile said, matter-of-factly.

"But I don't like fashion stuff," Jonah protested, shrugging again.

"I know. But we need people to do, like, all the other stuff — music, lights, the set."

"Do you like any of those things?" Cassie asked hopefully.

"Sorta," Jonah said, his hands in his pockets.

"Cassie, Jonah is the best artist! We need him to help. And *he* can get all of his friends to help," Etoile said.

Etoile was a girl on a mission!

"And, besides, I've known him forever and he has to do what I say. We're sort of like brother and sister — our mothers met in the hospital when we were born — isn't that amazing?"

"Totally!" Cassie said.

"Yeah," Jonah said, smiling suddenly, "she was, like, always crying and stuff. Such an annoying baby."

Etoile shoved him and they both laughed. "Okay, so sign up, right now," Etoile said.

Jonah took the pen off of the sign-up clipboard and wrote his name.

"Sign up some of the other boys, too. You know they'll do it if you tell them you are."

Obediently, Jonah wrote three other names down. "Okay? Can I go now?"

Cassie couldn't believe it. Four people! "Okay, the first meeting is tomorrow, after school," she said.

"And don't be late!" Etoile said.

Cassie laughed at how bossy she was with him. She didn't know Etoile had that side to her. "Thanks so much!"

Etoile was distracted by something, her eyes fixed straight ahead of her. "I think it worked."

Cassie turned to look. A trio of girls was headed directly toward the sign-up table. They were a grade older than Cassie and the closer they got, the harder her heart pounded in her chest.

But when they got to the table, they said four of the sweetest words Cassie had ever heard:

"Can we sign up?"

CHAPTER 11

Okay, Time Is Flying

Cassie didn't realize how quickly winter could go by, even when it snows so much. She had learned the art of not slipping on the ice and had even had a fun snowball fight with Etoile. Before she knew it, the plans for the Fash Bash Fashion Show (that was what she and Etoile had decided to call it, in a moment of pure inspiration) were coming together and there was even a hint of warmth in the Maine air. Cassie could not wait to bid *adieu* to the snow.

Things were moving along relatively smoothly. Cassie hadn't quite made legions of friends, but she couldn't worry about her social woes when there was so much work to do. Plus, she did have Etoile — and a motley group of volunteers. Some were secret fashion fans, some were just looking to add an extracurricular to their list, and some, well,

Cassie had no idea why they were there. And when Lynn Bauman — one half of Mary Ellen's Nightmare Sisters — signed up to help, Cassie almost fainted. Really. She didn't know what to do!

The Mary Ellen factor was a troubling one. She was automatically on the committee because of her involvement with the fund-raiser in the years before. But she never came to the meetings and she and Cassie didn't speak at all when they did see each other. Mary Ellen was doing an important job, working directly with the National Arbor Day Foundation. And Cassie was grateful that she was, so she could focus on the fashions.

Here's how everything was shaping up in Cassie's adorable Lisa Frank mini notebook:

✔Staff Assignments: All positions filled, including: Vice President of Polish, Secretary of Shadow, Treasurer of Gloss, VP of Blush, VP of Hair Products, VP of Dresses, VP of Cute Shirts, VP of Pants, VP of Accessories. And so far so good, there is some style in Maine!! Etoile=VP of the Entire Show. Me=President and VP of Shoes. Totally!

✔Girl Models: 11 outfits. Totally and utterly complete and all divine and springtastic! Total faves: pink and pearl Junko Shimada cotton dress with cap sleeves and totally amazing belt;

the classic Lilly Pulitzer Carolee dress; the way hip L.A.M.B strap bow gown.

✔Boy Models: 9 outfits, 8 totally and utterly complete. From cute and casual to dressy and dashing. Just one more.

✔Hair Products: done! Thanks to the fantastico Fabrizio. Texas in the house!

✔Accessories: in process, thanks to Lynn Nightmare's mother, who designs her own jewelry. Gorgeous corals and dangly pendants, glittery rings, and chunky necklaces.

✔Models' Makeup: deliciously bright and darling, shimmery and glittery! A frosty palette for a warm spring glow. And an artist from the mall makeup counter to help us on the night of the show! Can't wait to show those girls how to rock some gloss.

✔Polish: springy and flirty. About a zillion choices to choose from!

✔And, of course, shoes!! Just three pairs left to find.

✔Sets: bright and colorful. Being created under the guidance of Jonah, who is rocking it!

✔Music: The boys are tweaking and perfecting. All very sassy and poppy.

✔Teaching the models how to work the runway: yikes. Not as smooth as I was hoping. It's like they

417

all have a fashion-walk impairment. Etoile said they'll get it. I hope so!

✓Invitations and banners: in progress. Wording is genius. To the printer on Friday! Will be spectacular!

✓Tickets: Being printed.

The Fash Bash Committee was really working hard. And Cassie's parents and Etoile's parents — along with PV, Mr. B, and Rose Miller, the friendly cafeteria lady — were making sure that all the stuff stayed organized and on schedule. And even Erin, far away in Houston, was advising on spring fashion combos with the help of Cassie's camera phone.

Of course Cassie's favorite part of all of this was going to the mall after school with the staff, splitting up, and asking for clothes and shoe donations. They even got a tailor who agreed to hem the clothes for everyone. And to top it off, a few stylists from a salon agreed to do hair for the show.

On the final excursion to the mall, in search of the last three pairs of shoes, Cassie and Etoile walked together, sipping Häagen-Dazs Sorbet Sippers. They felt they'd deserved a treat.

As they walked past the mirrored fountain wall, Cassie stopped to reapply her gloss and Etoile sprayed her hair with a small pump bottle.

"What's that?" Cassie asked, her pointer finger creating a perfect swoop across her lips.

"It's hair spray."

"That's *so* not hair spray." Cassie stuck her hand in her purse and pulled out a big aerosol can. "*This is* hair spray!" She popped off the top and coated her hair with a cloud of mist.

Etoile waved her hand in front of her face. "Ew! What is *that*?" She coughed dramatically.

"This is hair spray! Not that silly little stuff you use."

"Cass, c'mon! Do you really think the girl who is running Fundraising Fashion Show to Save the Planet should really be using an aerosol hair spray? It's *so* bad for the environment."

Cassie covered her mouth in shock. Etoile was right. *Of course.* How had she never once thought of that?

Etoile handed Cassie the bottle. Cassie took it and examined it. It looked cute, all flowers and blue sky. "Fresh Botanicals Mist?"

"Try it." Etoile smiled at her reassuringly.

"I don't know. The word *mist* scares me a little. Does it do anything?" Cassie pushed the bottle back toward Etoile.

"Cass!"

Nervously, Cassie handed her Sorbet Sipper to

Etoile and sprayed the right side of her hair with an easy pump. She scrunched, then moved to the next section. Soon, she was enveloped in a mist of yummy freshness.

She smiled cautiously. "And it will really hold?"

"Totally!" Etoile said. "Isn't it delicious?"

Cassie turned and gave Etoile a big hug. "Thank you so much!"

Thrilled with her fresh-smelling hair, she gave her lips one more check before the two girls walked to the final frontier: the only shoe store they hadn't checked out.

"Okay," Cassie said to Etoile, "this is it. Keep your fingers crossed."

They walked in together and admired strappy little sandals, the most precious pair of espadrilles, and delicious green pumps.

"Hi, can I help you?" a very sweet-looking young woman asked Cassie. She wore a khaki hunting jacket with a starched white shirt underneath, perfectly worn-in jeans, and truly genius leopard-print flats. Her hair was pin-straight and luxuriously brown, with one thick blond highlight. Cassie thought she was probably in college.

"Hi, I'm Cassie." Cassie extended her hand and they shook. "And this is Etoile." Etoile gave a handshake as well. "We are both on the committee of Oak Grove's charity fashion show."

"Cool," the salesgirl said.

"We've been asking stores in the mall if they would donate some things for it. All of the proceeds are going to buy saplings for the communities in the country that need them the most," Cassie recited proudly.

"That's so great," the girl said. "So, do you guys have your eye on some shoes here for the show?"

"Yes," Cassie said.

The girl scanned the row of shoes in front of them. "Can I guess which you like?"

Oh, the Shoe Game! Cassie loved the Shoe Game! "Of course."

The salesgirl didn't hesitate for a moment. "You're doing spring, right? No need to let winter last any longer than it has to. Especially here in Maine," she said with an eye roll. She went directly for the espadrilles. "These."

Cassie nodded in total and complete agreement.

"Are all the clothes colorful and bright?" the girl asked.

"Yes," Etoile said, dazzled and delighted.

"Well, then, these are perfect." Cassie knew where she was headed. Uh-huh — to the strappy sandals. Each strap was a different bright color. So cute!

"You're a shoe psychic!" Etoile said. They all giggled.

"So, the last pair . . ." The girl looked around the store, deep in thought. Cassie felt relieved and excited all at once. This was really the last big thing to cross off the list.

"The last pair have to be these," she said, holding up a pair of spring-green pumps.

"How did you know all of this?" Etoile asked.

"You just know sometimes," she said, smiling. "Let me talk to the owner and I'll get these for your show." As she walked to the back, Cassie sat down and pulled out her notebook.

✔*Shoes — done!!*

CHAPTER 12

Does it Really Snow in April?

> *You are Cordially Invited*
> *to The Fash Bash*
> *a Celebration of the Fashions of Spring*
>
> *Saturday, April 14*
> *8 P.M.*
> *The Runway at the Oak Grove Gym*
> *Tickets: $5 at the door*
>
> *All proceeds will be donated to the*
> *National Arbor Day Foundation.*

It was the day before the big show and Cassie could feel the excitement in the air. Even though she still wasn't the biggest hit at Oak Grove, Cassie knew some people were looking forward to it. Especially the people on the Fash Bash Committee. But there was one person who clearly wasn't excited: Mary Ellen.

As she walked down the hallway, Cassie smiled at all of the signs Jonah and the boys had created. She was totally impressed with their work. The signs were all different colors, but Cassie insisted on one thing: teal in each one. (Of course!)

She was still waiting on Etoile's final answer about the jacket, but she knew it was going to be a yes. She could feel it.

She headed to the gym. The run-through was in just a few minutes. Jonah had told her that the set had the finishing touches on it and she was dying to see it.

As she opened the door to the gym, she gasped in utter amazement. The boy committee had created a stage and runway that would have any designer in Paris panting. The runway itself was painted a shiny deep blue, and a clean white screen hung at the back. Cassie wanted the backstage area to be the actual backdrop to the show, so the audience would be able to see everyone's shadows through the screen. The podium — and the mic! — were covered in marabou and crystals. It was all totally wonderful and gorgeous. Cassie wasn't surprised. She had even gotten her dad to help build the set on the weekends — and she knew what Paul could do.

Cassie wished Erin and the girls could come to see it all. She pulled out her camera phone and snapped a pic of the set to send to them.

Just then Mary Ellen walked in. Mary Ellen had freaked when she heard Lynn was on the Committee. They were still on speaking terms, but Lynn was not one of the favorites like she used to be.

Mary Ellen walked calmly across the gym. "So, this is it?" she asked Cassie, her words echoing.

"Yeah. It's looking so great," Cassie answered cautiously.

"Well, everything is all set with the Arbor Day Foundation. Principal Veronica just finished up a phone call with them. And we will send them *whatever* money the show makes next week." Mary Ellen made it sound like the show wasn't going to make any money.

Cassie wouldn't allow Mary Ellen to get in the way of her excitement. "That's fantastic. Thanks so much for all that you've done." She smiled and turned away then, excited to go backstage and see everything. Even the hair and makeup people were coming to the run-through today.

As Cassie stepped onto the runway, Mary Ellen said, "So, I guess you're not nervous about that huge snowstorm that's on its way?"

Cassie stopped, almost tripping but catching herself. *"What?"* How could it snow in April?

"They're calling for almost two feet." Mary Ellen had a look of sheer happiness on her face. "Good luck with the dress rehearsal." She turned dramatically, her frumpy tartan skirt twirling, and walked to the door — with a smile on her face, Cassie was sure.

Does it really snow in April?

There was no time to think about it now, because the Fash Bash staff was arriving. Cassie had to get them ready for tomorrow, snow or no, and she had to make sure they all knew how to work it down the runway. She'd shown them a thing or two and even assigned them to watch as much fashion show coverage on the Style Network as they possibly could, but she still wasn't sure they were ready. At the last rehearsal, one of the boys actually *fell off* the runway.

"Okay, guys, while we wait for hair and makeup to come, I thought we could practice our runway one last time." Cassie waited for a negative response but was surprised when they lined up. She looked at Etoile, shocked.

"All right," Etoile said, "Jonah, can you give us some music?"

"Sure," he called from backstage. In a moment, the gym was filled with a lively *thump-thump-thump*. Cassie sat back and watched as the models strutted down the runway. They'd been practicing! Each one had their own style, their own method of working the perfect sashay.

Cassie squealed with joy and grabbed Etoile's hand. "They're unbelievable!" she said.

"I told you they'd get it!" Etoile said.

They were both super-wowed by Lynn, who worked the runway better than any supermodel could hope to. She was the perfect combination of confidence and nerves, and her long legs cut perfect, sharp angles. Maybe it was time to give up on her nickname. No Nightmare could ever be so beautiful!

CHAPTER 13

Yup, That's Right, It Snows in April

The day of the show had arrived. Cassie opened her eyes and took a sec to admire her room. The Fash Bash was so time consuming but she really was so proud of how her room had come together. Two of the walls were a gorgeous teal, and the others were a warm, wonderful white. It totally made her feel like a robin in the nest, and she adored it. Her new bedding was really different from the way it was in Houston. There, she had pink island patchwork. But here in Maine, she wanted something more snuggly and cozy. She and Sheila opted for an amazing chocolate brown duvet and bright white sheets.

Divinity.

The rest of the room felt familiar and she was glad for some normality. She had her wooden vanity, with the stain on top from when she spilled nail polish remover on it; her tall dresser with the lattice doors; and her white desk and her big, fuzzy blue rug. That rug ruled. Just the perfect balance of soft and scratchy on bare feet.

She sprang out of bed with a satisfied sigh, slid on her marabous, and marched to the window. Snow or no?

Of course, Mary Ellen had been right. The ground, the trees, everything was covered in snow!

Cassie looked out the window at the snow falling. She had to admit it: It was beautiful. Sure, its effect on her shoe collection was unforgivable. Cassie had ruined almost every pair of shoes she adored, from her chunky Steve Maddens to her Kitson Lovebird sneaks. She had finally decided, after much thought and deliberation with Erin, to get a pair of duck boots. It was a super-difficult decision to make but she had to do it, for the preservation of her beautiful shoes. (And Cassie was no fool — she changed out of her duck boots the moment she got to school.)

Cassie and staff were due to report to Oak Grove by two P.M. There was a ton of hair and makeup and last-minute stuff to deal with. And snow!

She had her whole morning planned, starting with a peaceful breakfast with Paul and Sheila.

"So, the snow's not going to stop people from coming to the show, right?" she asked over a bowl of oatmeal.

"It's not, I promise you," Paul said. "Do you think that this is the first time these people have seen a snowstorm in April? They're used to it. And they all have the big cars to prove it!"

"And, I spoke to Etoile's mom this morning and they're ready to go," Sheila added. "She said nothing could stop them from getting there!"

Etoile still hadn't said a word about the jacket, and Cassie was nervous. Of course, there was a Plan B for the jacket but she didn't want to go with Plan B. When she finished eating, she went upstairs to call Etoile. She didn't want to put pressure on her, but her curiosity was getting the best of her. She grabbed her cell phone and saw that she had two new messages.

First, from Erin

You get 'em, girl! xox, Erin and the girls

Oh, what would she do without her Texas support team?

She clicked to the next message.

1 new picture mail.

Cassie loved picture mail. And she couldn't wait to see who it was from! She waited as the picture loaded. And then, finally, when the picture came up on her screen, Cassie squealed with delight: a fabulous, handmade, Etoile original jacket! Cassie couldn't believe it.

She dialed Etoile's number as quickly as she could.

The phone buzzed for a second before Etoile picked up. "What do you think?" she asked, a slight note of panic in her voice.

"I think you are a genius," Cassie said.

"Really? Are you sure?"

"I can't wait to see it in person!"

"I am totally nervous to show it."

"Don't be," Cassie said. "It will be fabulous and so will you, Miss Emcee."

Cassie wanted to be backstage, making sure everything was running smoothly. And she knew Etoile would do a terrific job up there.

"Okay, don't remind me!"

"I can't believe it's snowing, though," Cassie said, peeking out the window at the falling flakes.

"Why? I didn't really even think about it."

"Mary Ellen made it seem like it would be the end of the fashion show if it snowed."

"Cassie, come on, you're too smart to be that

431

gullible. It always snows like this in the spring. And look at it this way; it's even cooler to have a spring fashion show in the middle of a snowstorm!"

Cassie hadn't thought of it that way.

"You're right. You are SO right." Cassie looked at the time. "And there's only three hours till we have to be there!"

When she hung up, Cassie took her new yummy teal dress from her closet and laid it out on her bed. She'd decided to wear something lovely but functional, and this dress was it. It was light and flowy, with thick beaded straps, a fab flower right in the center, and silvery beading at the hem. It was dreamy. AND comfortable. She pulled her shoes out of the closet—and, of course, her duck boots.

Duck boots to a fashion show? She was *so* Maine!

CHAPTER 14

It's Fashion Time, People! Fashion Time!

Backstage was madness! It was really dark except for the hair and makeup room. There were clothes *everywhere,* and the sweet smell of natural mist hair spray wafted through every now and then. Half of the girls were getting their makeup done and the others were getting worked on by a hair stylist. Cassie made it a point to visit with everyone and see how they were doing. She had her camera phone in hand, so she could instantly document all of their beauty.

Then she stood behind Etoile, who was getting her brown tresses smoothed and flattened. Total roar! Her poker-straight hair fell perfectly around her face, making her brown eyes glow.

"You are gorgeous!" Cassie said, while the stylist did her thing.

"Thanks! I can't believe we're finally here! I can't

believe you pulled this off!" Etoile beamed from the chair.

"What I can't believe is how perfect this jacket is! You are brilliant!" Cassie stepped closer to the jacket hanging on the rack. It was the perfect combination of elegant and hip, with its denim jacket cut and its opulent sequin details. *Wow*.

"Thanks so much for making me do it. All of this is just so great!" Etoile beamed.

Cassie walked to the front of the chair and flung her arms around Etoile.

"All right, all right, enough, you two! There's work to do!" PV said as she walked into the room.

Cassie gasped. PV looked incredible. Her hair was out of the bun and curled just so. And instead of one of her sad suits, she wore a pink tweed blazer and matching skirt and heels. Heels on PV! And lipstick!

Cassie was stunned. "Look at you."

PV stopped and smiled. "You know, I like to dress up sometimes, too."

"Give us a twirl," Cassie said, spinning her index finger.

"No! Girls! No!" PV tried — in vain — to sound firm. She was blushing.

Etoile popped out of her chair. "Oh, please, Principal Veronica!"

434

And with that, PV gave the best, proudest outfit twirl in the History of Outfit Twirls. Cassie and Etoile applauded.

Just then, Mr. B came gliding into the room in a gray Calvin Klein suit. He had bought it himself and he just looked too debonair for words.

"Can I come in?" he asked.

"Of course, Robert," PV said.

"So, are you guys ready?" he asked, his smile toothy and happy.

Etoile and Cassie looked at each other. "We are totally ready!" Cassie said.

"Before we start," PV said, getting serious, "I want to thank you, Cassie, for your wonderful spirit. It's been a long time since we've had a student like you here at Oak Grove."

"Thank you so much," Cassie said, tears filling her eyes. Etoile grabbed her hand and squeezed tight.

Jonah came running through backstage just then. He looked perfectly arty in his black pants, black Converse, black button-down, and skinny red tie.

"Cassie, six minutes to showtime!" He stopped and put a headset on her so they could communicate throughout the show. Cassie loved wearing it. She felt like a pop star on her world tour!

Just before the show started, Cassie had

everyone stand in a circle and hold hands. PV and Mr. B were there; Paul and Sheila; Etoile's mom; Rose Miller; and all the parents who had helped. It was pep talk time.

"Okay, you gorgeous and glamorous people: The only thing left for all of you to do is to rock that runway and have some fun." She looked out at the circle of people and was so impressed by them. They all looked back at her with excitement in their eyes.

"Good luck out there. Break a leg. And thank you so much for all that you've done. This is just the best!"

"Two minutes till curtain!" Jonah said over the headset.

It was time.

"Okay, guys, places!" Cassie shouted, her heart pounding.

Cassie gave Etoile a giant hug. "Good luck!" she said.

"Wait! I have something for you," Etoile said, reaching into her purse. She extracted a simple silver necklace with a tiny star pendant on it. "My name might mean "star," but you really *are* one, Cassie."

Tears ran down Cassie's cheeks as Etoile put the necklace on her. "I am so proud to be your friend."

That was one of the nicest things that anyone had ever said to Cassie. Thank goodness for waterproof mascara!

"One minute, Cassie!" Jonah said.

They hugged again and Etoile ran off to the other side of the stage, ready to take the podium.

Cassie turned on her mic so Jonah could hear her. "Okay, Jonah, let's make some fashion history." She nodded at PV and Mr. B, who were going to do a very brief welcome. She pulled her turquoise bangle up on her arm.

"Houselights down," she said. She peered at the packed (*packed!*) auditorium from backstage. The lights went out and a hush fell over the room.

"Cue spotlights."

The lights went up and PV and Mr. Blackwell walked out. As they greeted everyone, Cassie did a last review of all the models.

Once she heard PV wrap up her intro, Cassie clicked her headset back into the "talk" position. "Lights out." She waited a few beats. "Spotlight up on the podium." She gave Etoile a thumbs-up from across the stage, and Etoile walked out onto the stage.

"Ladies and gentlemen, welcome to Oak Grove's Charity Spring Fashion Show, or as we like to call

437

it, the Fash Bash. Thank you all for coming to this important event. . . ."

Cassie walked the line of models, straightening a lapel, fixing a strand or two of hair, and running the lint brush over a few people.

When she heard Etoile say "Let's begin," Cassie ran to the edge of the screen.

"Here we go," Jonah said in Cassie's headset.

"Roger that. Cue music."

The music pumped out over the sound system.

"Stage lights down and swirling spotlights up."

The stage went dark for a moment and then bright pink, blue, and green lights popped up and swirled across the catwalk.

Cassie took the first model's hand, gave her a big smile, and mouthed, "Go."

Obediently, she strutted past the screen and onto the runway.

Etoile picked up right on cue. "This stunning Malicious Designs lace and cotton dress is not to be believed. It features an ultra-fab cut and a soothing, springy cream color that provides the epitome of chic."

Cassie watched from backstage. *Good pivot, good smile, and some fierce attitude.*

"Next up, we have a Betsy Johnson double silk stretch set. With its pleated skirt and wrap top, the dazzling pink lines will have you ready for anything this spring!"

Etoile handled it very well when her jacket hit the runway. She and Cassie had written the description together and decided that they would say it was created by "Star Designs." And it got quite a reaction from the audience, worn with a fitted pair of Ralph Lauren boy shorts. Cassie was so excited for Etoile. She was going to make sure to tell the school newspaper that Etoile had designed it.

Model after model, each was perfectly poised, smiling, and stunning. Cassie was so excited and so focused on the timing that she was shocked when they got to Lynn, the last model of the show. Lynn was rocking her L.A.M.B. Strap Bow Gown. She was a vision on the runway. As Cassie peered from the sideline, she saw Mary Ellen in the audience. She was sitting with Deirdre Nightmare and some of her other cronies, looking happier and more excited than Cassie had ever seen her.

Once Lynn made it backstage, Cassie sent all of the models out for a final bow. As they filed out, laughing and smiling, Etoile spoke into the mic.

"Before we end," Etoile said, "I would like to introduce you all to the star of this show. She said she wasn't going to come out on the stage, but I think we can get her out. . . . Ladies and gentlemen, put your hands together for the toast of Oak Grove, President of the Fash Bash Committee and VP of Shoes!"

Cassie was frozen.

The audience applauded and everyone backstage joined in.

Okay. I have no choice. I have to do this.

Etoile continued, "I present to you Miss Cassie Cyan Knight!"

Cassie took a step through the curtains, the bright spotlight hitting her in the face.

She paused for a second, and the audience went wild. Etoile and the models clapped like crazy.

"You get 'em," Jonah said on her headset.

Cassie's smile grew larger and larger. She walked to Etoile and grabbed her hand. Together, they walked down the runway. And when it was Cassie's turn to take center stage, she put her hands on her hips, laughing.

And created a brand-new Life Rule.

Life Rule #58: You can do anything you want to do. No matter what you might think is in the way.

A cheer came from the audience and Cassie

waved. She grabbed Etoile's hand again and they bowed.

"How are we ever going to top this?" Etoile said over the noise.

Cassie squeezed their hands tight. "Oh, I have an idea or two."

The girls turned together then and walked the length of the runway.

As they bowed with the models, PV hurried to the podium. "Ladies and gentlemen, I want to let you know that because of all of the hard work — and your support — we have raised more money than we ever have in the history of the Oak Grove fund-raiser!"

Cassie was stunned. Incredible!

"And it is because of the dedication of one young woman," PV continued, "that all of this was possible. Please, let's give her another round of applause. . . . Miss Cassie Knight."

The audience applauded like mad and soon they were chanting, "Cassie! Cassie!" Cassie was overwhelmed. She never thought it would happen like this. She looked out at the crowd and bowed, grateful, once again, for waterproof mascara.

Paul walked to the foot of the stage and handed Cassie an enormous bouquet of roses. "We're so proud of you, Cass," he said, as she leaned down to take them from him.

Everyone on the catwalk applauded and shouted before they ran backstage. In the midst of a flurry of hugs and congratulations, Cassie saw Mary Ellen talking to Lynn. Mary Ellen looked nice, in a Laura Ashley-ish flowered dress and a matching headband. She would have been a perfect model for the show, with those long legs and perfect skin. Cassie hesitated for a moment and then decided to go and say hello.

"Hey, Lynn!" Cassie said. "You were gorgeous out there! That dress was made for you."

Lynn blushed. "Thanks so much. And thank you for letting me help. I had so much fun." She caught herself and looked at Mary Ellen nervously.

"Thanks for coming," Cassie said, courageously, to Mary Ellen.

"I came because Lynn was in the show." Mary Ellen didn't make eye contact.

"Well, we couldn't have done it without her and her hard work," Cassie said, proud of Lynn for standing up to Mary Ellen.

Cassie was about to turn away, but before she did, she said to Mary Ellen "I really like your dress. The colors are pretty."

It looked like she was trying to fight it, but Mary

Ellen's face brightened up into a smile. "Thanks." Her cheeks flushed. "It was really a good show. And thank you for raising so much money. I don't know how you did it."

"How *we* did it. We did it together!"

"Thanks," Mary Ellen said, this time sincerely.

Hmm, Cassie thought, *there is hope for her!*

She wanted to say something else, wanted to tell Mary Ellen to lighten up and maybe try some lip gloss and not judge people right away. But, instead, she took a deep breath. *Not yet*, she thought. "Thanks again for all of your help," she said. She gave Lynn a quick hug and walked toward another group of people.

Just then, her phone buzzed in her purse, and she flipped the phone open. It was a text from Erin, of course.

So?? Are we smiling??

Cassie turned around and saw all of the Fash Bash Committee standing together, laughing and talking, still floating on clouds. How could she be more lucky? Her best friend from Houston was texting her, and her new friends in Maine were all standing around her, celebrating their first success together. Cassie's heart swelled. She had so many terrific people in her life. And they loved Cassie for being *Cassie*.

She texted back:

We are more than smiling! We are happy! xo

And with that, she flipped her phone closed, scrunched her hair, and sashayed over to the group.

About
the
Authors

Mimi McCoy was never a cheerleader, but she had friends who were. Over the years, her school mascots have been the Vikings, the Bears, and the Wildcats—she's thankful to have never been a Mule. Mimi lives in Brooklyn, New York.

Laura Dower has never fake-swallowed a worm (like Jeff) or been a carnival leader (like Taryn). But she did have a longtime crush on a boy who lived next door. She's the author of more than 70 books for kids, including the series From the Files of Madison Finn. She lives in New York with her husband, two kids, and laptop computer. Check out her Web site: www.lauradower.com

Francesco Sedita was born in New York City and has been writing since the second grade. He has an older sister, who liked to beat him up and still does sometimes. His first foray into the world of "showbiz" was playing the title role in the preschool production of *Frosty the Snowman*. His grandparents came and he cried throughout the entire performance, especially when the sun was trying to melt him. The next year, he was cast as Pirate #7 in the kindergarteners' rendition of *Peter Pan* and had one line, said in unison with all of the other pirates: "Yo ho, yo ho!" The sun, who had melted him in the previous year, had the starring role of Wendy.

Francesco lives in Brooklyn, NY. To learn more about him, the latest Miss Popularity book, and Cassie Knight, visit www.francescosedita.com.

candY
APPLE

TURN THE PAGE FOR
MORE DELICIOUS
CANDY APPLE
STORIES!

HOW TO BE A GIRLY GIRL IN JUST TEN DAYS
by Lisa Papademetriou

Nicolette Spicer ("Nick" to her friends) is a tomboy through and through. Everything changes when she meets Ben — but he seems to go for girly girls. So when Nick's best friend suggests a makeover, it sounds like a great idea… Or is it?

DRAMA QUEEN
by Lara Bergen

Charlie never dreamed that auditioning for the junior high's musical would involve so much drama! She's stuck baby-sitting her little sister at rehearsal, the school's diva has it in for her, and the cutest guy in school gets picked to play the lead. But when the curtain finally goes up, the spotlight falls on something no one expected — especially Charlie.

THE
BABYSITTING WARS
by Mimi McCoy

Kaitlyn is the top babysitter in Marshfield Lake—until super-sitter Nola moves to town and starts stealing Kaitlyn's clients. Now this isn't just babysitting, it's war! But how far will Kaitlyn go to defend her turf?

TOTALLY CRUSHED
by Eliza Willard

Annabel is thrilled to find a red carnation at her locker on Valentine's Day—pink ones are from friends, but red ones are from crushes! But when it turns out to be from her best guy friend, things get messy. Annabel's perfect Valentine's Day might just turn into a perfect disaster!

I'VE GOT A SECRET
by Lara Bergen

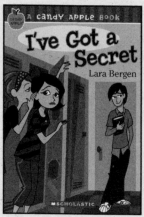

Shy Amanda Mays had the time of her life at summer camp. She was outgoing, she made new friends, including popular Allie, and she even (accidentally) let everyone think she had a boyfriend back home. A harmless white lie—she thought. But now Allie's moving to Amanda's town! What happens when Amanda's secrets are revealed?

CALLIE
FOR PRESIDENT
by Robin Wasserman

When Callie Singer finds herself accidentally running for student council president, she doesn't take it too seriously—Brianna Blake, the most popular girl in school, will definitely win. Then Brianna humiliates Callie in front of the whole school and steals her best friend. Callie may be the underdog, but she's not going down without a fight!